the Keepers' Council

THE KEEPER'S SAGA: BOOK FOUR

the Keepers' Council

Kelly Nelson

WALNUT SPRINGS PRESS

For my mom Kris,
whose request for one more chapter led to an entire book.

Text copyright © 2014 by Kelly Nelson
Cover design copyright © 2014 by Walnut Springs Press
Interior design copyright © 2014 by Walnut Springs Press

Walnut Springs Press
4110 South Highland Drive
Salt Lake City, Utah 84124

Printed in the United States of America.

ISBN: 978-1-59992-970-5

THE KEEPER'S SAGA

The Keeper's Calling

The Keeper's Quest

The Keeper's Defiance

The Keepers' Council

Acknowledgments

First and foremost, thank you to my mom for asking for more when she finished *The Keeper's Defiance*. Without her I would never have imagined the events that make up the first part of *The Keepers' Council*. The last half of the book came about when Linda, my amazing editor, heard about these extra chapters and asked me to add enough for a full-length novel. And thank you—the reader. It is exciting to have so many of you join with me in the Algonian adventure. Your emails and words of praise are inspiring. Thank you to Garry and Linda at Walnut Springs Press for believing in Keepers and counters. I appreciate their friendship and support of my writing career. Thank you to the staff at Brigham Distributing for scheduling book signings and getting my book where it needs to be when it needs to be there. Thank you to Tracy Anderson of Anderson Photography for the beautiful graphic design work on the cover. A special thanks to all the Costco managers who have welcomed me into their stores and helped promote The Keeper's Saga. Most importantly, thank you to a loving Heavenly Father who hears prayers and from Whom all great ideas originate.

Characters

Chase Harper—the Protector; the Protector's Keeper (born Feb. 17, 1994)

Ellen (Ellie) Elizabeth Williams—Chase's girlfriend (born May 28, 1845)

Jessica Harper—Chase's twin sister

Joe and Jennifer Harper—Chase's parents

Steve and Marianne Harper—Chase's uncle and aunt

Adam—Chase's cousin

Amanda—Chase's cousin

Garrick Eastman—the Guardian; the Guardian's Keeper (born Oct. 8, 1944)

Rose Adams—Garrick's deceased wife (born Sept. 16, 1791; died Aug. 24, 1818)

Davy Adams—Perception's Keeper; Garrick's adopted son; married to Sylvia (born Jan. 6, 1812)

Master Archidus—the Master Keeper; king of Algonia

Lord Arbon—deceased king of Shuyle; Archidus' older brother

Lord Dolosus—son of Lord Arbon and heir to the Shuylian throne

Legard—a Sniffer; Lord Arbon's second in command

Marcus Landseer—Algonian soldier who killed Lord Arbon and rescued Chase

Wickliff—an old elf; father of Creation's first Keeper, Courtenay

Segur—Algonian soldier

Aiton—Algonian soldier

Barhydt—Algonian soldier who is part sorcerer

Azalit—daughter of Archidus

Brierly—Marcus Landseer's younger sister

Carol and Lyman Gibson—owners of the mercantile in Vandalia, Illinois

Shahzad—the last of the magi; Perception's new Keeper

Mei-Lien—Illusion's Keeper from San Francisco

Raoul Devereux—Wisdom's Keeper from Paris, France; nicknamed Wise Wolf

Kalipsia—an elf woman; Creation's new Keeper

Castile—a sorcerer; Propulsion's new Keeper

Perry—scribe to the Keepers' Council

Leitner—an Algonian elf soldier

Nebus—an Algonian sorcerer soldier

Cecilia—an elf healer and owner of the apothecary shop in the Elf Province

Ravinia—a witch employed by Lord Dolosus

Places

Algonia—kingdom of Master Archidus

Cadré Unair—fortress city of Algonia

Capstown—hometown of Marcus and Brierly

Shuyle—kingdom of the former Lord Arbon

Valley of Tierran—main entrance to Shuyle

Susack Plain—grassy plain in the center of the Borderlands

Saddle Pass—northern gap in the Shuylian mountain range

Dragon's Lair—portal between the old world and Shuyle

Witches Hollow—portal between the old world and Algonia

Provinces of Algonia

Central Province

Wine Province

North Farming Province

West Farming Province

Southern Province

Shipping Province

Elf Province

ONE

U of O

"Drive safe, Son," my dad called.

I set my last bag on the back seat and pulled out my keys. "I will."

With the window down, I waved as I backed my Camaro out of our driveway in Hillsboro. *College, here I come.* I didn't anticipate it with as much enthusiasm as I'd expected to a year ago. The idea of leaving home wasn't new—I'd been on my own more times than I could count during the last year. School was now a means to an end. I'd worked construction all summer, but the thought of swinging a hammer forever didn't appeal to me. I needed an education to make a good living.

Last week, I'd asked the girl of my dreams to marry me. I met Ellie Williams after I found my counter buried in a cave in Zion National Park. When I touched a button inside of it, I went back in time to 1863. That was where I ran into her for the first time. Long story short, I brought her back to the present and we fell in love, so now I had responsibilities.

According to my birth certificate, I was eighteen and a half. Yet I felt much older. And if you added all the months I'd spent in other times, I had actually lived longer than that. I called New York home in 1817 when I worked construction building the Erie Canal with Garrick the Guardian, a Keeper. I'm a Keeper as well.

My counter is Protector, so I'm Protector's Keeper, or just the Protector for short.

My girlfriend Ellie worked for a daycare center, and her employer loved her. I doubted there was anyone better with kids than Ellie. I had left town without saying goodbye to her, but it didn't bother me. I would drive my Camaro three hours to Eugene, Oregon, find my dorm room, unload my gear, and then use my counter to come back and see her when she got off work. Nothing would really change for me, except I'd be at school all day instead of work. I'd still see Ellie every night. That was nonnegotiable.

My mom was with my twin sister Jessica, helping her settle in at Oregon State University. Both my parents were Oregon State grads, so I was rocking the boat by crossing our state's Civil War lines and going to the University of Oregon. Although I'd been offered a wrestling scholarship at OSU, I couldn't turn down a full-ride track scholarship at U of O. Tossing a javelin around would sure beat spending my college career with my head in another wrestler's sweaty pits.

With my dad swamped in teaching responsibilities at Portland State University, I headed off to college alone. I had assured my parents it didn't bother me. And truthfully it didn't. Ellie was the one I wished was coming with me. Unfortunately, I would have to wait until next semester for that. I was counting down to December 29— my wedding day. I had tried for a Thanksgiving-weekend wedding, but my mom had put her foot down. She wanted things to be perfect, and perfection took time, or so she said. I was starting to wish Ellie and I had tied the knot along with Davy and Sylvia when we were in Vandalia, Illinois, for their wedding. He was Garrick's adopted son. Davy had almost succeeded in marrying Ellie, when they thought I'd died in Lord Arbon's dungeon. Luckily, I'd found her in time to put a stop to that.

A few hours later in Eugene, I left Franklin Boulevard and turned onto East 13th Avenue. After glancing at my directions, I signaled for a left turn onto Beech Street. Carson Hall would be my home for the next few months. I hauled my two bags up a flight of stairs. My dorm looked comfortable enough, each side of the room a mirror image of the other. I tossed my bags in the closet and flopped onto the bed. Home sweet home—for now. I exchanged text messages with Ellie for an hour before a skinny dude with black-rimmed glasses dragged a heavy suitcase into the room. My roommate.

"Hey," I muttered.

He extended his hand to me. "Hello. I'm Robert David Murphy, from Sacramento, California."

I rolled over and shook his limp hand. "I'm Chase Harper."

Robert methodically unloaded his bags, starting with his laptop. His parents came into the room, each carrying a box. After a quick introduction they helped him unpack. Robert hung his pressed clothing in the closet, sliding the hangers so the spacing between them was even. He made his bed with pinstriped sheets and a navy-blue comforter. Watching their frenzy of unpacking and organizing left me feeling a little behind.

"I better get the rest of my gear," I mumbled. I went out and grabbed two boxes from my car, then retraced my steps up to my room. After making my bed and plugging in my laptop and printer, I pronounced my unpacking finished. I wouldn't worry about my clothes—they'd get unpacked as I wore them. I pulled out my cell phone. Ellie wouldn't be off work for another two hours.

My roommate's parents said goodbye and left. Robert sat down on his bed and asked me, "What's your major?"

"I'm not sure yet. Maybe something in the computer industry— my uncle has a good job with Intel. He does all right. My dad's an accounting professor. I suppose I could be a CPA. I'm taking required classes this semester while I figure it out. How 'bout you?"

He smiled. "Either physics or mathematics, with a minor in history. I've completed most of my required courses through the IB program at my high school. I have thirty-two college credits."

I nodded. "Whew, that's a lot." I knew where I would go for help with homework.

"Have you bought your books yet?" Robert asked.

"No, have you?"

"Not yet, but I want to do that today so I can start looking through them. Should we walk over to the bookstore before dinner?"

I shrugged my shoulders. "Sure, why not?"

I followed my roomy across campus, wearing a Hilhi Spartans wrestling T-shirt, faded blue jeans, and basketball shoes. In contrast, he carried a map of the school in the front pocket of his collared shirt and had a planner tucked under his arm. Robert maintained a nonstop one-sided conversation as we walked. This guy talked like he had a computer for a brain. At that moment he was giving me the U of O history lecture—founder of the university, first building erected on campus, that kind of stuff.

We bought our books and started the hike back to our room. When his scrawny muscles looked like they were about to give out, I offered to carry his books, hoping he wouldn't be offended. With no apparent shame, he handed me his two bags. He'd bought nearly twice the number of textbooks as I had. He was taking seventeen credit hours and had picked up two extra books—one about U.S. history and the other about ancient European history—just for fun. I rolled my eyes at his idea of fun. If I wanted to learn any more about history, I'd take a trip with my counter and see it for myself.

Once the books were stacked on his desk, Robert turned his lamp on and began reading. He slipped into his own world, and it was as if I didn't exist. I made an effort to look at one of my books, but it didn't hold my interest. I paced the small room, my left hand curling around the gold counter in my pocket, my cell phone sitting in the palm of my hand. Ellie would be off work in twenty minutes.

"I'm going out for a bit," I said.

As I reached for the doorknob, Robert said, "You should see this. I think I found a long-lost relative of yours."

I looked over his shoulder at the black-and-white photo he pointed to in his U.S. history book. The grainy quality was consistent with other 1800s photos I'd seen, but there was no mistaking the three faces staring back at me. Thomas Macaulay leaning against the mule Old Sal. Garrick, his chin propped on the top of his shovel handle. And me, holding the chain we were about to hook onto the stump of an old oak tree.

I smiled, remembering how grateful I was the guy had picked us for a photo. Exhausted from heat and long days, we had been happy to stand still and rest for a few minutes.

"Which one?" I asked, messing with my roommate.

Robert dropped his finger onto the page directly over my face. "That one. He could be your twin."

"Nah, he couldn't be *my* twin. My twin's a girl. Her name's Jessica and she has brown hair."

Robert looked up at me. "You have a twin?"

"Yeah, but she's at OSU." I backed away. "Hey, I'll see you later tonight."

"Should I wait for you to get back to go down to the cafeteria?"

"No, I'll get something to eat while I'm out."

I closed the door behind me and walked down the hall, grinning. Garrick and I had made history. Enough reminiscing. For now I needed a quiet place to disappear. I stopped by the bathroom. It was empty at the moment, but for my return trip there would be no guarantees. I wandered down a flight of stairs and found a janitor's closet. After glancing in both directions, I opened the door and stepped into the darkness. The pale-blue light from my counter illuminated the small room as I set the dials. I raised my thumb to press Shuffle, but my phone rang, startling me. I dug it out and slid it open. "Hello?"

"Chase, where are you now?" my mom asked.

"Um . . . Carson Hall, the building where my dorm room is."

"Have you met your roommate yet?"

"Yeah. His name's Robert. We went to the bookstore together and got all of our books. He's one of those really smart guys—a little nerdy, but nice."

"That's good. I'm glad you like him. Jessica's all settled in and I'm driving home now. I just wanted to make sure you're safely there."

I scratched my head. "I'm here," I said with a pang of guilt, knowing I wouldn't be for long.

"Love you, honey. Call me after your first day and tell me how you like your classes."

"Sure thing, Mom. I love you too."

After sliding the phone back in my pocket, I pressed Shuffle and Go. I wondered if the shuffling was even necessary now that Lord Arbon was gone. Life as a Keeper had been relatively uneventful the past several months. There had been no sign of Sniffers, and I hadn't been plagued by Archidus' errands either.

Last week when I left Garrick in Vandalia, Illinois, in 1834, he hadn't heard from Archidus in over a year. Maybe life had finally returned to normal. Sometimes I worried about Legard and regretted he had gotten away. While searching for Ellie and Davy, Garrick had attacked Legard in the Ohio cabin. At the time I was so worried about finding my girlfriend, I had no desire to pursue my nemesis when he had disappeared. Now I wondered if we should've gone after him.

In my modern clothes, I felt out of place in a couple of the shuffle zones and averted my gaze as I darted into the shadows. On the last shuffle, I squatted on my haunches and envisioned the dumpsters behind the strip mall. The daycare Ellie worked at was in the last building. I'd scoped out the dumpsters last week in anticipation of this. As expected I appeared out of sight, with the dumpster in front of me. Slowly I stood and stepped into the open. My bike was chained to a rack. I'd started to teach Ellie to drive this summer, but she wasn't comfortable with it yet.

I leaned against the wall and texted my cousin Adam while I waited. Ellie soon left the building. She walked to the bike and turned the numbers on the lock, never once looking in my direction. Feeling mischievous, I pulled out my counter, focused on the space directly behind her, and pressed Go. Immediately, I reappeared and grabbed her waist.

She screamed, dropping the bike helmet, and tried to bolt out of my grasp.

I laughed. "Ellie, it's me."

She hit me in the shoulder. "Chase! You scared me half to death. What are you doing here? I thought you were leaving for college today."

I smiled. "I did leave. But I'm back. I was bored down there without you."

She smiled. "Were you now?"

I sighed, pulling her closer. "It's going to be a long semester."

"Well, look on the bright side—at least you can easily visit."

I picked up the helmet and bent to unlock the bike for her. "Yup, and I will, too." Pushing the bike with one hand, I offered her my other. "Are you hungry?"

"Yes, are you?"

"How 'bout we go across the street and get some Chinese?" I said.

After we talked for over an hour in the restaurant, I walked Ellie the two miles to where she lived with my aunt and uncle. I stopped a few houses away and watched until she entered the garage. Then I darted between a rhododendron bush and the fence and returned to the janitor's closet at the University of Oregon.

I pocketed my counter and turned the knob. The door banged into something, and a startled scream came from the other side. I stepped into the hall. "Sorry about that."

A pretty blond stood next to another girl, who had one hand on the door and the other over her mouth. "That was freaky," she said.

"Sorry, I didn't realize anyone was there. Are you okay?"

She laughed. "I'm good. I just wasn't expecting that. What were you doing in there?"

I glanced in the closet. "I . . . I was looking for something . . . uh, some cleaner for my . . . for the mirror in my room."

"Did you find it?"

Is this girl the hall police or something? "No, it's not a big deal, though. I better go." I started to leave.

"Wait, what's your name?"

I kept walking but turned slightly toward her. "Chase Harper."

She jogged to catch me, her friend following. "I'm Jenna Brady. Are you a freshman?"

"Yeah."

"Where are you from?"

"Hillsboro—west of Portland."

"I know where that is. I'm from Beaverton. What high school did you go to?"

I had reached the stairs. She was sticking to my heels better than my first dog. "Hilhi."

"This is my friend Cynthia. She and I went to Jesuit."

"That's nice. I thought this was a guy's wing."

"Oh, it is. We're just visiting."

Jenna put her hand on my arm. "You should visit our dorm. There's a party tonight at Walton Hall by the sand volleyball courts. It'll be fun."

Is she asking me out? She's definitely flirting. "Thanks anyway, but I'm engaged."

"What? No way. Didn't you say you were a freshman?" Now Jenna and Cynthia seemed more interested than ever.

"Yeah, I am, but I finally found the girl of my dreams and I don't plan on losing her again."

"Where is this lucky girl?"

I'd reached the door to my dorm. "Hillsboro. Nice meeting you two. See you around." I stepped into the room and closed the door.

Letting out a deep breath, I shook my head at Robert. "Women."

"What about them?"

"The ones you want have a way of slipping through your fingers. The ones you're not interested in pop up at every turn."

Robert stared at me. "I've never had that problem. I don't give women much thought, though. Do you have a girlfriend?"

I kicked off my shoes and sat on the bed. "Actually, I have a fiancé. Her name's Ellie Williams. We're getting married in December."

"Wow! I don't mean to sound critical, but aren't you a little young to be getting married?"

I smiled. "We don't think so, plus she's older than me." *Quite a bit older, actually.*

"When do I get to meet her?"

"Maybe I'll bring her down here one of these weekends."

TWO
Shotgun

By the end of the first week, I had slipped into an easy routine—go to class, do homework, exercise, and then visit Ellie before bed. Although I was at the University of Oregon on a track scholarship, it wasn't my first love. But I was good at it. Regular team practices would start soon, and for now I hit the gym and jogged laps around the campus on my own.

Getting Robert as a roomy was a stroke of luck. He never questioned my frequent and unexplained absences. He was more than willing to offer his advice on any complicated homework that came my way. And he was easy to get along with.

On Sunday, after the second week of school, my phone rang in the middle of the night, waking me. I pulled it off my desk and said hello.

"Chase, you have a visitor."

I rubbed my face, trying to figure out what the heck my mom was talking about.

"Chase, did you hear me? That friend of yours is here in our house looking for you."

I sat up in bed. "What are you talking about? What friend?"

Mom exhaled loudly. "One of your magical friends. That man who was here last spring."

"Wickliff?"

"He didn't say, but I don't like waking up to some man knocking on my bedroom door."

"Is he an old guy with a long beard?

"No, he's the young one."

I smiled. "Garrick? How's he doing? What does he need?"

"I'll go hand him the phone, but please tell your friends they can't just walk into our house in the middle of the night. He's lucky I didn't call the police."

"Mom, he didn't walk into the house. He probably appeared in my bedroom, expecting to find me sleeping. Let me talk to him."

"Here he is," my mom said.

Robert mumbled and rolled over, so I stepped out of our dorm room, not wanting to wake him. "Garrick?"

"Hey, little brother, where are you?"

"College. What's up?"

"I have a favor to ask. I need someone to ride shotgun for me on my next haul. I'll pay you regular teamster's wages, if you'll come back and help."

I rubbed the sleep out of my eyes and yawned. I wasn't as excited as my roomy about starting another school week, so a little delay wouldn't bug me. "When do we leave?"

"We'll pull out from my place in Vandalia at first light on August 11, 1834."

The idea of hangin' with Garrick took root. "Count me in."

—◈—

Garrick and I had been on the road to St. Louis for three days. His son Davy's wife had been sick, and Garrick said he thought she was in the family way. With none of the other guys they usually hired available for this run, he had asked me.

Once the horses were watered and hobbled, I gathered wood and built a cook fire while Garrick prepared our simple meal. By

Shuylian-dungeon standards it was a feast, and my mouth watered at the savory smell. Garrick handed me a plate of food and plopped himself down on a log. I sat on Davy's waterproof duster and leaned against a tree. After practically inhaling my food, I said, "I was wondering, where did you get your counter?"

Garrick glanced up from his plate. "Grandpa Eastman."

I thought back to when I'd found my counter. "Did you know what it was when he gave it to you?"

Garrick chuckled. "Oh, I knew all right, and so did my cousin."

"Sounds like there's a story behind that."

"I reckon so."

I swallowed the wad of biscuit I'd been chewing. "Well, come on. Spit it out. It's not like we've got anything better to do tonight— no TV, no phones, no radio, no computer."

"Been a long time since I've watched a television program." Garrick smiled. "Sometimes I miss stretching out on the couch for an episode of *Bonanza*. That'd sure beat this here tree trunk."

"What do you need to watch that for? You're practically living *Bonanza*." I laughed, thinking an episode of *Duck Dynasty* would beat *Bonanza* any day.

Garrick laughed, then plucked a piece of grass and chewed on the end. "Here's a bedtime story for you, little brother. I was fourteen the first time I heard about Keepers and counters. Grandpa Eastman owned a cattle ranch outside of McAllen, Texas. Once we each turned twelve, my cousin Andrew and I would spend our summers working the ranch with him. Since Andrew was two years older than me, he heard the story before I did.

"For the last three generations the counter had been passed from grandfather to oldest grandson. Family tradition dictated the counter should go to Andrew. All the stories Grandpa told us—the idea of another world, Archidus being betrayed by his brother, the Sniffers, the responsibilities of being the Guardian—fascinated me, but at the time I wondered why he even bothered telling me any of it. The counter would go to my older cousin, not me. When I asked Grandpa about it, he said, 'Just because the counter has always gone to the eldest grandson doesn't mean that will be the case in the future. It will go to the one best qualified to do the job. That may be Andrew, or it may be you. Old Master Archidus will have a say in it as well.' After that, Grandpa rested his hand on my shoulder and squeezed. 'Time will tell. You look tired. Y'all better get some sleep. Mornin' comes early 'round here.'

"After Grandma passed away, Grandpa poured all of his energy into teaching us boys everything he knew. I learned horses, ropin' cattle, swords, and guns. Grandpa whittled wooden swords for us to practice with and taught us to use pistols and rifles. Before he'd take us into town for sodas and supplies at the end of the week, we had to write each Algonian symbol and what it meant on a piece of paper. Then we'd burn it in the wood stove.

"By the end of my fifth year at the ranch—Andrew's seventh— my cousin became rebellious. He picked up smoking and a few other bad habits. He didn't want to work and basically gave my grandpa more trouble than he was worth that summer. By the next spring, Grandpa was sick with cancer. He sold the ranch and moved into town with Andrew's mom. I missed the ranch, but I missed being with my grandpa even more. We had grown close over the years, and in some ways I was closer to him than to my own dad. My parents lived a couple of miles from Andrew's, so each day I'd ride my bike over there and sit at Grandpa's bedside."

Garrick tossed a stick onto the bed of coals. Sparks jumped into the sky and then cooled to ash. "No one could tell stories like him. He'd have me hanging on every word."

"When did your grandpa tell Andrew he was giving you the counter?"

"He never did. Andrew had graduated high school and spent all his time working at the auto-body shop in town or seeing his girlfriend, so he wasn't around much. After Grandpa got sick, he never talked about who would get the counter. Andrew assumed he would get it and so did I, so there really wasn't much to talk about. Grandpa never let the counter out of his sight, though. When his time drew close, he clutched it in his pale, bony hand. Once Andrew tried to pry it out of his fingers, but even in a near coma Grandpa was too strong. Or maybe that was Archidus and his magic at work.

"I remember the night Grandpa passed away like it was yesterday. He hadn't eaten anything in almost a week, and he hadn't spoken in over two weeks. Each breath seemed to rattle his chest, and more than once I thought he'd stopped breathing only to have him suck in another lungful of air. It was nearing midnight, and I had dozed off in the reclining chair next to his bed when he said my name. I bolted up and grabbed his hand, looking into his eyes. They were bright and clear, not glazed over like they had been for the past few weeks. His voice was strong when he set the counter in my hand and said, 'You are the Guardian now. I expect you to be a good one.' As soon as the counter left his possession, his head fell back on the bed. His breathing became even more labored as I knelt next to him. I cried when I realized it was the end.

"I dried my eyes and called to Andrew and his mom so they could be with him too. When he drew his last breath, or at least what we thought was his last breath, my aunt left to call her brothers with the news, leaving Andrew and me alone in the room. He pulled down the blanket and reached for our grandpa's hand that had clutched the counter. Andrew saw it was gone and became livid, swearing up a storm as he searched the bed for it. When I showed him the counter and told him Grandpa had said I was to be the next Keeper, Andrew slammed me against the wall. I could smell liquor on his breath as he yelled and threatened me. I tried to talk some sense into him, but that only made him angrier. He punched me in the stomach and threw me to the ground. He had a good twenty pounds on me, and I think I was in shock. The counter fell from my hand, and Andrew kicked me before I could grab it.

"He opened the counter and scowled. It had remained dark. I hadn't touched any of the buttons yet, so if it wasn't lighting up in his hand, my grandpa wasn't dead after all. Sure enough, Grandpa exhaled. Andrew walked to the bed and said, 'Die already, old man.'

"The meanness in my cousin's voice as my grandpa struggled to take one last breath drove me to action. He'd given me the responsibility of the counter, and here I was lying on the floor like a whipped pup. At that moment, I knew more than anything that I wanted to make him proud. I jumped to my feet and tackled my cousin. I pulled the counter out of his hand, but couldn't get away from him until we rolled into a nightstand and a lamp fell on his head. I scrambled toward the door and clicked open the counter. It lit up in my hand and I pressed the Go button. Grandpa had the coordinates set for that day, so my efforts to get out the door were instantly rewarded. I disappeared then reappeared in the hall outside his room. Andrew's mom collided with me. She had tears streaming down her cheeks as she yelled at Andrew and me to stop fighting.

"The sensation of using the counter for the first time had left me dizzy. Andrew grabbed it from my hand, and of course it didn't light up for him. At that point, I think he realized he'd lost, because he threw the counter down the hall, then shoved his mom and me aside and stormed away. I didn't feel like a winner at all, because I knew then and there I'd lost one of my best friends. A few days later, Andrew and I stood on opposite sides of our grandpa's grave, both of our faces black and blue from the beating we'd given each other."

The sound of crickets filled the night air as Garrick finished his story. I could barely make out his features in the light of the dying fire.

"Did Andrew ever forgive you?" I asked.

Garrick shrugged. "He hasn't spoken to me since."

THREE

The Errand

Three weeks later, at the beginning of October, I drove home to spend a real weekend with Ellie. Of course my parents thought I was spending it with the family. Sure, I would be with them, but I'd have Ellie by my side, too.

That first night, I was sleeping soundly in my own bed when Master Archidus intruded. I saw myself standing in the hallway of a home I didn't recognize. Sad voices filtered through the partially closed door in front of me.

"Good night, Papa. We'll let you rest now," a woman said.

A raspy voice answered, "Good night."

The sound of approaching footsteps sent me scurrying behind an open door across the hall. I listened as the family retreated into the kitchen. I made sure the hallway was empty and tiptoed into the old man's room. Whom had I been sent to visit? He didn't seem to be in danger from anything, except the frailties of old age. I pushed the door open. Counter coordinates flashed before my eyes—June 25, 1896, St. Louis, Missouri—before I could see the man.

I sat up, wondering what kind of errand Archidus wanted me to do. Within minutes, I was dressed in my frontier clothes and setting the counter. I contemplated telling Ellie where I was going, but it was after one o'clock in the morning. She'd probably be sound asleep.

Whatever Archidus wanted, it didn't look particularly treacherous, but I'd go prepared anyway. I'd already learned that lesson the hard way. I pulled my sword and Luger pistol out of the closet, then decided the gun was enough and tossed the sword on my bed.

I set the counter to match what I'd seen in the vision and imagined the vacant hallway. Out of habit, I pressed Shuffle and Go, then disappeared. My counter favored certain times and locations. I had shuffled often enough that I began to recognize some of them. So, although it was unpleasant, it wasn't totally unexpected when I appeared standing on the water in the middle of what I guessed to be the Pacific Ocean. The air shimmered around me while I sank.

Kicking my feet, I shot to the surface. One hand patted my pocket, checking on my counter, while the other lifted the pistol out of the sea. Smiling at the memory of Ellie here with me, I treaded water. She'd be relieved to hear she missed this trip.

The familiar shimmer moved before my eyes, and despite my best efforts to keep my feet beneath me, I staggered when making the abrupt transition from swimming to standing on dry ground. I would have preferred the solitude of a hot desert, but instead I stepped into a throng of people making their way toward the security checkpoint in an airport.

"You're soaking wet," a man next to me said.

"Sorry," I mumbled.

A woman screamed behind me. "He's got a gun!"

Glancing up, I realized I still held the loaded Luger pistol over my head. The guy in front of me turned and grabbed my arm. He wrestled with me for possession of the weapon. The concussion of the pistol firing through the terminal's ceiling sparked an onslaught of screaming and yelling.

"Drop your weapon and get down on the ground," a security guard yelled over the commotion. I'd be in custody within seconds, if I didn't disappear. I threw a hard left jab into the man's face. He toppled back, stumbling over his bag. Then I pushed the women behind me out of the way as I ran from the guards. Appearing in this airport was really getting old. I doubted they'd shoot me for fear of hitting someone in the crowd, but my heart raced at the thought of a bullet sinking into my back.

I darted into one of the airport shops and ducked behind a rack of magazines. I pulled my counter out and hit Shuffle again. After a seemingly never-ending line of shuffles, I appeared in the vacant hallway in 1896 and stepped behind the open door in anticipation of the family leaving the old man's room. Water dripped from my clothes onto the polished wood floor. The room cleared out, and the hum of voices grew quieter as the people walked the other direction.

I stepped from behind the door and entered the man's room, my wet boots squeaking with each step. His shock of white hair went in every direction. His face was thin, his eyes sunken and closed in apparent sleep. Suddenly his mouth moved. "Harper, thank you for coming."

I crossed the room and bent over his bed. His brown eyes opened, and a weak smile touched his lips. Before I could speak, he said, "You're younger than the last time I saw you."

"Davy?"

"It's me. I don't look so good now, do I?"

"What's wrong? Was that your family?"

"I'm old, Harper. Gettin' old ain't for sissies. Maybe Garrick had the right idea—avoid it as long as possible." Davy's dark eyes fluttered closed.

I looked around the room. "Archidus sent me, but I don't see what I can do. Is there anything I can help you with?"

"Take the counter. My Sylvia's been gone for twenty years now. I miss her terribly. I never did tell her about it. Kept it a secret. Never told my children, either. I didn't want to risk burdening them with what Ellie and I went through . . . with what you went through."

Davy raised a trembling hand, his wrinkled skin hanging loosely from the arm I remembered as strong and muscular. "It's in the top drawer. Please take it. Then I'll be free to leave this world and find Sylvia."

Fighting a wave of emotion, I pulled open the drawer and dug through the clothes until my hand clutched the familiar shape of the counter. When I returned to the bed, Davy took the counter from me and clicked it open. The familiar light lit his face.

"I never used it after I got married. I wouldn't risk leaving my wife. I wonder now if I missed out."

I didn't want him dying with regrets. "No, Davy. You did it right. There's nothing more important than taking care of your wife and family."

His gnarled hand grabbed mine, and he pressed the counter into it. "Thank you, Harper. Please find someone to keep this. It's not the legacy I want to leave my children."

"I will. When I walked in here, you said the last time you saw me I was old. What did you mean?"

"Fourth of July, remember? You, Garrick, and me—we meet every year. We've never missed an Independence Day."

"Were Ellie and I happy?"

He didn't respond. His eyes closed, and he struggled for another breath. I laid my hand on his shoulder. "Thank you again, for keeping her safe from Legard when I couldn't. I'll never forget what you did."

Almost imperceptibly his head nodded. He sucked in air and then lay still. I waited for his next breath while hot tears brewed behind my eyelids. A voice from the hallway brought my head up. "Where'd all this water come from?"

I dropped to the floor behind the bed. The trail of seawater would lead the woman straight to me. I retrieved my counter as the woman entered the room.

"Is someone in here?" she asked.

She was greeted by the rattle of what I had to assume was one of Davy's final breaths, and then I disappeared.

The dam holding back my tears burst on the first shuffle. Fortunately, I was alone. In that moment, I glimpsed my own mortality. I'd faced my death before, but this was different. If

I didn't die tragically in a desperate struggle for life in some other time or world, I would most certainly grow old and face the horrible ordeal of a slow death by old age. My eighteen-year-old brain had never faced the idea before, and it was hard to accept. I eventually found my way back to my bedroom and collapsed on my bed.

I slept fitfully, waking every hour to monitor the progress of the numbers on my clock. During a brief stretch of sleep, Archidus sent another vision. In this one, I dropped into Witches Hollow. Counter coordinates flashed before my eyes. I didn't see a date, only a location. Northern Mexico.

Luckily, I'd fallen asleep fully dressed because before I awoke, Archidus yanked me into the dreaded abyss separating our worlds. It led to one of two places—Witches Hollow or the Dragon's Lair. Half asleep, I dropped onto a thick carpet of moist leaves. I rolled over and climbed to my feet. Witches Hollow.

After getting my bearings, I started up the path toward the fortress city, planning to give Davy's counter to Archidus. A shot of pain through my head stopped me in my tracks. I bent over, grabbing a tree for support, as the counter coordinates of northern Mexico again flashed before my eyes. But the vision continued. I dropped onto the sand amid a cluster of Bedouin-type tents. A camel's call shattered the quiet night.

I stood and surveyed the area, unsure where to go. Archidus' voice pierced the darkness. "Find the last of the magi. He will be Perception's Keeper."

My mind came back to me, along with the throb of a headache. I took another step toward the fortress city—bad idea. Pain hit my skull and sent me stumbling onto my hands and knees. Again the vision of the tents played through my mind as the voice said, "Find the last of the Magi. He will be Perception's Keeper."

My counter blurred before my eyes as I set the coordinates to northern Mexico and pressed Go. I'd never used my counter on the new world, but I could only guess it would take me to the tent village. The shimmering cleared, and the braying of a camel felt like a knife stabbing my already-throbbing head.

I started to stand when I heard the crunch of approaching footsteps. Someone stepped on my back, driving my face into the rocky sand. Two sets of strong hands wrenched my arms behind me and tied cords around my wrists. I spit out dirt as they dragged me to my feet. Why had Archidus sent me here incapacitated with a splitting headache? I really didn't appreciate his sick sense of humor.

"I need to see the last of the magi," I said. "Can you take me to the last of the magi?"

A slur of foreign words assaulted my eardrums.

"Magi? I need to see the last of the magi," I tried again, slower this time. It appeared useless—they didn't understand me.

The full moon cast pale light over the tent village. The men who held me captive wore sabers at their waists and turbans on their heads, their flowing robes fluttering in the night breeze. We marched past the camels, secured with stakes, to the farthest tent. The men lifted the flap, pulled me inside, and tied me to the tent pole. Then they hurried out, leaving me alone.

I sat quietly until the painful throbbing in my head subsided. *Who was the last of the magi, anyway? And what were those guys saying?* With this language barrier, I'd be lucky to escape with my life. Could the message have been a trap? If it wasn't from Archidus, I was a sitting duck. Could Legard have been behind this? The thought of facing him again—of never returning to Ellie—sent me into a frenzy. I pushed myself to my feet and fought against the pole, shaking the tent like a hurricane. If I toppled the tent, maybe I could work myself free.

One of my captors burst in, yelling at me in that language I didn't understand.

I shook my head at him. "I need to see the last of the magi."

My request was met with an angry scowl. The man raised his saber and struck me with the metal hand guard. I licked my lips and tasted blood. His spit flew into my face as he yelled the same phrase he'd used earlier. When I remained silent, he nodded in approval, so I figured the words meant "shut up."

Slumping onto the woven mat, I fought to keep my wits about me. Images of my time in Arbon's dungeon came at me with full force. I doubted I could hold up under the pressure of another dungeon ordeal—I'd crack for sure.

I took a deep breath. I wouldn't think about that now. I could last until morning. My mom always said things looked better in the morning. At least they hadn't taken my counter or Davy's, although that could change once the guards notified whoever was in charge around here. I closed my eyes and replayed the memories I'd thought of a million times in Lord Arbon's dungeon, falling into the old routine of withdrawing to the safety of my head.

FOUR

The Last Magi

I woke to the turban guard standing above me barking orders. My neck ached as I lifted my head. He stooped to cut the cords binding me to the pole and then dragged me to my feet. He shoved me ahead of him into the pink glow of sunrise. A second guard pointed out the direction I was to walk, and they marched me through the village. Shirtless little boys left their mothers and followed, until the guard waved his sword in the air and yelled at them.

We stopped in front of the largest tent, and I think the turban guard told me to wait. Fortunately for me they now used hand gestures with their verbal commands. The sun made its brilliant debut while I stood there. My shoulders sagged and I groaned inwardly. Ellie. My mom. They'd stress out when they found me missing this morning. They would most likely guess my fate. My frontier clothes were missing from the closet, and my sword and pistol lay on the bed where I'd tossed them the night before. *What a shame I didn't actually live long enough to marry Ellie.*

A woman opened the tent flap and motioned for the guards and me to enter. When my eyes adjusted to the tent's dim interior, I stood facing the man I hoped was their leader. These people appeared to be descendants of the Arabs—medium to dark skin, flowing robes and turbans, and veils over the women's faces.

I waited as the guards exchanged small talk with the leader before their animated hand motions made it evident they were telling the story of my capture. When they finished talking, their leader turned his attention on me. "Tell me why it is you sneak like a thief into my village under cover of darkness."

English—he speaks English. The voice had a heavy accent, but I understood the words. I sighed. "I was sent by Master Archidus of Algonia to find the last of the magi. Can you help me?" Until I knew who he was, I didn't want to reveal my identity. It was a miracle they hadn't searched me and found both counters hidden in my pockets. Although the cords binding me to the tent pole had been cut, my hands were still secured behind my back, and I couldn't reach my counter.

"I know of the last of the magi. Who seeks him and why?"

"I'm a messenger from Archidus. He requests his . . . services, on behalf of Algonia," I answered, still uncertain how much information to give.

"I will submit your request to the last magi. But the decision to grant you audience will be his."

I smiled in relief. "When will we get his answer?"

"Two days." The man spread his arms and grinned. "So, you will be my guest while we wait. If the answer is no, well"—he shrugged his shoulders—"I decide then what to do with you. Maybe you die, maybe not. We shall see."

He turned to his guards and gave an order. The guard closest to me pulled a knife from his belt and cut the cords from my wrists. The other guard left, hopefully to take my message to the magi. The leader motioned to the place next to him. "Come, sit and eat."

I rubbed my wrists as I walked to the cushions lying on the floor. A feast of fruits and flat breads was spread on the mat in front of him. "Thank you. What's your name?" I said.

"I am Chief Haman of the desert people. What do you call yourself?"

My stomach growled, and I picked up a clump of grapes. "Chase Harper."

I ate my fill, and then Chief Haman walked me through his village, spouting off an endless stream of stories and facts. I wondered if he would allow me to walk out of here after everything he'd told me.

That night, I ate dinner in the chief's tent with his family. His wife peeked through her veil at me more times than I could count, while his daughters hid their mouths behind their hands and giggled. I couldn't help but notice the ever-present guards. They may have cut me free, but it was clear I was still a prisoner.

When night fell, they returned me to the same tent from the night before. In my absence, someone had furnished it with pillows. I dropped onto the cushions and tucked one hand beneath my head, then pulled Davy's counter out of my pocket. It hadn't changed in the seventy or so years he'd had it, and my mind flashed back to the fateful day I had collected it from Ruth during World War II.

I opened the cover. Perception's pale light welcomed me— invited me to touch it and become its Keeper. But I turned away and closed it.

I took my own counter from the other pocket and looked longingly at the Return button. But it wouldn't get me where I wanted to go. It might get me closer, but nothing on my powerful counter could take me to Ellie's world. The fear that Legard was behind this had evaporated throughout the day. The chief seemed like a good man. Protective of his people, yes, but I didn't think he was in league with the likes of Legard.

I slept soundly that night, waking at first light to the sound of camels braying. My second day with the desert people was much like the first. The chief loved to talk, and I'd bet he had grown tired of sharing his stories with the same people. He was more than willing to fill my ears with his tall tales.

"You know," he said as we sat in the sparse shade of a tree late in the afternoon, "it has been years since my people visited Algonia. Too wet up there. And cold. It's enough to make an old man's bones ache. I like it here. We get a decent crop along the river's edge. The land is not as fertile as in Algonia, but it's peaceful. There is much fighting in Algonia. Between those two brothers, it's nothing but trouble. You've heard of Lord Arbon, have you not?"

I gazed across his village at a group of young boys wrestling in the sand. "Yeah, I've heard of him."

"He fights his brother's people. Fighting, fighting, fighting—they are always fighting each other. I don't get involved. Better to stay here. But you, my friend, must have traveled a long way to search out the last of the magi. The desert is difficult to cross. Not many Algonians—or Shuylians, for that matter—think it worth the trip. So tell me, how did you get here?"

"Like I said, Archidus sent me. You know he's a sorcerer don't you?"

The chief scratched his chin and studied me. "Yes, of course."

"So, I got here by magic."

—◆—

We were sitting cross-legged around the dinner mat later that evening when horses thundered into the village. Standing abruptly, Chief Haman spoke to his family and added the word "stay" for my benefit.

The chief exited his tent. The snorting of horses and the stamping of hooves mixed with a rush of foreign words. I watched the tent flap, wishing I could see what was happening on the other side of the canvas. The family continued eating as if nothing was amiss.

Chief Haman's guard pulled aside the flap, and a tall man with a shaved head and ebony skin entered. The chief stepped in after him and must have asked his family to leave because they quickly exited the tent as the newcomer sat across from me. Like a lighthouse on a moonless night, the whites of his eyes made a stark contrast against his dark skin. He was royalty, no doubt about it. The way he moved. The way he dressed—like a modern version of one of the three wise men—was as fine as any I'd seen in the new world.

The man studied me for a moment before speaking. "You wished to see me?"

"Are you the last of the magi?"

He nodded. "My name is Shahzad. Many years have I studied the heavens and the laws of the land. There were once five of us, but now I am the last. What message does Archidus send? I know him well, but it has been at least a hundred years since we have spoken."

I smiled at the softness of Shahzad's voice and the sincerity in his expression. With his fancy robes, I expected him to be arrogant, yet he didn't seem that way at all. "Are you a sorcerer?" I asked.

A slight smile turned his mouth. "I am."

"Have you heard of the counters?"

His left eyebrow lifted. "I have, but that is something I've not spoken of in ages. My grandfather was one of the original seven who formed the new world and left a counter as his legacy. In the beginning, my father served on the Keepers' Council and held a counter. But why would Archidus send you all this way to ask me about counters? He too was once a Keeper on the council. Could he not have told you himself everything you wished to know?"

My fear of revealing my true identity dissolved. I stared at Shahzad in awe. "Archidus sent me because I'm the Protector. I was told to find you and offer you the counter Perception. You're supposed to be its Keeper." I pulled the counter out of my pocket.

Shahzad's brow furrowed as he stared at the gold device. "But what of Lord Arbon? The council decided it wasn't safe to have the counters on our world. He is much too powerful and the risk is too great."

News must not travel very fast on this world. "Arbon is dead. We have nothing to fear from him." I tried again to hand the counter to Shahzad.

Looking skeptical, he sat back and folded his arms. "How would one such as you know that? Arbon and his army would be nearly impossible to defeat in battle, and his skill with magic would make him difficult to kill."

I smiled at him. This *was* something I knew. "Maybe, but poisoned with a tasteless, odorless substance, slipped into his wine late at night while surrounded by his army and within the safety of Shuyle, it would be possible. He would never expect it."

He straightened his spine. "Who could do such a thing? A Shuylian traitor?"

"Marcus Landseer, an Algonian captain, working undercover as a Shuylian soldier. He poisoned the wine, waited until the second watch of the night, killed two guards, and then cut off Arbon's head. The captain barely escaped with his life. Even in death, Arbon's magic was powerful. Marcus was sliced open when he severed the leather cord holding Arbon's two counters, Propulsion and Creation."

"And you know all of this how?"

I leaned forward. "I was there. I saw it with my own eyes. I dragged Marcus's bleeding body through the woods to safety and pried open his grasp to release the counters. I was the first to open them and see their light—the sign that confirmed Arbon's death."

Shahzad smiled. "In that case, I would be honored to assume my father's legacy." He laughed then, his eyes twinkling in delight as he reached forward to take the counter. "So, it has come back to my family after all these years."

I let out a deep sigh as Perception's counter once again left my possession. The bits of information came together in my mind like pieces of a puzzle. "Your father was the first Perception's Keeper?"

"Yes. And my grandfather had the perception with which the new world was hidden from the old. It is his counter I now hold. There is an old prophecy, telling of a time when the seven counters will come together and our world will again be united and ruled by the Keepers' Council. Perhaps that day is nearer than I imagined."

I picked up a piece of bread. "Maybe so."

Shahzad filled his plate and smiled a white-toothed grin. "Tomorrow we journey together to Algonia, my fellow Keeper."

"With our counters, we can go tonight." I appreciated Chief Haman's hospitality, but I had no desire to be here longer than necessary. I could only imagine what Ellie was going through. Hopefully, she still wanted to marry me after all this.

Shahzad gave me a stern look. "It would be impolite to call on Archidus this late in the day. Tomorrow morning we will see my old friend."

Impolite? I shook my head. *When is Archidus ever polite when he calls on me? I should give him a piece of my mind the next time I see him.* He couldn't keep yanking me out of my world without a moment's notice. I had a life too. I would endure one more night in this sweltering tent village, and then I was going home.

Shahzad must have informed Chief Haman and his guards that I didn't need watching over any more. My credentials as the Protector seemed to grant me free access to the village, and I wandered through the maze of tents and animals once the sun set. What a waste of my three days at home. I imagined the conversation between my roomy and me. "What did you do over the weekend?" he'd ask. I'd answer, "Nothing much. I sat sweating through my clothes in tents at an oasis in the middle of the desert for three days, waiting on some magi guy. How about you?"

I'd looked forward to this weekend for too long. I wouldn't roll over and miss it without a fight. As soon as I got back, I'd use my counter and return to Friday night. I wanted a do-over.

—✦—

Early the next morning Shahzad's voice awoke me. "Protector, it is time. I prefer to get an early start when I travel."

I groaned, reluctant to leave sleep behind. "We could've gone last night, you know. That would've been an even earlier start."

His deep laugh resonated through the tent. "Come, Keeper. I'll prepare the horses."

I pulled on my boots and checked the location of my counter before standing. Still half asleep, I staggered into the cool of early dawn. I jogged to catch Shahzad. "Horses? Who said anything about horses? I'm using my counter to get there." No way was I riding a horse all the way to Algonia.

Shahzad kept up his brisk pace. "Who said anything about not using our counters?"

"But you said you'd prepare the horses. I don't think we need horses."

"I disagree. And I'm not about to abandon my horses at this oasis. They are two of the finest steeds this side of the border."

The man wasn't worth arguing with. I'd follow along for now, but if we weren't on our way to Algonia soon, I'd part company with him and use the Return button on my counter. It should take me to Witches Hollow. From there I'd find the fortress city and demand Archidus send me back to the old world.

"You ride the gray. Here's a saddle." I took the armful of tack he offered me and saddled the dappled-gray gelding. Dancing in anticipation of the ride, the Arabian horses had delicate faces with soft, wide-set eyes.

Shahzad climbed into his saddle before I finished with mine. It had been a long time since I'd ridden. The last time was in Algonia, with Marcus, Brierly, and Garrick. I climbed onto the animal's back and found I'd missed the feel of a horse beneath me. Maybe I *would* ride with the magi for a while.

He chuckled. "Now for our counters. I'll meet you at the fortress city."

I looked up from adjusting my stirrups to see the magi and his horse disappear into thin air. I smiled as I pulled out my counter, clicked it open, and pressed Return. The air shimmered. The gelding pranced beneath me at the sensation. Clutching the reins, I closed my counter and stuffed it in my pocket.

We appeared in Witches Hollow. The horse raised his head and neighed, probably unhappy at suddenly being separated from the herd.

He felt like a rocket about to explode between my knees. I guided him to the path and gave him his head. Dirt sprayed the trees of Witches Hollow as he galloped away. I lowered my head next to the gelding's neck. The speed brought a rush of adrenaline as I dodged low-hanging branches and jumped my mount over fallen logs. The horses had been a good idea. I'd be at the fortress city in no time.

We burst through the trees into the open. I galloped the horse to the entrance in the city's massive wall. After sliding to a stop at the gate, I jumped down. The Algonians had been busy since I'd left here. I pounded on their new wooden door.

The peephole slid open. "The Protector, here to see Master Archidus," I said.

The heavy door opened with a creak, surprising me. I had expected to either sit and wait or climb the rope ladder to enter. I mounted my lathered horse and trotted through the gate.

The guards closed the door behind me and went back to their business, completely ignoring me. I'd show myself to the castle, I guess. The high-strung Arabian pranced up the cobblestone streets. As we neared the courtyard his ears pricked forward and he let out a shrill neigh. Another horse answered. I peered ahead and saw Shahzad walking through the castle door. *He beat me here.*

A groom stepped forward to take my horse when I dismounted. I thanked him, then jogged through the doorway. I ran my fingers through my sweaty hair and attempted to brush the dirt off my clothes. "Hey, Shahzad, wait up, man."

He finished speaking with the butler, who told him Archidus was waiting for us upstairs. I had worked up a sweat, but the magi looked totally relaxed. "Where did you go?" he asked me.

"Witches Hollow. How about you?"

"The gate to the city. Did I not tell you I'd meet you at the fortress city?"

I fell into step next to him. "Yeah, I guess you did."

We showed ourselves to the great hall and knocked. I squared my shoulders and tried to stand taller. I should tell Archidus that

I expected a day's warning if he ever yanked me back to Witches Hollow again, then demand to be sent home at once.

Archidus' guard opened the door and bade us enter. The Master sat at the head of the table with a feast spread before him. "Come in, Keepers. I've been expecting you."

One look at Archidus and I bit back the reprimand on the tip of my tongue. He had aged years instead of months since the last time I'd seen him. When he moved to greet the magi, the Master's previously confident stride was a limp, and his salt-and-pepper hair was more salt than pepper. Azalit hadn't exaggerated when she said her father nearly died. Clearly he still hadn't returned to full health.

"Shahzad, my old friend and the last of the magi, 'tis good to see you again," Archidus said, offering his hand.

"It has been too long, my friend. Is the council being reunited?"

Still clasping Shahzad's wrist, the Master smiled at him. "Not yet, but soon. First, let me get our young Protector on his way. I perceive he is unhappy with me at the moment."

I lowered my head. "Sorry."

"There is no need to apologize. It warms my heart to see you well. There was a time I feared you were lost. But you have returned to us, and we are grateful for your victory. Wickliff never tires of telling your story. You're welcome to food and drink before you leave, if you wish."

I surveyed the table and picked up two star-shaped rolls sprinkled with sugar. "Thanks. I'll take these for the road." I walked toward the door. "You'll send me back once I get to Witches Hollow?"

"Of course."

I paused. "Do I have to walk? Or can I use my counter?"

"The counter is fine. Shahzad, show him, please."

Shahzad took my counter, adjusted the tiny globe, and returned it to me. "This is the location for the fortress city or Witches Hollow. Use your mind to place yourself where you wish to appear."

When my fingers touched the counter, it lit up again. Shahzad had placed the pinpoint of light over what I knew was Tennessee.

"Thanks, Shahzad. It was nice meeting you. Master Archidus, I'm glad to see you made it home safely, sir." I nodded farewell and pressed Go.

Immediately, I appeared at Witches Hollow. I closed my counter and waited to be sent home. I took a bite of a sugar-sprinkled roll. Before I finished chewing, I was plunged into the abyss. I dropped onto the edge of my bed, which immediately erupted in a scream.

"Chase! Is that you?" Ellie's frantic voice filled the darkness as she clutched at my arm.

I pulled her to me. "It's okay. It's me. What are you doing here?"

She let out a muffled sob against my chest. "Waiting for you. Where were you?"

The sweet smell of her hair was intoxicating. I smoothed it away from her face and kissed her. Focused on her lips, I forgot her question until she put her hand on my cheek and turned her face aside. "Chase, please tell me where you went."

I dropped the rolls behind me on the bed and held her face in my hands. "Algonia," I said, picking up kissing where I'd left off. "I missed you."

She wiggled away again. "Why didn't you tell me you were going? You always tell me when you leave. You have no idea how devastating it was for me to find you gone."

I flipped on the lamp next to my bed. "I'm sorry. I didn't know it was going to happen like that or I would have."

Ellie wiped her eyes. "At least you're safe. That's all that matters now."

I picked up the roll I'd started eating in Algonia, took another bite, and then offered the rest to her. "Are you hungry?"

Her face brightened with recognition. "The star rolls—my favorite." She took a bite and closed her eyes while she chewed. "How do you suppose they make these? I tried many times to duplicate them in Vandalia, but could never get it quite right."

I smiled. "Magic. If you can't make them they must be made with magic." Watching her savor the sweet roll gave me an idea. I picked up the second roll and held it behind my back, while I got off the bed. "Ellie, I'm going to the bathroom. I'll see you in a minute, okay?"

She ate the last bite of the roll and licked the sugar from her fingertips. "Thank you. That was delicious. You should tell your mother you're back. She may have been even more worried than I."

I stood near the doorway, enjoying the sight of Ellie in my bed. "I'll take care of my mom. Don't worry."

We exchanged smiles, and I stepped into the hall. I would definitely take care of my mother's worries—I'd go back and erase them altogether.

I slipped into the bathroom and pulled out my counter. After setting the date for Saturday and envisioning Ellie's room in the early morning, I pressed Go. I shimmered into the past and left that alternate reality behind.

FIVE

Reinforcements

The blur cleared and I stood in the spare room at my cousin Adam's house. Ellie's even breathing told me she was still asleep. I sat on the rocking chair in the corner. Suddenly she awoke and saw me.

"What are you doing?" she asked.

I walked to the side of her bed. "Are you hungry? I brought you something. I believe it's one of your favorites." I offered her the star roll.

She gasped. "Where did you get this?"

I smiled at her. "Algonia."

She turned the roll over in her hand. "How did you know they're my favorite? Davy knew, but I don't recall you and I ever talking about it."

I chuckled. "I have my sources. Try it. See if it's as good as you remember."

She took a small bite and closed her eyes. Chewing slowly, she let out a sigh. "Mmm . . . yes, it is as good as I remember. Maybe even better."

I sat next to her. "I'm glad you like it. Now, what should we do today?"

She narrowed her eyes as she looked me over and touched my lip. "Whatever were you doing in Algonia? Were you in a fight?"

I wrapped my hand around hers. "It's nothing. I wasn't in a fight. I just got hit once before they knew who I was. Friday night Archidus sent me to collect Davy's counter when he passed away in 1896."

Ellie froze, her eyes wide as she stared back at me. "Oh no."

I shook my head. "It's okay. I was sad at first too, but he was an old man. He'd lived a full life and was ready to die. He was surrounded by family and loved ones." She seemed to think for a minute, and I thought I saw tears gathering in her eyes. "You'll see him again," I said. "I promise. We'll go back in time and see him and Sylvia when they're young. We'll see them each year, so it will be like we grew old with them."

Ellie nodded. "You promise?"

"Of course, when have I ever let you down?"

That got a chuckle out of her. "Well, I don't recall you informing me that you were going anywhere last night, let alone Algonia."

"I didn't tell you because it was the middle of the night, and I figured it would be a quick trip. But then Archidus pulled me back to Witches Hollow. He didn't tell me in advance, just yanked me out of my bed and sent me on a wild-goose chase to find the guy I was supposed to give Davy's counter to."

Worry clouded Ellie expression. "How long were you gone?"

"Not long—about two days," I said, rounding down.

She ran the tips of her fingers across my hand. "I'm glad you're back safely. I can't imagine the horror I'd feel should I find you missing someday."

I leaned in and kissed her. "I'm glad I am too."

—⬥—

My weekend at home was everything I'd hoped for. During the week, I regularly used the counter to see Ellie, but it was a relief to hang out in public with her. Usually, I had to sneak around so my aunt and uncle wouldn't get suspicious. They still didn't know about the counter, and I'd decided to keep it that way. Ellie and I rode horses, filled out our wedding-gift registry, and went to dinner and a movie.

Sunday night I drove to Eugene, parked my Camaro, and walked into Carson Hall. As I neared the door to my dorm, I heard girls laughing in the room. Hadn't Robert told me he wasn't much of a ladies' man? I thought about leaving and coming back later. But this was my room, and I was tired. They'd have to take their party elsewhere. I unlocked the door and opened it.

"You're back," a familiar voice said. "We've been waiting for you."

This spelled trouble. Apparently, the pretty blond I'd met outside the janitor's closet hadn't given up on me. In another lifetime, I might have been interested, but not now. Not after meeting Ellie.

"Jenna . . ." I said. She crossed the room and opened her arms to hug me. I dodged past her and tossed my gym bag on the bed.

Sitting by Robert on his bed, Jenna's friend Cynthia had her flirt-o-meter cranked up to high. Poor guy didn't realize the only reason she was here was to get Jenna through my door. With my back turned, I tried to ignore the girls. But Jenna made it impossible when she ran her hands across my shoulders and said, "You feel tense. Sit down and I'll give you a massage."

I shook my head. "I am tense. But you're why. You should leave. And take Cynthia with you. Robert and I have to get to bed," I said sternly, giving her my coldest shoulder.

But her hands didn't leave my back. "Chase, what's the matter? Why are you in such a bad mood? Girlfriend problems?"

I spun around and grabbed her wrists. I sniffed her breath. It smelled like alcohol. "Are you drunk?"

She frowned as she pulled away. "I just had one tiny drink . . . or maybe two. But I am not drunk."

Pulling her alongside me, I walked to where Cynthia sat next to Robert. She whispered in his ear, while he tried to tutor her on math. I slammed Cynthia's Algebra book closed and handed it to her, then pulled her to her feet and marched her out the door with Jenna. "Good night ladies," I said. I closed the door and locked it.

"Are you tired?" Robert asked, looking a bit disheveled, like Cynthia might have run her fingers through his hair.

"Tired of them." I hitched my thumb over my shoulder at the closed door.

Robert adjusted his glasses and straightened his shirt collar. "They seem like nice girls."

"They're too pushy for my taste. Robert, there is a way better girl out there for you."

He shrugged his shoulders. "So, how was your trip?"

I smiled at the thought of my long weekend and the unplanned detour to Algonia. "It was real good. Thanks for asking." I lay back on my bed and tucked my hands under my head. "And you?"

He grinned across the room at me. "It was good. Jenna and Cynthia needed help with their math, but Jenna couldn't stop asking questions about you and your girlfriend."

"I've got to get her to back off. This crap's gonna drive me crazy," I muttered.

"No one's ever seen this fiancé you keep talking about. You can't blame them for being skeptical. And it is kind of weird for a college freshman to be engaged. Don't be mad at me for repeating this, but they're starting to wonder if you don't like girls."

I shot out of bed like a bullet. "Why would they think that?"

Robert leaned away as I towered over him. "They don't understand why you don't notice any of them, I guess."

I stepped back and sat on the bed. "That rumor has got to stop tomorrow. I'm not going to have people thinking that. But how?"

"Start going out with some of the girls."

I looked Robert in the eye and frowned. "I'm engaged. I can't cheat on Ellie, plus I wouldn't want to."

"Then maybe you should get her down here."

— ❖ —

Jenna's pestering never let up. She conveniently went to exercise at the same time I left for track practice. Although she acted surprised to bump into me, I knew it was intentional, and every day she talked my sullen ear off the whole way across campus. I lasted two weeks before I decided to bring in reinforcements.

I texted Ellie. "Can u come down here 4 a few hours?" While I dressed for track, I waited for her reply. My phone soon vibrated with the response. "I think I can get off work early. What's wrong?"

I typed, "Wait 4 me behind the daycare. Be there in 5."

I darted upstairs to the janitor's closet and set my counter. After pressing Go, I appeared by the dumpsters. Not a soul was in sight, so I slung my gym bag over my shoulder and walked to the door. It stood partially open, and I heard Ellie say, "Thanks, Susan. I appreciate you letting me go early. Good night."

When my fiancé rushed out the door, I pulled her into my arms. "Thanks, Ellie."

Her lips turned down in a frown. "What's the emergency? Is something wrong?"

I smiled at her, still trying to figure out how to explain my girl problems. "I need somebody to protect me."

Ellie laughed. "What could I possibly do for a big, strong guy like you?"

After scanning the area for bystanders, I looked down at my counter. "Hopefully a lot." With my arm around her, I pressed Return. Darkness enveloped us when we appeared in the closet.

"Where are we?" Ellie whispered.

I felt for the door handle but didn't turn it. "We're in the janitor's closet in my dorm. There's this girl named Jenna who's trying to make me her next conquest. I've done nothing to encourage her—I swear. But she won't leave me alone. I don't think she believes I'm really engaged. I need you to hang out for a while. Maybe if she sees me with you she'll get it through that dumb-blond head of hers that I'm not interested."

When Ellie didn't respond, I pushed the door open to let in some light, wondering if she was upset. Her expression was unreadable. "Should we get out of the closet?" I said.

She stepped into the hall. "I don't understand why you're so angry about this."

I followed her. "Who said I was mad?"

"I haven't heard you sound this upset in a long time, if ever."

I grabbed her hand and led the way down the hall. "Maybe I am mad. The whole thing's stupid. Why can't the girls leave me alone?"

She laughed at me. "Chase darling, if you weren't so dashingly handsome I'd understand your complaint. As it is, you'll get little sympathy from me. Are you forgetting *I'm* one of those girls who can't leave you alone?"

She was irresistible when she flirted, and I smiled. "But you're different, Ellie. I don't want *you* to leave me alone." I opened the door to the dorm building for her. A gentle rain fell on the sidewalk. Wrapping my arm around her shoulders, I pulled her next to me. We walked around the corner, and there was Jenna, as predictable as the sunrise. I turned and whispered in Ellie's ear. "That's her—black yoga pants, white U of O dance-team sweatshirt, standing near the steps."

Ellie glanced over her shoulder and flashed an amused smile. "Looks like she's stalking you."

I rolled my eyes and averted my gaze.

"Should I stake my claim?" my fiancé asked with a grin.

"Please do."

As Jenna closed the distance, Ellie went up on her tiptoes to kiss me. With that kiss, the blinders went on and I became oblivious to everything except her. I buried my fingers in her curls and held her there, kissing her soundly, until Jenna's voice broke the spell. "Hey, Chase."

I stopped kissing Ellie but let my eyes linger on her for a moment. "Yeah?"

"Are you going to introduce me?"

No, I thought. But that would be rude. "Jenna, I'd like you to meet my fiancé, Ellie Williams."

Ellie, ever the polite one, said, "Jenna, it's nice to meet you." Then she turned to me. "Chase darling, don't we need to get you to track practice?"

"Yeah," I muttered, trying not to laugh at the stunned expression on Jenna's face.

"Well, come on then." Ellie put her arm around mine and propelled me past Jenna.

I glanced over my shoulder when we were out of earshot. Jenna stood rooted in place, the drizzle of rain ruining her perfect hair. I chuckled at how easy it had been for Ellie to set Jenna straight. Now, hopefully she would stay out of my life. "Thanks, Ellie. You're awesome."

"You're welcome. After the last year and a half, it's in my best interest to protect you," she said in all seriousness. "I can't afford to lose you again, for any reason."

"Don't worry. No girl could ever replace you."

I stopped at the edge of the track. Other runners were warming up, and I saw the javelin coach glance in my direction. I hadn't thought through my plan beyond having Jenna meet Ellie. "Well, do you want me to take you back before I go to practice?"

"I can wait for you. I'll look around the campus. And then maybe we can get something to eat tonight."

I dug the key to my room out of my gym bag. "If you want, you can hang out in my room. Go back to the building we came from—room 237. Knock before you go in, in case Robert's in there."

Ellie took the key and kissed me goodbye.

"Where r u?" I typed into my phone. Practice had gone over. It was dark by the time coach let us go, and I hoped Ellie had safely made her way back to my room. I slid my phone open at the first hint of vibration. It was a message from her. "I'm in ur room talking to Robert." I replied, "Good, I'll be there soon."

I dropped the phone in my gym bag and jogged across campus, wondering if her appearance had shocked my roommate. I took the stairs two at a time, anxious to see Ellie.

SIX

December 29

My mom had threatened me within an inch of my life if I was late for my own wedding. Since Ellie and the bridesmaids had hair appointments on the morning of the big day, I'd jumped at the chance to play a little basketball with Adam at the high school gym. Our one-on-one gradually expanded to five-on-five as some of the members of this year's high school team joined us.

I passed over my tuxedo and the extra one we'd rented in a slightly bigger size, choosing instead to put on my frontier clothes. I ran my fingers through my hair, brushing off the excess water from my shower. I pulled out my counter and set it for Vandalia, Illinois, July 4, 1835.

It's true, I had procrastinated. I should have asked Garrick a long time ago to be my best man, but there had always been something else to do. It was now or never, and I wouldn't hear the end of it if I didn't invite him to my wedding.

Imagining his cabin in Vandalia, I pressed Shuffle and Go. Once I landed in the first shuffle zone, I relaxed. Now I had all the time in the world. When the shimmer cleared after my last shuffle, I saw the cabin. Davy's wife Sylvia was taking laundry off the line next to the house.

"Sylvia, happy Fourth of July," I said.

She whipped her head around and then smiled. "Mr. Harper, where'd you come from? If I didn't know Davy and Garrick were so fond of you, I'd think you were up to no good, sneaking around behind me like that."

As she turned to face me, I could see she was expecting a baby. I walked toward her and picked up the laundry basket. "Sorry, I didn't mean to startle you."

She massaged her lower back. "I'll finish that later. Come sit on the porch and I'll get you something to drink."

I started pulling clothes off the line and folding them. The fabric was warm and slightly stiff after hanging in the hot sun. "You sit down and let me get the rest of these. You might have to refold them, though. I'm not doing as good a job as you."

Sylvia breathed a sigh of relief as she eased herself into the rocker on the porch. "Thank you, Mr. Harper. Frankly, I don't care how they're folded at this point."

I pulled the last of her clothes off the line and carried the basket to her. "When do you think Garrick and Davy will return?"

"Any day now. They made an extra run to St. Louis last week. Garrick mentioned you might be visiting. He said you should wait for him here."

I sat on the steps and rested my elbows on my knees. "When's your baby due?"

"Another month or so. I'll confess I'm a wee bit nervous. I had an aunt who died giving birth to her first."

Childbirth in 1835 definitely had its risks, but I wasn't worried for Sylvia, because I knew she would live to be an old woman. And I'd heard multiple children saying goodbye at Davy's bedside. I smiled. "Sylvia, everything will be fine. You'll have lots of children. Just wait and see."

She rested her hands on her stomach. "I do hope you're right."

—◈—

Two days later, Garrick and Davy pulled into the yard with their empty wagon. I had offered to help out, so Sylvia put me to work on Davy and Garrick's unfinished projects around their cabin. But even with keeping busy, the waiting nearly killed me. My wedding should have been two days ago.

When I heard their horses enter the yard, I left the dinner table. Garrick and Davy climbed down from the freight wagon. "Hey, you're late," I yelled.

Garrick turned at the sound of my voice. "Little brother, I was afraid we'd missed you." He wrapped an arm around me. "I'm sorry I wasn't here. One of our best customers had a shipment delayed out of New Orleans. We couldn't leave St. Louis without it."

Davy nodded in my direction as he left what he was doing to greet Sylvia, who had followed me outside. I waved and smiled, then turned to Garrick.

"I've been here for two days doing your chores. You owe me."

Garrick started tending to the team. "Anything. You name it."

I unhitched the second gelding in the string for him. "Come with me for a day. I'm getting married, and I want you to be my best man."

My friend grinned. "Sure, I'd love to. It's about time you tied the knot. I thought you'd never get around to marrying that girl."

"Yeah, me too. I thought I'd be stuck waitin' for you forever."

Garrick dropped his voice a notch and grinned. "Don't go complaining to me, Harper. You know you could've jumped ahead and found us."

We turned the horses loose in the corral and slung the tack over our shoulders. "Like that would work. How was I supposed to explain popping in and out every day to Sylvia?"

"You could've figured something out."

"Truth is, Sylvia looked like she could use a hand around here."

"Yeah, business has been booming for Davy and me. We've been out of town more than we should. I'll finish up with these horses, and then we'll go get you married."

After we fed the stock, we sat down to dinner. Davy had declined my invitation to attend the wedding, as he didn't want to leave his wife. He pushed his plate away, offered Sylvia his hand, and said, "Take a walk with me? It'll be a beautiful sunset tonight."

She smiled. "The dishes need doing."

"They can wait. I'll do them when we return. Come on, I've missed you."

She slid her chair back. "All right then." They strolled out of the cabin, hand in hand.

Garrick picked up the pail and started for the door. "I'll fetch some water and get cleaned up. Then we'll take off."

"Let's leave now. You can clean up at my house." With Davy and Sylvia gone, I spoke freely. "It'll be faster—hot shower, soap, shampoo, deodorant. Plus, I'm tired of waitin' for you."

Garrick looked out the open door, probably making sure Davy and Sylvia hadn't turned back. "Okay. Are you taking us or am I?"

I pulled out my counter. "I will."

Garrick dropped his hand on my shoulder. Without any hesitation, I pressed Shuffle and then Return.

We appeared in the Sahara Desert. Gusting wind whipped orange sand into our faces. It pricked our bare skin like the tips of a hundred pins. "Aren't you glad you waited to shower?" I yelled over the roar of the wind.

Squinting his eyes, Garrick turned his back to the onslaught of sand. "Don't be so smug. You're not always right."

We shook the sand off of our clothes during the next four shuffles and ultimately returned to my bedroom.

"When is this wedding?" Garrick asked.

"Now. We've got less than half an hour to be at the church. You shower upstairs. I'll run down to my parents' bathroom." I pointed to the extra tux. "That one's for you. I guessed on the size, so I hope it fits. See you in a minute."

Garrick kicked off his boots and smiled. "You sure know how to give a guy advance warning."

I dashed downstairs and ran past my dad. He was fastening the cuff links on his shirt. "What're you doing now?"

"I need to shower," I replied.

"I thought you just got out of the shower."

I turned on the water and stepped into the spray. "I need to shower again," I yelled.

Garrick and I showered and shaved in record time. We stood side by side buttoning our shirts when my dad walked into the room. He looked surprised at the sight of my best man, but he recovered quickly. "Good to see you again, Garrick." He paused, watching us put on our bow ties. "Um, Son, do you have any questions for me? Since . . . well, you know . . . with it being your wedding night."

Both my dad and Garrick looked at me, waiting. "No, Dad, I think I got it."

He released a visible sigh. "Okay, good. We'd better leave soon or your mother's not going to be happy."

"We're almost ready. I'll follow you in my car," I said.

Garrick and I hustled to the Camaro, and I followed my dad's BMW out of the driveway.

Garrick cleared his throat. "Little brother, have you ever been with a woman before?"

I looked across the car at him. From his expression, it was clear he wasn't joking and expected an answer. "No," I said.

He smiled that mischievous grin I'd seen a hundred times before. "Then I don't think you 'got it,' little brother. Let me educate you."

—◆—

Garrick had my rapt attention until my dad's tapping on my car's windshield brought me back to reality. I rolled down the window.

"What're you still doing in the car?" my dad said. "Your mom sent me out to find you. You having second thoughts? Because if you are, we don't have to go through with this. You know I always thought you were too young to be getting married."

I pulled my keys from the ignition. "Dad, I'm not having second thoughts. I'm coming."

Garrick opened his car door. "Come on, little brother. Let's go get you married. By the way, you didn't give me enough time to get you a wedding present. So I think I'll let my older, richer self take care of that." He grinned. "I did good on the graduation present, don't you think?"

"Yes, you did—I love this car. But just having you here is a present. So don't worry about it."

The two of us ran into the church and took our places.

It was impossible not to fidget—standing there on display, in front of all my family and friends. My insides felt like they were on a roller coaster. How much longer would it be until Ellie came out to stand across from me? That was bound to improve things. At least half of the eyes would shift to her, if not all.

The bridesmaids entered first—Lauren, one of Ellie's friends from school, followed by my cousin Amanda, and then my twin sister Jessica. Garrick gave my shoulder a reassuring squeeze when the wedding march began.

Ellie entered on the arm of my uncle Steve, whose house she had stayed at for the past year. My eyes, along with those of everyone else in the room, followed her graceful walk down the aisle. She was the picture of perfection with her fancy updo and a shimmering veil draped over her shoulders. She held a bouquet of lilies, and the train of her dress seemed to float along the floor behind her. She lifted her dress and stepped up next to me with a smile. I winked at her.

I don't remember a thing the pastor said in the way of advice. I was too distracted by the beautiful bride before me.

"Do you, Joseph Chase Harper, take Ellen Elizabeth Williams to be your lawfully wedded wife . . ." Finally, all the waiting, all the searching—and all the praying that I'd find her before Legard did—had paid off. Ellie would be my wife, just like I'd imagined so many times before.

The pastor finished the question, paused, and then cleared his throat as he looked at me. "Yes, I do," I said.

He then turned to Ellie. "Do you, Ellen Elizabeth Williams, take Joseph Chase Harper to be your lawfully wedded husband, to cherish and to hold in sickness and in health, till death do you part?"

Ellie smiled at me through her veil. "I do."

"Then by the power vested in me by the state of Oregon, I pronounce you, Joseph Chase Harper, and you, Ellen Elizabeth Williams, husband and wife, legally and lawfully wedded. Mr. Harper, you may kiss the bride."

Slowly, I lifted her veil and pushed it gently over her head. I stepped closer and raised my hand to her cheek. Although I'd kissed her more times than I could count, this kiss felt different. It was sweeter, full of love and the promise of sharing our lives with each other. Oblivious to my surroundings, I lingered, savoring the kiss until Ellie pulled back. "I love you," she whispered.

Before turning to face the crowd of well wishers, I whispered back, "I love you too."

The rest of the day rushed by in a whirlwind of wedding festivities. When everything was over, my dad pulled me aside and said, "You got everything arranged for your trip to Hawaii, right?"

"Yeah, Dad, I got it all figured out."

Ellie and I darted through a rainstorm of rice to my newly decorated Camaro. White letters reading "JUST MARRIED" covered the back window. We drove out of the parking lot with a line of clanging cans behind us. Garrick stood next to my mom and Jessica. He'd find his way home. Who knows, maybe he'd stick around a while.

"Where to now?" Ellie asked.

I looked across the car at her. "Honeymoon, but I want it to be a surprise."

I had reservations at the Grand Wailea Resort in Maui. Ellie and I would enjoy a week of honeymooning on sandy beaches, with midnight walks under the moonlight, listening to the crash of the surf. I'd treat her to the finest dining, and if she felt so inclined, perhaps I'd teach her to swim. I didn't drive to the airport, though. I returned home and parked my car in the shop, hiding it behind closed doors.

I grabbed Ellie's bag from the back seat and opened her door. She laughed. "This is some big surprise."

I kissed her. "Just wait. I'll be right back. I've got to get my stuff."

She folded her arms against the chill of the shop and smiled. "I'll wait here."

Moments later, I dashed out of the house. I set the counter coordinates for the island of Maui, today's date. I slung my bag over my shoulder, picked up Ellie's, and offered her my arm. I had scoped out the lay of the hotel last week. I envisioned the dark, foliaged area near the parking garage and pressed Go.

"It's warm here," Ellie whispered a few seconds later as she reached to touch one of the exotic plants. "Where are we?"

The sound of an approaching security guard patrolling the grounds in a golf cart kept us hidden in the shadows. I waited to answer my wife's question. After the guard passed, I led Ellie to a rock path lined with lights and brilliant purple flowers with oversized green leaves. "Welcome to Hawaii, Mrs. Harper."

Ellie leaned her head against my shoulder. "I certainly like the sound of that."

After we checked in, the clerk behind the massive mahogany desk handed me two key cards and a map of the resort. "You're in room 657." He pointed at the large brass doors of the elevator. "Take the elevator to the sixth floor and turn right. Congratulations and enjoy your stay, Mr. and Mrs. Harper."

As we waited for the elevator, I watched Ellie. She lifted the purple-and-white lei they had given her to her nose, breathing in its sweetness, and then followed me. Wonder lit her face as she scanned the elegant furnishings of the hotel lobby. Fancy water fountains and sculptures were set in shallow pools of water running the length of the large room. A bell sounded as the elevator opened, and I stepped in.

The full skirt of Ellie's wedding dress brushed against my legs as she walked past me. I dropped our bags and wrapped my arms around her. We kissed until the bell signaled we were stopping. I moved away, leaving her face flushed. We had stopped on the fifth floor. When the door opened, two girls probably in their early teens stepped into the elevator. They stared at Ellie. When the door opened on the sixth floor and we stepped out, one of the girls said, "You're really pretty. I like your dress."

Ellie smiled and thanked her. The doors closed behind us and we were alone. "Chase, I've never seen such elegance in all my life. I never dreamed a place like this existed. What year are we in?"

I stopped in front of room 657 and slid the key card in and out of the slot. The small light flashed green, and I opened the door. "The present. It's still our wedding day."

A ceiling fan turned slowly, casting dancing shadows across the room, while a Hawaiian melody played from the TV. Pink flower petals dotted the pristine white comforter. Two chocolate mints lay on each pillow. I set our bags down and went into the bathroom, leaving Ellie to peruse the room at her leisure.

As I turned off the light in the bathroom and stepped into the hall, she walked in from the balcony and closed the glass door. Her white shoes lay in the middle of the floor. Her veil had been draped across a chair. She walked to the edge of the bed and picked up one of the flowers. "It's beautiful here."

I set my suit coat on the arm of the chair and removed the burgundy bow tie. After dropping it onto the tux, I undid my top button and my cuff links. I crossed the room to her, clearing my throat. "Not as beautiful as you are."

My mind raced through Garrick's lesson on women. I kissed my way down her neck while she unbuttoned my shirt. She slid it off of my shoulders, her fingers tracing the line of muscle down my biceps. I set my knee on the edge of the bed, planning to lower her onto the petal-covered mattress. I'd waited so long for this. It almost seemed too good to be true.

SEVEN

Reconvene

I felt myself suddenly yanked away from Ellie and plunged into the dark abyss. It *had* been too good to be true. When I was released from the darkness, I stumbled forward and fell to my hands and knees. I slammed my fist into the ground. "Dang it, dang it, dang it! You have got to be kidding me," I yelled. I dropped my head into my hands. "I'm going to kill him for this."

Garrick's laugh resonated behind me. "Good luck with that, little brother."

I jerked my head around and climbed to my feet. In no mood for his teasing, I said, "What're you laughing at?"

He pointed at my shirt, hanging from my elbows, and let out another round of laughter. "It doesn't look like you made it far."

I yanked my shirt back on and began buttoning it. "Knock it off. What are we doing here, anyway?"

Garrick pulled off his bow tie and stuffed it in his pocket. He undid the top button on his shirt. "Don't know. What are *you* doing here?"

"Shut up."

A grunt sounded on the other side of Witches Hollow. Garrick and I turned to see Raoul Devereux—Wisdom's Keeper—climb to his feet.

Garrick crossed the hollow and shook his hand. "Wise Wolf. How you doin', man?"

"Good," Raoul said. "And you?"

"Never better." Garrick pointed at me. "But Harper isn't too happy. Archidus pulled him away from his honeymoon."

I slumped onto a protruding root, wanting nothing to do with their small talk. From the way Garrick was laughing and talking you'd think he'd just opened a birthday present, but for me this was the last place I wanted to be, especially tonight. There had better be a good reason for this. I needed to get back to Ellie. She would not be happy about me disappearing.

The cheerful banter between Raoul and Garrick continued until another Keeper dropped into the center of Witches Hollow. It was Illusion's Keeper—Mei-Lien, the sharp-tongued, karate-chopping Chinese woman from San Francisco. She climbed to her feet and brushed the dried leaves off her pantsuit and asked, "What is the meaning of this?"

We all had the same question, and none of us knew the answer. I stood and left the hollow, taking the path leading to Cadré Unair, the fortress city. I set a furious pace, leaving Garrick and the others behind. A few minutes later, I remembered my counter and the lesson I'd received from Shahzad. I pulled it out, set the globe for that spot near Tennessee, and pressed Go. I focused on the steps of the castle. I wouldn't be swayed from my determination to return to Ellie.

I reappeared outside the fortress gates instead and wondered if Master Archidus had some kind of shield to keep people from popping into the fortress city by magic. I raised my hand and banged on the door. The guard opened the peephole. "What's yer business in the capital city?"

"I'm Protector's Keeper and I need to see Master Archidus. It's urgent."

"You may enter."

The heavy doors creaked and groaned on their hinges. The way opened before me, and I marched into the capital city. It wasn't long before I set foot in the castle. No one bothered to question me as I found my way to Archidus' great hall. Having summoned all four of us here, there was no doubt he would be expecting a visitor. The guards saw me coming and swung the door open. I stormed into the room. Five individuals sat at the table—Archidus, Wickliff, a blond-haired elf woman, a finely dressed man in his thirties, and Shahzad.

The Master gave me a wry smile and motioned toward the four empty chairs. "Welcome, Protector. Please take a seat. It is good to see you, although I perceive the feeling is once again not mutual."

I didn't accept his offer to sit. "No, it is not. I demand to be sent back at once. Whatever you're doing here will have to wait a week."

"I'm sorry, but it is not feasible to wait. The New Year is but three days hence. The Keepers' Council has been reconvened and must be ready to depart on the first day of the New Year. And whether you like it or not, you are a member of the council, so your attendance is mandatory."

"Then I'm going to have to resign, or quit, or whatever you do to get out of it. I just got married, and I've got commitments on the old world. I can't have you popping me back here anytime you want. That's just not going to work for me anymore."

Archidus' smile faded as he stood and approached me. "You forget, Keeper, that as a human this is not a calling from which you may resign. Your resignation would require your death. Considering what you left behind on the old world, I doubt that is desirable to you. This is now an annual sacrifice you will be expected to make."

I sighed in frustration. "How long do you need me?"

"A month or so."

I groaned. I couldn't leave Ellie hanging in Hawaii. She would be stuck there with no money and a fake I.D., which I doubted could survive airport security and get her home. This time there was no Davy to watch over her, either. "I can't leave my wife where she is now. At least let me go back and get her to a safe location. Please, just let me take her home first and then I'll come right back. I promise."

Archidus rubbed his hand over his neatly trimmed beard. But before he answered, Wickliff cleared his throat. "Sire, may I offer an alternative answer to the problem at hand?"

Archidus turned to Wickliff. "Certainly."

"Perhaps we should bring the girl here. She's been in Algonia before and is somewhat familiar with our world and our customs. It would be a quick solution, and one I think would be acceptable to the Protector." Wickliff winked in my direction. I smiled and turned to hear Archidus' verdict.

"Are you volunteering to get her?" the Master asked

Wickliff chuckled. "Of course. I'd be delighted to fetch the girl, assuming you are willing to send me to where you collected the Protector, or allow me to take him along. Otherwise, I may spend an exorbitant amount of time searching out her whereabouts."

Archidus shook his head in amused dismay. "Protector, you bend my will like a wet reed. Never in our history has there been a more complicated Keeper than you."

Now I was amused. "Thanks. I'll take that as a compliment."

Archidus chuckled as he turned to Wickliff. "I will send you back to the old world. Get the girl and bring her to the castle. She can wait in one of the guest rooms. Tell her the Protector will be sent to her when we're finished with him."

Wickliff nodded. He took three steps toward the door and vanished. I imagined he reappeared in Witches Hollow. Archidus closed his eyes and his brows furrowed. With any luck, Wickliff would soon show up in the hotel room and explain my disappearance to Ellie. I could only hope she would take it well.

A while later, the other three Keepers strolled into the room. "Garrick the Guardian, you are much younger than I expected. Did I not pull you from the same year as the Protector?"

Garrick smiled. "You did, sir, but my twenty-four-year-old self was visiting there for Harper's wedding."

"Ah, I see. With two of you to choose from, it doesn't surprise me that I pulled the most familiar version of the Guardian back to Algonia. Welcome."

Garrick stepped forward and clasped wrists with Archidus. "Thank you, Master. But why exactly are we here?"

"All in good time."

Introductions were made, and we were instructed to take a seat at Archidus' table. The blond-haired elf woman was Kalipsia, Creation's new Keeper, and the finely dressed man was a sorcerer by the name of Castile, Propulsion's new Keeper. Everyone else met Shahzad, Perception's Keeper.

Within the hour Wickliff returned. I breathed a sigh of relief as he nodded in my direction. He had found Ellie, and she was somewhere in the castle waiting for me. I relaxed into my seat and stretched my legs out under the table.

We were instructed on the finer points of Algonian history and customs. This included a detailed explanation of why we were summoned, what was expected of each Keeper, and the duties of the council. Lunch and dinner were served to us in the great hall, and both Garrick and I were yawning as the hours dragged by.

I had noticed the times and seasons in Algonia didn't match up to those in Oregon. When it was summer here, it was winter there. When it was morning here, it was night there. So this day lasted forever. Twice I fell asleep during the lecture, only to have Master Archidus clear his throat and wake me with one of his mind tricks— some kind of magic probe that sent what felt like a low-voltage shock of electricity through my brain. Before we were dismissed, he assigned an Algonian servant to each of us to show us to our rooms.

The servant with me stopped before a closed door. "If you require any services, pull the bell cord over the bed and Heather will assist you." He bowed before turning to leave.

I opened the door quickly. If my wife wasn't in there, I intended to chase down that servant and make him find her for me. The room was filled with the pale glow of the setting sun. Ellie's golden curls lay across the pillow. Her eyes were closed in sleep. I stepped into the room and shut the door. Her wedding gown hung from a hook on the wall, and both of our bags sat on the bench below the window. As I moved toward the bed, her eyes fluttered open. "Chase?"

I leaned over, resting my hand on the bed next to her. "Yeah, it's me. I'm so sorry. I had no idea that was going to happen. I just—"

Ellie raised her finger to my lips and smiled. "Shh. Wickliff explained everything. You have no idea how good it is to be here and have you with me. I was so lonely the last time I slept in this bed. I thought I'd lost you then. But now—" Her fingers moved to the buttons on my shirt. "Where were we, darling?"

—✦—

I woke to the sound of Ellie pulling the curtain aside. She stood with her back to me. The pink glow of early morning filtered into the room. She leaned closer to the window. I smiled, perfectly content to lie in bed and watch my wife. She unhooked the latch on the window and pushed it open. The sound of birds warbling in the trees filled the room, and a breeze fluttered the curtain, carrying with it the smell of lilacs. "Hey, beautiful," I said.

She spun around and smiled. "Good morning, sleepyhead."

I tucked my hands behind my head and chuckled. "Come back to bed."

She meandered across the room and crawled under the covers. A light knock sounded at the door. "Who is it?" Ellie called.

"It's Heather, dear."

Ellie sat up and scooted to the edge of the bed. "Come in."

"What now?" I whispered, rolling my eyes.

"Breakfast, most likely. I'm starving."

The door opened slowly, and a woman carrying a large tray of food stepped in. "Where will you take your meal?"

"The bed, please," Ellie said.

Heather gave me an amused smile and raised her eyebrows. "I see you found your Keeper, Miss Ellie."

"Oh yes, I most certainly did. Chase, I'd like you to meet Heather. She was like a mother to me the last time I was here. And Heather, this is my husband, Chase Harper, also known as the Protector."

I didn't usually meet new people from the comfort of a bed, but I leaned forward and offered her my hand. "It's nice to meet you, Heather."

She shook my hand and then pointed at a blue card on the food tray. "There's a summons from his majesty. He often gets an early start on the day's business, so you may want to take a peek at it before you eat. Wouldn't want you to be late, sir."

I reached for the paper. "Why am I not surprised?"

Heather turned to face Ellie. "I'll be back in an hour to help you dress. I've the perfect gown for you." She turned and walked to the door. "Enjoy your breakfast. If you should require anything before then, ring the bell, dear."

EIGHT

The Council

I marched through the corridors of the castle, my boots clicking against the stone floor. Heather had delivered a stack of Algonian clothing, a pair of boots, and a sword. I had wanted to ignore the blaring blue card with the yellow wax seal, but Ellie opened it anyway. The summons from Archidus required my audience in the great hall immediately following the morning meal. Garrick exited his room ahead of me. "Guardian," I called out to him.

Stopping to wait, he smiled and raised his eyebrows. "Hey, little brother, how you doin' this morning?"

"Good."

"Good? That's all you've got to say?"

I chuckled. "That's all I got to say. How are you this morning, big brother?"

"Not as good as you, but it's nice to be back here. I kinda missed it. I need to find Marcus, though. There's something I want to ask him."

"What's that?"

Shahzad stepped into the hall before Garrick could answer me. "Greetings, fellow Keepers. May I presume you slept well?"

"We did. How about you?" I said.

"Very well indeed."

My second day in Algonia passed much the same as the first. All seven Keepers were trained in the intricacies of Algonian law and the responsibilities of the Keepers' Council. In ancient times the council met annually to tour the land. They stopped in each province, and their visit was cause for a great celebration as the Keepers paraded into the village. Traditionally, on the first night in each province, a large feast was prepared for local dignitaries and council members. In the days that followed, the council would meet to hear grievances and pass judgment on any undecided local cases. In effect, the Keepers' Council was the final court of appeals in the new world. A group of advisors, soldiers, servants, and cooks would accompany the council. As a boy, Shahzad had joined his father on the tour of Algonia when he served on the original council. Shahzad predicted the trip would take about five weeks.

Master Archidus declined the position as advisor to the council due to his poor health and his responsibility to manage the affairs of the kingdom. Wickliff took the assignment in his stead.

A military contingent was assigned to accompany the council and assist in providing protection. Since Garrick's and my primary duties were to guard and protect the council members, we were relieved to know we weren't alone in the assignment.

After three days of intense training, we prepared to depart the capital city. The Keepers were measured and fitted with Algonian clothing—fancier clothes than I'd previously worn there. Heather supplied my wife with a trunk full of dresses that would rival the best gowns of the Victorian Era, or so Ellie said.

On our final day in the great hall, Archidus announced, "You leave tomorrow at first light. Have your trunks packed and left outside your doors before you retire for the evening." The king smiled and looked directly at Garrick. "My new head commander, Marcus Landseer, and his squadron will serve as your escort through Algonia. I perceive that decision meets your approval, Guardian. And you, Protector? Are you also in favor of Commander Landseer leading your guardsmen?"

I nodded my agreement.

Archidus stood. "Then all is settled. Keepers, may you be wise in your counsel and safe in the discharge of your duties. Farewell till we meet again."

A chorus of appreciation and goodbyes erupted around the table. We rose to our feet and took a turn clasping wrists with the Master Keeper and king of Algonia.

I stood behind Garrick when he held Archidus' wrist. "Where is Marcus now?" Garrick asked.

"He was to arrive in Cadré Unair today and will be camped with his men down on the green," Archidus answered.

"Thank you, sir."

I clasped wrists with Archidus and smiled at him. "Thank you for letting Ellie come with me."

"You are most welcome. Have you enjoyed your stay at the castle?"

"Yes, sir, I definitely have. And Ellie really enjoys being here."

"That is good to hear." Archidus lifted his head to look beyond my shoulder, a troubled expression on his face. "Watch over the Guardian. I perceive there is cause for concern."

Caught off guard by the king's last comment, I followed his gaze to the door. Garrick exited the great hall and disappeared around the corner. I looked back at Archidus, but he had already turned to bid Shahzad farewell.

I hustled out of the room and ran down the corridor, which came to a T. "Garrick?" I yelled.

"Yeah?" His voice echoed from down the hall to the left.

I ran to where the hall turned. "Wait up, brother. Where are you off to in such a hurry?" I closed the distance between us.

"I'm going to find Marcus before dinner. Want to come?"

At the edge of the city, we found the large field where the army drilled and practiced. The green also doubled as a camp for troops laying over on their way to assignments. A handful of cook fires burned along the perimeter, leaving the humid air hazy. Garrick stopped the first soldier he came to. "Excuse me, have you seen Marcus Landseer?"

"The commander is at the blacksmith's. That way." The soldier pointed to a building with a large stone chimney.

Marcus was a whirlwind of activity, barking orders left and right. He had horses to be shod, weapons to get repaired, and wagon wheels that needed replacing.

Garrick strode over and slapped him on the back. "Marcus."

The commander whirled around, his scowl melting into a warm smile. "Garrick the Guardian. I didn't expect to see you until the morrow, my friend."

"I couldn't wait. It's been too long. So you're in command now?"

Marcus glanced down and nodded. "'Tis the king's excuse to give me more work, 'tis all."

"Congratulations, though. You deserve the promotion." Garrick acted as if he had something else to say, but he suddenly turned away and clamped his mouth shut.

I stepped closer and clasped wrists with Marcus. "It's good to see you again. I hear you're going with us tomorrow."

"I am. Follow me while I finish checking on our horses."

We tagged along for the next hour, helping where we could and making small talk. I would've bet money that Garrick had something specific he wanted to ask Marcus, and I finally grew tired of waiting. "Garrick, spit it out, brother. I know you've got something else to say, and I'm ready to get back to the castle to have dinner with my wife."

That got Marcus's attention as well as Garrick's. "What can I do for you, Guardian?" the commander asked.

Garrick shot me a dirty look before turning to Marcus. "I'd hoped for some word on your sister."

I raised my eyebrows in surprise, while the commander laughed. "Brierly? Why didn't you just say so? Last I heard she was well, but I've not seen her in quite some time. She is at home with my father in Capstown, the capital of the Wine Province. I believe that is our third stop. If you're inclined to see her, I can arrange a meeting."

"Do you think she'll remember me?"

Marcus appeared to consider the question. "After the passage of this much time, I may need to provide you with an introduction." Garrick looked dumbfounded—clearly that wasn't the answer he was hoping for. But the commander burst out laughing as he slapped him on the shoulder. "Are you daft, man? Of course she remembers you. I'll take you to see her myself as soon as we arrive in Capstown."

Garrick sighed as he smiled back at him. "Thank you."

—✦—

Two days after leaving Cadré Unair, we entered Greenwood, the capital of the Farming Province. The whole town turned out to wave miniature Algonian flags as we rode down their streets, and it reminded me of Hillsboro's Fourth of July parade. We waved and smiled at the enthusiastic crowd.

That night the Keepers' Council attended a dinner celebration with the local magistrate, the sheriff, and the area's prominent landowners. Word had gotten around about my imprisonment in Shuyle, and Marcus's attack on Lord Arbon. The townsfolk peppered us with questions about our escape. Although I'd rather not be reminded of those dark days, I somehow told the stories without triggering any attacks of post-traumatic stress disorder.

Early the next morning, a soldier knocked on my tent pole and informed me that the first case was to be brought before the Keepers' Council in one hour. I dressed, ate, and joined Garrick and Marcus. We walked to the edge of our camp, where a large tent had been erected. The council members sat around a horseshoe-shaped table.

Cases were brought before the council that the local magistrate had been unable to resolve, or those involving people from different jurisdictions. Most were easily resolved through the process of inquisition. Shahzad and Wickliff could both read minds, so if either the plaintiff or the defendant submitted to inquest via magic, the truth was quickly determined.

Wickliff, Raoul, and Shahzad took the lead in deciding cases. Raoul had a knack for understanding and applying the law. No doubt the magic from his counter, Wisdom, had rubbed off on him. Shahzad, Wickliff, and the elves had a wealth of experience, gained through their unnaturally long lives. As a skilled sorcerer, Shahzad knew how to fully tap the magic of his counter, Perception, so he could perceive intentions and decipher what he saw when he read people's minds.

Garrick and I stood guard with Marcus and his men, listening in on the proceedings. If the defendant wasn't present, the job of finding him or her fell to us. We were sent to bring in one guy who didn't show up to a case involving a dispute over property lines. Wickliff used his skills to extract an image of the man's property from the plaintiff, and then he put the image into our memories. We set our counters and disappeared, each taking two soldiers with us. It felt strange to be disappearing with someone other than Ellie, and in front of an audience, no less.

We appeared at the property Wickliff had shown us and found the man working in his barn. He resisted at first, but once we said we were Keepers, he came with us. I'm sure the four burly soldiers guarding our backs helped persuade him as well.

Late in the afternoon, we had a strange case. We heard the two hot-tempered men arguing before we could see them. In the middle of their debate, they stepped into the tent. Shahzad rang the gong and demanded silence. He pointed to the man on the right. "What complaint do you bring before the Keepers' Council?"

"Thank you for hearing me, sir. My name is Alfred. Inferno, my prized stallion, which I raised from birth, disappeared a fortnight ago. After making a thorough search of the surrounding area, I found him on this man's property, covering his mares. Thinking that perchance my horse had simply run away, I went to this man's door with the intent to claim my animal and offer thanks for corralling him. But this man refuses to return Inferno and instead claims to have purchased the horse. The man is a thief, and I don't doubt he's hiding his crime with these lies."

Shahzad nodded his acceptance of the testimony, then pointed to the defendant. "What defense do you provide the council?"

"Sir, I tell no lie. The stallion in question belongs to me. I purchased him from a horse trader, and I have the bill of sale to prove it." The man handed Shahzad a piece of parchment. He read it and passed it to the other members of the council. Mei-Lien, Illusion's Keeper, slid the paper in front of Garrick and me. It read: "Sold one sorrel stallion to Thomas the elder of Greenwood." It was dated and signed. The scrawled signature at the bottom was unreadable.

"Are either of you opposed to inquest by the council?"

"Nay, sir," said the plaintiff and defendant at the same time.

In turn, Shahzad grasped the men's wrists and viewed their memories. Wickliff did the same. The old elf smiled as he released Thomas's wrist. "You both speak the truth."

"Does the horse have any distinctive markings?" Shahzad asked.

"He's solid brown," said Thomas, the man who had purchased the stallion, "but built like an ox, with enough muscle for two, and he has a temper to rival Hades."

"He is brown," Alfred said, "with no white marks, but his color is more like burnished copper, especially in the sunshine. He is built like an ox. He's fast as the wind, and in the wrong hands he might act like Hades to show his displeasure. But Inferno has a heart of gold and is gentle as a kitten. Ask this man if the horse he bought has any scars."

Shahzad looked at Thomas, who answered, "None that I've seen, but I've not owned the animal very long."

Alfred's chin jutted out and he took a step forward. "Inferno has a scar on his belly from getting hung up in the fence as a foal. It runs a hand span near the inside of his left hind leg. Have someone see if the stallion does not have a scar to match the description."

Shahzad said, "The Protector and the Guardian will check the horse."

We stood and received our directions to the property from Shahzad. Marcus came with us, and we disappeared.

The farmyard was well kept. Behind a small barn filled with hay stood a beautiful stallion and five mares. Garrick took the coil of rope off the nail and climbed the fence. He lassoed the horse on the first try. The stallion danced around, shaking his head. The mares trotted away. Garrick calmed the horse enough for Marcus and me to get close, but as soon as anyone touched the horse's belly, or bent to look, he kicked. The hind foot swung so fast and wide that it clipped Marcus's helmet, leaving a small dent and giving the commander a headache.

"Let's pick up a front foot to keep him from kicking," I said.

Garrick held up the animal's left front hoof while I tried to see the scar, but the horse reared up, yanking free.

"Old Thomas is right about the temper like Hades," Garrick said. "He's downright mean."

My mom had raised one of her horses from a foal. That mare was as sweet as could be to my mom, but if anyone else tried to ride her, she'd pin her ears and throw up a buck. I was starting to wonder if this horse had the same temperament. "So," I said, "let's see if Alfred is right. We'll take the horse to him and see if he can be as gentle as a kitten."

"Smart one, little brother," Garrick said. "We don't even know where exactly we are, and you expect us to drag this wild animal all the way back?"

I pulled the rope away from him. "Give me the horse and I'll show you how." With one hand resting on the stallion's neck, I slid my hand in my pocket and pulled out my counter.

NINE

Verdict

I imagined the open space outside the council's tent and pressed Return. I figured the stallion would freak if he reappeared inside surrounded by strange people. As it was, he fought the rope around his neck, dragging me across the dirt and nearly breaking free as we reappeared. The commotion brought people hurrying out of the tent.

Alfred spoke in a soft voice as he came from behind me and took the rope. "Whoa, Ferno. Calm yerself now, lad."

With a rope burn across my left palm, I was more than happy to pass the lead off to someone else. As I joined the crowd of spectators, Thomas said, "You brought the horse here? Are you daft?"

Inferno had quit moving away and seemed to be studying the man holding his rope. Where the stallion had given Garrick and me the wild eye, he lowered his head toward the man in front of him. The animal's whole demeanor changed, and he stepped close to Alfred and nuzzled his chest.

Garrick and Marcus hustled through the tent opening and stopped next to me. I cleared my throat. "Case solved—the horse belongs to Alfred."

Marcus, holding his helmet under his arm, scratched his head. "Would you look at that."

"I'll second that decision," Garrick said.

Thomas stepped forward. "But I bought that horse. I paid good money for him."

The stallion pinned his ears back at Thomas. Alfred raised a finger and looked his horse in the eye. "No," he said firmly, and then turned to other man. "Well, he's probably covered a few of your mares by now, and you'll have some nice foals come spring. That should make up for it. But this here's my horse, whether you paid money for him or not."

Thomas's face was turning red, but before he started talking, Shahzad raised his hands. "Quiet. May I touch the stallion?"

Alfred nodded, and Shahzad rested the palm of his hand on the horse's forehead. Perception's Keeper stood quietly with his eyes closed, as if listening intently. The silence stretched on for a couple of minutes. When Shahzad lowered his hand, he smiled. "The Protector is correct. The horse does indeed belong to Alfred. I have seen it in the animal's memories. He was stolen on the night of the new moon by a horse trader, who then sold the animal to Thomas. The fault in this case lies with the horse-trader-turned-thief."

When Shahzad paused, Raoul said, "The laws of the Realm state that stolen goods cannot legally change hands, hence the bill of sale is unenforceable and non-binding on the two parties. Thomas, you have the right to bring a suit against the horse trader for the price you paid for the horse. Add your name to the roster and we will hear your case in turn."

The man muttered to himself as he walked back to the tent to talk with Perry, the scribe in charge of the schedule books.

"So, am I free to leave with my stallion?" Alfred asked.

Shahzad extended his arm. "Of course. He is a fine animal and loyal to his master."

Alfred smiled. "My thanks to you, sir." We watched as he led the horse away—as docile as a kitten, just like he'd described.

Garrick slapped me on the back. "Way to go, Harper. That was some trick. I didn't know we could do that."

I smiled. "Shahzad taught me that one."

The council didn't get to Thomas's case until late the next day. He and Shahzad worked with an artist to draw a likeness of the horse thief. Garrick and I searched several locations with our counters, but he was long gone. The council had the artist draw up "Wanted for Horse Thievery" posters, which were sent to the various provinces. I figured they must be the Algonian equivalent of an arrest warrant. Other than that, there wasn't much we could do. When the horse thief was eventually found, he would be forced to return Thomas's money and serve time in the dungeon.

On our final day in Greenwood, a young woman brought a case against her former brother-in-law. Her sister, the man's wife, had passed away the year before. The woman claimed he was a drunkard and a brute, and that his son was suffering as a result. She asked the council to intervene and allow her to raise her sister's child. The woman said she had no proof but feared her sister may have died at the hand of her husband, and she didn't want her nephew to fall victim to the same fate.

As she testified before the council, she twisted the edge of her apron between her fingers and shifted her weight from foot to foot. Long brown hair hung past her shoulders, shadowing half of her face, and her eyes seemed focused on the dirt in front of her rather than the council members.

Shahzad asked, "Will you submit to inquest via magic?"

"What is that, sir?"

"Wickliff the elf and I will each place our hands on your wrist and view your memories as they relate to this case, allowing us to see what you have seen in regards to your brother-in-law."

"Will it hurt any?"

"No, it will not."

She stepped forward and extended her hand. Shahzad's brow furrowed as his large brown hand circled her wrist and covered a purple bruise on her arm. The longer he maintained contact with the woman, the sterner his expression grew. When he released her, he abruptly stood. "Show me your face."

She pulled her hair back, fear showing in her eyes as she raised them to meet his. A dark bruise circled her left eye. "Protector, Guardian," Shahzad said, "go at once and bring me this man and his son." At his demanding tone, Garrick and I jumped up, our swords clanging against the wooden stools. We knew the drill by now and walked to him, hands extended.

"Come here, child," Wickliff said to the woman.

Shahzad clasped our wrists and showed us a run-down cottage where a big man took a swig from a jug and wiped a dirty hand across an even dirtier black beard. Finally, he showed us a small boy about the age of Davy when I'd first met him in New York, 1817. But this boy was too thin. His worn clothes hung crookedly on his gaunt frame, exposing bony shoulders.

Our counters were already set to this province, and anything within the area could be accessed with those coordinates. Garrick had his counter out before I finished processing what Shahzad had shown me. Garrick dropped his hand on my shoulder and pressed Go, transporting us to the scene without Marcus or our usual backup of soldiers.

We appeared near the house in a yard full of knee-high weeds. A broken-down fence enclosed a paddock. A horse with matted fur covering a protruding rib cage stood listlessly near a turned-over water bucket, along with two goats and a cow that looked like they were in similar states of neglect. "This guy should face charges of animal cruelty along with the child abuse," I said.

Garrick didn't say a word, just marched to the door and banged his fist against it, rattling the doorframe.

A voice from inside yelled, "Go away!"

"Open up. I need to see your son. You've got some answering to do," Garrick yelled back.

I stepped next to him and tried to go for a more diplomatic approach. "We are the Protector and the Guardian. We represent the Keepers' Council and are here on official business. Sir, you need to open the door."

"Keepers' Council, my eye. I be minding my own business here, and you should be minding yers. Now take yerself off me land."

Garrick stepped back, raised his foot, and kicked the door in. He held out his elbow to block the door from bouncing back when he charged in. It took a moment for my eyes to adjust to the dim interior as we moved into the back room. The man we were after darted toward the table and reached for a dagger. Garrick was faster. He grabbed the man's collar and spun him so they faced each other. He slammed his fist into the man's chin and threw him to the ground.

Movement in the corner of the room caught my attention. A small boy climbed from behind a chest and ran out the door. Garrick left the man where he'd fallen and followed the boy. I turned to the man. "Stand up. We're taking you to see the council."

The man climbed to his feet and spit on me, a disgusting glob of saliva that landed on my chest. I never should have looked down to wipe it off.

Like a linebacker, the guy barreled into me. All I saw was a dark blur as his head collided with mine. He sandwiched me between the wall and his shoulder, his breath reeking of alcohol. Although we were about the same height, he must have had a good seventy-five pounds on me.

I fought back, using my knees and my fists, all the while trying to keep my sword out of his possession. Both of us were holding the pommel, and if it came out of the scabbard, I wanted to make sure it wasn't in his hand. I felt the warm trickle of blood under my nose.

I heard the sound of boots on the wooden floor as Garrick rushed in. He pulled the man off me and laid into his stomach like it was a punching bag. When the man doubled over, gasping for air, Garrick pulled his head up by a fistful of curly black hair. "What kind of man are you?" Garrick yelled. "How dare you lay a hand on that boy? Or a woman for that matter. Pick on somebody your own size."

For good measure, Garrick landed a swift blow to the man's nose. I heard the crack of cartilage and the guy screamed, covering his nose with his meaty hands.

I drew my sword and wiped my face with the sleeve of my shirt. "Let's take him back to Shahzad."

Garrick grabbed the man by the shirt collar and dragged him out the door. The boy scrambled up into the branches of an overgrown apple tree. "Watch him," Garrick said to me as he released the man into my custody.

Garrick stood at the base of the tree and talked in a soft voice, urging the boy to come down. He asked him about the woman who had come to the council, and we learned her name was Aunt Penny. The boy also admitted that his father sometimes hit Penny when she told him what to do. "Would you like to live with your aunt Penny?" Garrick asked.

"Oh yes, sir. She's real nice, and she feeds me sweets when Father ain't looking."

Garrick smiled. "Well, come on down then. I can take you to her. I'll bet she can cook you up something mighty fine for supper tonight."

"What about my father? He won't like me going to Aunt Penny's. Says I gotta do my chores every day."

"Your father can do his own chores for a bit. Your aunt Penny needs your help now."

The little boy climbed down and put his hand in Garrick's. As they walked closer, I saw what had made Garrick so mad. The boy's face and arms were covered in bruises of various shades.

Anxious to bring the kid's father to justice, I pulled out my counter. "I'll meet you back at the tent."

Garrick nodded as he pulled out his own counter and knelt to face the little boy.

With my sword tip against the man's ribs, I touched him with the back of my hand and pressed Go. The man flew into a rage at the sight of Penny when we reappeared. She cowered away from him as Marcus and two of his soldiers rushed in to restrain him. Shahzad didn't ask for permission before he wrapped his hand around the man's wrist. Maybe for criminals suspected of violent crimes, he didn't have to.

The man cursed and tried to pull away as Shahzad viewed his memories. Perception's Keeper scowled at what he saw. Stepping away, he said, "Wickliff, this inquisition requires a second witness."

Wickliff stepped forward, and soon he too frowned at the man's memories. Garrick appeared with the small boy in his arms. As he bent to set him down, the accused cursed Wickliff. The little boy clung to Garrick's neck. I was reminded of the years Garrick spent raising Davy. He sure was good with kids. "Hey, little man," he whispered. "Look over there and tell me if you recognize anyone."

The boy turned. He saw his aunt and ran across the tent to wrap his arms around her legs. She must have been so focused on her brother-in-law that she hadn't noticed the boy. She lifted her nephew and hugged him to her chest. I blinked back tears. What a relief to see the kid with someone who would love him.

Wickliff cleared his throat as he stepped away from the accused. "This is more grievous than we had thought. This man has neglected his son and beaten him. He inflicted injury on the woman offering to help him. He did the same with the boy's mother, and she died as a result of those injuries. Situations such as this demand my attention on a personal level as well as a judicial one. It is unconscionable that a woman should die at the hand of the one who should protect her. Since she was unable to bring a case against her husband while she lived, I hereby do so on her behalf. Bartholomew son of Draper, I find you guilty of the murder of your wife and propose to the council a punishment of death by hanging. Shahzad, do you second my proposition?"

"I concur with Wickliff's findings and second the proposition. Are there any on the council who disagree with the charge or punishment?"

None of the council members spoke.

"The sentence will be carried out immediately," Shahzad said. "Take him away."

By the expressions on Wickliff's and Shahzad's faces, I didn't doubt they had seen something disturbing, and I felt nauseous as I returned to my seat. I didn't envy Marcus and the job he had. The man fought the soldiers all the way out the door.

The woman we now knew as Aunt Penny said, "May I take my nephew and go home?"

Shahzad stepped aside and raised his arm, clearing a path for her. "Thank you for bringing this matter to the council's attention. I hope you will give the boy the love and care he should have received from his father."

The woman smiled as she curtsied. "Oh, I will, sir. Thank you, sir."

TEN

Capstown

Toward the end of our second week touring Algonia, we neared the outskirts of Capstown. We rode in pairs down the road, and Garrick was talking to Shahzad directly in front of Ellie and me. Garrick held his counter in front of him, studying the globe. "So where are we now?" he asked Shahzad.

Perception's Keeper opened his counter, which he wore on a thick gold chain around his neck, and fiddled with the globe inside. "Here." He extended it for Garrick to see.

Garrick leaned closer and looked at it before setting his counter. "Is that right?" He held it out for Shahzad's inspection.

"Yes, that is correct."

Garrick nodded and went back to studying his counter.

Both of our previous stops had followed the same pattern—grand parade through town, welcome feast with local dignitaries, and a day or two of hearing cases and passing judgments. Ellie roamed among the locals, although never without an armed escort. As my wife, she was treated like royalty. Only one other Keeper had been accompanied by a spouse—the elf who was Creation's Keeper traveled with her husband, also an elf. He was good-natured and quick-witted.

I scanned the growing crowd as we paraded onto the streets of Capstown, clearly the smallest of the towns we'd visited so far.

Garrick fell back next to Ellie and me, and our horses continued prancing between lines of cheering townsfolk. Children waved and jumped up and down in excitement. They seemed to direct their waves at Ellie, who looked like a princess in her fancy gown, riding sidesaddle on the flashy white horse Marcus had given her. I may have been biased, but I'd bet her beauty could draw anyone's attention. Her fine upbringing in Boston's 1860s society hadn't failed her, either. Wherever we went, Ellie, along with Creation's Keeper, seemed to steal the spotlight, and Capstown was no different. I was content to hang back and watch her shine.

We were nearing the other end of town when I noticed Garrick wasn't smiling anymore. "What's the matter?" I asked.

With a furrowed brow, he looked at me across the back of my wife's horse and gave a half smile. "It's nothing."

As the crowd began to thin, Ellie gasped. Her wide eyes and fearful expression met my curious glance. "I just saw Legard," she said.

My pulse quickened. I scanned the area as I fished my counter out of my pocket. "Where?"

She pointed off to the right. "He was standing next to that cottage, but he disappeared as soon as I looked at him."

There was nothing out of the ordinary next to the cottage, so I looked behind me. Wickliff seemed relaxed and unconcerned. So did the other elves in the group. I shook my head. "Legard wouldn't be in Algonia. It was probably just somebody who looked like him."

"I know what I saw, and it was Legard."

I couldn't think of a reason Legard would be watching us parade into Capstown, but I figured it wasn't worth arguing over. "Okay. It looks like he's gone for now."

"Shouldn't we warn Wickliff or something?"

"I'll talk with him, but I doubt Legard will do anything here."

We halted in a grassy clearing west of town. Capstown was a series of rolling hills covered by grape vineyards and surrounded on all sides by dense forestland. Marcus's soldiers, along with the numerous servants accompanying us, began at once to set up our camp. Strangely, Garrick never dismounted. He rode around following Marcus as the commander issued the final orders to his soldiers. It was then I remembered we were in Marcus and Brierly's hometown. When Marcus finished with his men, he waved at Garrick, and the two of them galloped down the dirt road into the woods. By the time we needed to leave for dinner, they hadn't returned.

The council members and advisors, all dressed in their finest, gathered at the edge of camp to board carriages. I wore a fancy suit coat with pants tucked into knee-high black boots polished to a high shine, and a ridiculous tie around a starched collar that practically choked me. Ellie looked like Cinderella going to the ball. I held her hand as she stepped up into the carriage, but before I followed her, I looked in the direction Garrick and Marcus had gone. There was no sign of them where the road disappeared into the darkness of the forest. I frowned as I took the seat next to my wife.

She leaned closer. "You don't think Legard found them, do you?"

Before we dressed for dinner, I had asked Wickliff how easy it would be for someone like Legard to come into Algonia. The old elf assured me they were watching for Legard, and the Algonian gatekeepers or Archidus would surely have sensed his presence had he crossed the border. But Ellie was so sure of what she had seen that I didn't have much luck convincing her otherwise.

"I'm sure Garrick and Marcus are fine." I forced a smile. They were armed and they were together, I reminded myself. If anybody could take care of themselves, it was those two. They had made it safely across Shuyle to rescue me, so surely they wouldn't get into trouble in Marcus's hometown.

We stopped near the largest building on the main street and entered a large pavilion lit with torches and candles. The wine was plentiful, and servants wandered among the guests, handing out glass after glass of the dark red liquid. Ellie and I declined, but before long the laughter got louder and the comments more brazen. There was an endless stream of questions from the locals. Evidently my exploits in Shuyle had been well publicized, and in many cases exaggerated. Ellie seemed nervous after thinking she had seen Legard, and all the talk about Lord Arbon didn't help. These folks were big talkers and more prideful in their attitudes than what I'd seen in the first two villages. It didn't take long before their boasts got on my nerves.

It was fully dark by the time the lord of Capstown tapped his wine glass with a knife. Grateful to have an excuse to end my conversation with some of the locals, I turned my attention to him. "My fellow dignitaries and I are pleased to welcome the members of the Keepers' Council to Capstown, the wine capital of Algonia and the finest town on the border."

We all politely clapped in response. "We invite you all to be seated. Dinner will be served—" The lord's words trailed off as his gaze turned to the pavilion entrance. At the disapproving glare he sent in that direction, I turned. Garrick had entered with a timid-looking and elegantly dressed Brierly hanging onto his arm. Her beauty could rival any of the women in the room, but she was clearly afraid, and she walked a half step behind her escort. Garrick, on the other hand, confidently strode forward, took a glass of wine off of a servant's tray, and offered it to Brierly.

Whispers buzzed around us. Two men, one of whom I knew to be the son of the Lord of Capstown, confronted Brierly. In a voice loud enough for everyone to hear, he said, "You harlot. You think it will be quickly forgotten that you consorted with the enemy? Your kind isn't—"

Garrick thrust his fist into the man's jaw, silencing him on impact. The man stumbled back into the crowd. The other man swung wildly in Garrick's direction. The Guardian ducked and then gave the man an uppercut to the stomach that left him doubled over and gasping for air. When they both recovered and stepped forward for round two, Garrick danced between his attackers, throwing jabs into their faces.

Boxed in by the crowd, I didn't make it very far as I tried to get to my brother. Marcus pulled his sister behind him and drew his sword. His men rushed forward to break up the fight, but he raised a hand in warning. The commander seemed content to let Garrick handle things his way. When both accusers spouted blood from their noses and clutched their bruised ribs, Marcus called an end to it with one word: "Guardian."

Eyes blazing, Garrick lowered his hands and took a step back, surveying the crowd. "You're fools! All of you are nothing but a bunch of hypocrites. Look at you. You come here tonight to honor the Keepers, and yet you would scorn the woman who saved the life of one of them. How dare you ridicule the one who helped kill Lord Arbon? That single act turned the tide of war in your favor and brought peace to your lands. Without *her* we wouldn't be here celebrating tonight. Without *her* your men would still be fighting the Shuylians. They'd be dying one by one on the battlefield instead of feasting on fine wine." Garrick picked up another glass of wine and threw it on the ground at the feet of the two battered dignitaries, glaring at them. "Get out. I'll not eat with the likes of you. Either you leave, or I will."

A strained silence filled the pavilion. The two men looked at the lord of Capstown. I'd bet he shared their sentiments, yet his pride and desire to preserve the peace must have won out. He raised his hand and motioned for them to leave. The two men grumbled to each other as they fled the tent.

Garrick squared his shoulders. "Anybody else got anything to say to Miss Landseer?" If silence could somehow become quieter, it did. Bloody-knuckled Garrick made a formidable barrier, and not a soul made a sound or moved a muscle.

The lord of Capstown cleared his throat. "Ladies and gentlemen, there's no need for a minor disturbance to disrupt the pleasures of the evening. Please be seated and dinner will be served."

Like a flock of birds, the crowd moved toward the tables. Garrick wiped the back of his hands across his pants and turned his attention to Brierly. Marcus sheathed his sword and stepped aside. He took his guard's stance by the exit and glowered at the townsfolk. Gradually, the people seemed to relax as they took their seats. I picked up Ellie's hand. "I want you to meet someone."

I led her to where Garrick stood with a protective hand on Brierly's back. She looked mortified. He gently urged her forward, but she resisted, saying. "I should leave. I knew this wasn't wise."

"We aren't going anywhere," Garrick said. "You belong here as much as any of us do."

I smiled at them. "Brierly, it's good to see you. I'd like you to meet my wife, Ellie."

Brierly curtsied. "It's nice to meet you, my lady."

Ellie wrapped her arms around Brierly. "I've heard so much about you, I feel as if we are already the best of friends. Thank you for taking care of Chase in that dungeon. I'll forever be grateful to you and your brother, as well as Garrick, for his safe return."

Brierly's expression relaxed into a smile. "You're welcome. I'm pleased I could be of assistance."

"Come and sit by us," Ellie said.

Wickliff, Shahzad, and Raoul waited behind us for their turn to speak with Brierly. Wickliff extended his hand. "My dear girl, it is wonderful to see you again."

Brierly nodded. "Thank you." By the time she had been introduced to everyone on the council and had received their expressions of gratitude, she and Garrick appeared more at ease. The council members gathered at one end of the table to enjoy the feast spread before us. Garrick's eyes never left Brierly.

Shocked at the discriminating remarks made against her, I watched the townspeople—the disparaging glances they sent her way, the whispered comments behind raised hands. Despicable. She should have been given a warm welcome after surviving her captivity in Shuyle and successfully escaping. But instead she'd been despised for the indiscretions she'd been forced into.

We finished eating and said our goodbyes. Our carriage drove us back to camp, where Garrick, Marcus, Brierly, Ellie, and I sat in the large group tent and talked well into the night.

After Ellie yawned for the third time, I stood and offered my hand. "It's late. We should get to bed."

She put her hand in mine. "We should."

The others rose as well. "Good night, you guys," I said. Ellie and I left, followed closely by Garrick and Brierly. I glanced over my shoulder to see them move out of sight behind the carriage. I assumed they climbed aboard, but Garrick later informed me they never set foot in the carriage.

ELEVEN

Revenge

The way Garrick told the story, he set his fingers on the handle of the carriage door, reluctant to end his time with Brierly. "Would you consider walking?" he asked her. "It's a beautiful night—nearly full moon, starry sky."

She slipped her arm through his. "I'd love to walk with you." They hadn't gone far before she said, "Thank you for defending my honor. Or the pitiful shred of it that's left. I sometimes wonder what is worse—the cruelty of the Shuylians, or the scorn of my own people. Perhaps I shouldn't have done what I did."

Garrick took a deep breath. "And if you hadn't done what they demanded? What then? What would have happened in Shuyle if you'd fought them?"

In the moonlight, he watched Brierly shrug her shoulders and frown. "I would have been killed."

"That's what I thought. Then you did the right thing, because I want you alive."

"I don't know. Sometimes I think death would be a more pleasant alternative to this. The only good that came of my rescue was my mother seeing me before she died. It broke her heart when they took me. And my father—he needed my help caring for her during the last months of her life."

Garrick waited, sensing Brierly had more to say. Keeping her eyes on the ground in front of her, she finally continued. "Those men tonight, and others . . . they've tried to visit me. They expected me to turn to harlotry. But I've disappointed them. If it weren't for Marcus and my father, I may have been forced into it by necessity, to make enough money to buy food. There is no other way for someone like me to earn her keep.

"As it is, Marcus sends his pay home for Father and me. It is more than enough, and I put away the extra. But if my brother takes a wife someday, he'll have need of his salary. I also fear he may be injured or killed in battle. What would become of us? Well, no matter. I'm certain you don't need to be burdened with my worries." She squeezed Garrick's arm and smiled. "Tell me, did you ever find your son?"

Working to control his anger over the injustices Brierly had endured, Garrick didn't answer.

She stopped and raised her hand to her mouth. "I'm sorry. Did he . . ." She shook her head, obviously assuming the worst.

"No." Garrick wrapped his arm around her. "Davy's fine. I found him. He's married now, with a baby on the way. We work together, hauling freight by wagons on the old world. For me it's been three years since I was here last. Brierly, not a day's gone by that I haven't thought of you."

She looked at him. "I've thought of you too, Keeper."

When they arrived at the cottage, Garrick opened the door. "Well, here we are. If it's all right, I'd like to call on you tomorrow, as soon as I can get away from my duties. You'll be here?"

"Of course. I never leave the house. Where else would I go?"

Garrick leaned closer. "Then I'll see you soon." He drank in the beauty of her face until she stood on her toes and kissed him. "Good night, Brierly," he whispered.

She went inside and closed the door. Garrick stood at her doorstep, thinking for a moment. With his decision made, he left. Feeling the effects of the long day, he jogged along the road, anxious to get back to camp and his bedroll.

Deep in thought, he missed any telltale signs of movement in the forest around him. Suddenly, four men jumped out of the brush. Armed with clubs, they fell on Garrick. He drew his sword, but one of his assailants restrained his hand, while another battered his shoulder with a heavy, iron-spiked club, shattering the bone and drawing blood. Garrick's right arm dropped limply to his side, the sword slipping from his unresponsive fingers.

Their leader beat Garrick's face with a hand covered in gold rings. He was the same man who had humiliated Brierly at the feast. "Who do you think you are, Keeper? Parading that harlot into our town like she's royalty. Did you enjoy yourself at her house tonight? That Shuylian harlot has a lot of nerve taking you in after rejecting me." A wicked laugh erupted from the man. "But don't worry. We'll teach her a lesson once we're through with you." He turned to the other men. "Finish him off. And make it look like a robbery. I'll not have him live to talk."

Garrick swung his left fist, but it did little good against their numbers. Another man cracked his club into Garrick's knee, dropping him face first onto the dusty road. Dizzy from pain, he reached across his body with his left hand, searching his pocket. The gold counter tumbled out onto the dirt. His trembling hand slid across the ground and pressed the latch. One man grabbed Garrick's wrist, reaching for the glowing device. Another let his club fall onto the back of Garrick's head. Finally, his thumb found the Shuffle button.

Garrick and the man holding his wrist disappeared. The sudden change of venue shocked the man into releasing his hold. Reeling from the pain, Garrick pulled the counter closer to his body and pressed Shuffle again.

TWELVE

Request

I lay in bed next to Ellie, listening to her breathing. Her head rested on my shoulder, and I mindlessly ran my fingers along her arm. Sleep had eluded me. I was wide awake and restless. The only thing holding me still was my wife. If I moved or got up, I'd most certainly wake her.

What sounded like a pained moan came from outside my tent. I lifted my head to listen. "Harper."

At the sound of Garrick's voice, I flew out of bed and stumbled over my boots, trying to pull my leather breeches on.

"Chase, what's the matter?" Ellie's sleepy voice asked.

"It's Garrick." I threw back the tent flap. The pale moonlight revealed dark splashes of color on his light clothes. His right arm lay twisted at a grotesque angle.

"Marcus," I roared. My voice echoed through the quiet camp. The commander had mentioned that he had the second watch tonight. If I'd judged the time correctly he would be standing guard by now. I dropped to my knees. "Garrick, talk to me. What happened? Who did this?"

I heard the guards running toward us through the dark. Garrick moaned. Blinking his bloody eyelids, he tried to look at me. "Brierly," he breathed out.

Marcus dropped to his knees next to me, followed by Ellie. "What?" I said. "Brierly didn't do this."

"Guardian, where's my sister?" Marcus demanded.

Garrick's counter fell from his left hand and he clutched my arm. "Save Brierly," he said before slipping into unconsciousness.

Marcus bolted to his feet and pointed at one of the night guards. "Get me two horses." Turning to the other he ordered, "Call the healer." To me, the commander said, "Let's go."

I jumped to my feet and grabbed my boots, shirt, counter, and sword from the tent and pulled them on. Ellie followed me and lit the candles, then gathered a washcloth and basin. She touched my arm. "Be careful."

Shahzad must have heard the ruckus, because when I turned around he was helping Marcus carry Garrick into my tent. Ellie sat next to Garrick and began cleaning the blood from his face. She grimaced when she pulled the torn fabric away from his battered arm.

"I'll be back as soon as I can," I said as I left the tent with Marcus.

The commander mounted up and galloped away. I took the reins from the guard and followed. It was probably a mile from our camp to Brierly's cottage. We ran our horses the entire way. Marcus jumped from his horse's back before it slid to a stop. He raced through the broken door.

I dismounted in front of the cottage and listened. A woman's scream echoed through the trees.

"No!" Brierly cried.

I ran behind the cottage, following the sounds of her struggle. Marcus burst from the back door and drew his sword. Garrick's attackers hadn't taken Brierly far. We pushed through the tree branches and found her and three men in a mossy hollow. They appeared to have just begun tormenting her. At the sound of us crashing through the trees, they turned in our direction.

Marcus rushed forward. The closest man raised his club, and Marcus cut off his arm. The torch he held fell to the dirt. The man holding Brierly had large gold rings on his fingers and wore finer clothing than the rest. I recognized him from the feast. He shoved her to the ground and ran deeper into the woods.

While Marcus finished off the man who'd lost his arm, I drew my sword and faced the other one. He threw a bottle of wine, but I ducked and it shattered against the tree behind me. The man drew his sword and our blades clanged against each other until Marcus ran behind my opponent and swung his sword, taking off the man's head. My opponent crumpled at my feet. I dropped my arms to my side and stared at Marcus. His justice was brutal and quick.

He helped his sister to her feet and looked at me. "Keeper, take her back to my tent. I'm going after the other one." As soon as the words left his mouth, he disappeared into the woods.

Brierly's shoulders shook with a sob, and she buried her face in her hands. My heart raced. I hated the sight of blood, but her crying compelled me to action. I stepped over the decapitated body, retrieved the torch, and walked to Brierly.

"Are they dead?" she choked out.

I wrapped my arm around her. "Who? These guys?"

"No. Garrick? My father?" She pointed to the woods. "Perhaps now even Marcus. Everyone who's ever meant anything to me will be gone before this night ends." The torch's glow between us showed the despair in her expression.

"Garrick's not. He sent me to get you."

Her head shot up, but it was shaking back and forth. "But they said they killed him. They said I would never see him again."

"They lied. Garrick used his counter to disappear. He's injured, but alive. Marcus sent for a healer before we left."

Brierly turned toward the house. "But what of my father? He was in the cottage. Did you see him?"

"No. I never went in the cottage."

She lifted her skirts and broke into a run. "Father," she cried.

I ran after her. One flickering candle, sitting precariously on the edge of the table, lit the small room. In the dim light, I watched Brierly fall onto her knees next to an old man lying slumped against the wall. I tossed the sputtering torch into the cold hearth and carried the candle closer. Brierly dropped her head onto the man's chest and sobbed. I felt for a pulse, wondering if there was any way to save him. I pulled the man flat onto the wood floor and tilted his head back, intent on giving him mouth to mouth and CPR. But his neck wobbled in my hands. The gray hair fell away from his face, and lifeless eyes stared back at me.

I was no coroner, but I guessed they had broken his neck. I looked at Brierly and shook my head. Words escaped me at the pain I saw in her face. I stood and picked up an overturned chair, then slumped onto it. Tears burned my eyes as I listened to her mourn her father. She should have been safe here. This was her home. She had worked so hard to get back to Algonia, and for what—this?

After some time, Brierly pushed herself to her feet, weariness evident in her every move. She took a towel and dipped it in the basin, then washed her face, dabbing carefully at a cut on her lip. Her dress was ripped, but fortunately still intact. I shuddered at the thought of what would have happened if we'd arrived any later.

She breathed out a deep sigh. "I'm ready."

I tied Marcus's horse to the hitching post so it wouldn't follow us, and we rode back to camp in silence. The glow of multiple candles illuminated the canvas of my tent. I swung my leg over the horse's neck and slid onto the ground, then helped Brierly dismount. "Let me check on Ellie and see if they moved Garrick."

Brierly nodded and wrung her hands in front of her. I pushed aside the tent flap and entered. Garrick still lay unconscious on our bed. Ellie sat next to him, while an elf healer bent over the mangled shoulder. I pulled aside the flap and said, "Brierly, he's in here."

She followed me into the tent. At the sight of Garrick's injured body, her eyes again filled with tears. His shirt and one pant leg had been cut away from his flesh. The healer shook a white powder into the wounds. Ellie stood and offered her seat to Brierly, who picked up Garrick's left hand and pressed it to her lips. Her tears trickled down her cheek and onto his fingers. "I'm so sorry," she said quietly.

The broken bones were covered in a poultice made of crushed red leaves. The healer wrapped Garrick's leg, shoulder, and head with bandages, all the while whispering incantations of healing. I slipped my arm around Ellie and watched the process.

When the healer finished, he pulled two vials from his bag and offered them to Brierly. "Once he awakens, have him drink these. One is a bone-growth stimulant, absolutely necessary if these bones are to mend correctly. The other is liquid energy. It will speed the healing and ease his pain. It's the knock on the head that has him passed out right now, but I did get enough potion down his throat to take care of the swelling on his brain. I expect by midday tomorrow he'll at least be awake. I'll return first thing in the morning to check on him."

We thanked the healer before he closed his bag and left the tent.

— ❖ —

Exhaustion overcame all of us. Ellie and I lay on a blanket on the floor of the tent. Brierly slumped forward, still holding Garrick's hand, and rested her head on the pillow next to him. I slept until he moaned in his sleep. Brierly raised her head. She dipped a cloth in the washbasin and wiped the sweat from his brow. Several of the candles had burned out, leaving only two flickering flames. I closed my eyes again, knowing Garrick was in good hands. Ellie still slept soundly next to me.

"Brierly," Garrick said in a raspy voice.

"I'm right here. Can you drink something? It's a potion from the healer."

"Did they hurt you?"

"No, I'm fine. Marcus and Chase came. Can you lift your head?"

At Garrick's agonizing groan, I sat up. He had managed to raise his head enough for Brierly to pour the contents of the first vial into his mouth. "That's good," she said as he swallowed the liquid. She lowered his head onto the pillow.

"I need . . . to talk . . . to you," Garrick managed to say between labored breaths.

"Not now. You have one more vial to drink and you need to rest. There'll be time for talking later."

"No."

Brierly slid her hand beneath his head. "One more time. This one is liquid energy. You'll not like the taste of it, but you'll love how it makes you feel. Now, please drink it all for me."

I'd heard that tone of voice before—in the dungeon when she had doctored my mangled flesh. She was forcing a cheerful tone when she probably wanted to cry at the brutality Garrick had suffered.

Garrick complied, groaning as he again lifted his head. He swallowed the medicine, and Brierly stifled a sob. "I'm so sorry, Garrick. I never should have gone with you. I knew better than to antagonize those men. If I would have stayed home, none of this would have happened."

"Don't say that. The fault is mine, not yours. Listen to me. Brierly, marry me, please?"

She shook her head. "You don't mean that. The healer said you're not right in the head. You're in no condition to make an offer like that. You should rest now."

"I decided before," Garrick mumbled. "I was going to court you first, but it doesn't look like I'll be doing much of anything for a while. Brierly, say you'll come away with me and be my wife."

"After everything I've . . . no, Garrick, I'm no good for you. Why would you want me, when you could have any maiden in Algonia?"

"I don't love the maidens in Algonia. I love you."

"But what of my past?"

"What of it? It's in the past. We all have pasts."

Brierly still shook her head at Garrick's proposition. "I'll not answer this question now and have you come to your senses tomorrow and regret it. I want to hear it from you when I know you're well."

He chuckled. "Fine, but I'm not going anywhere."

Now it was Brierly's turn to laugh. "I can plainly see that."

Garrick nodded to the empty spot on the bed next to him. "You should lie down and get some rest."

She did as he suggested. It was quiet after that—until Marcus came back. Angry yelling woke all of us except Garrick. I left the tent to see what the ruckus was about. The man who had fled into the woods now walked behind the commander's horse, fighting the ropes that restrained him. It surprised me that Marcus had let the man live, although his face was battered. Brierly took one look and retreated back inside the tent. Marcus yanked on the rope as he dismounted, then waved to the guards. "Chain him up and post a guard. But put him far enough away that I don't have to hear him whine."

I met Marcus as he turned toward the tent. "My sister," he said. "Where is she?"

I looked over my shoulder. "In there, with Garrick and Ellie."

He marched past me into the tent, and I stepped in after him. Brierly moved into his embrace. Marcus wrapped his bloodied arms around her and pressed her head to his chest. "I'm sorry," he whispered.

She tipped her head up to look at him, tears glistening in her eyes. "Father—did you see him?"

"I did. We shall go back at daybreak and bury him. And then you will go with me when I leave here. I'll not be coming back again, for this is no longer my home. Come, you should rest."

Brierly looked at Garrick and shook her head. "I'll stay. I can rest here. But go sleep, Brother. You must be exhausted."

Marcus surveyed the room. He nodded at me and dropped to one knee by the bedside. With his hand on Garrick's good arm, he said, "Take care, my friend. And get well." The commander stood and addressed his sister. "I'll come by for you in the morning."

We again lay down to rest, hoping for a little more sleep before dawn.

Marcus and Brierly rode out of camp with a small, armed guard. They returned later with all of her belongs packed on the back of a horse. The duties of the council required my time for most of the day. But when I was free of my responsibilities, I returned to my tent. A servant sat with Garrick.

"Where are Ellie and Brierly?" I asked.

"They went to clean and prepare themselves for the evening meal," the servant replied.

"Thank you. I can stay with him now."

The servant stood and bowed. "Certainly, Keeper."

Although Garrick had watched me come in, he now looked as if he might have dozed off. I slumped onto the chair next to him and whispered, "Hey, brother, how you doin', man?"

With his eyes closed, I didn't expect an answer. But he slowly turned his head. "I've been better. How you doin', little brother?"

I smiled. "Compared to you, I can't complain."

"Have you seen Brierly?"

The lack of sleep had caught up to me, and I yawned. "Not since this morning."

"Is she okay?"

"I think so. But those men killed her father, and it shook her up pretty bad."

"I need to talk to her," Garrick said. "She didn't want to come to the dinner last night, and I should have respected her wishes. I had no idea she would be treated so badly. She tried to tell me, but I didn't listen."

"Do you remember talking with her last night after I brought her back?"

"I talked to her?"

"Yeah, in the middle of the night. She gave you your medicine. You don't remember? You had a whole conversation with her—a deep conversation."

Garrick gave me a puzzled look. "What are you talking about, Harper?"

Had Brierly been correct? Had he really not been right in the head? What he said had seemed impulsive, even for him. I scratched my head, speechless.

Brierly didn't know I'd overheard. If Garrick never said another word about it, she wouldn't need to be embarrassed if I kept it quiet. I leaned back. "You were asking her questions is all. If you don't remember, it's no big deal."

For a moment Garrick lay still, then he started to laugh. "What kind of mindless idiot do you take me for, Harper? Of course I remember. A guy doesn't forget something like proposing to the woman he loves."

I shook my head at him. "You worthless tease! If you weren't already hurt, I'd sock you one."

"Serves you right for eavesdropping on a man's private conversations with a woman."

Annoyed at being duped, I raised my voice to say, "Don't go having your personal conversations in my tent if you don't want me to hear them."

"You could've taken *my* tent. It was completely empty, you know. No need to—"

Ellie and Brierly pushed through the tent flap. "What's the meaning of all this yelling?" my wife asked. "Chase, perhaps this conversation will hold for another time? Garrick needs to rest."

"We're not yelling," Garrick said.

"Yeah, we're just talking," I added.

Ellie walked to where a brush sat on a small table. "Then that's mighty loud talking. I'll guarantee I heard raised voices. What do you think, Brierly?" Ellie put the brush to her wet hair and pulled it through the tangle of curls.

Brierly smiled at Garrick. "Most certainly, voices were raised."

He tried to smile back, but the swelling on the side of his face yielded a lopsided grin. "But only in jest, I assure you."

"You look well this afternoon," she said. "Are you feeling any better?"

"Much better. I can't move my leg or my right arm, but my head is clear. Last night you wanted to hear my request when I was well. Am I sufficiently well enough that you'll take my proposal seriously?"

Brierly stood as still as a statue, her face pale. I think she fully expected he wouldn't remember a thing from the night before. Ellie, who hadn't overheard the proposal, looked at Garrick in surprise.

When Brierly didn't say anything, he forged ahead. "I don't have a ring, and I can't go down on one knee and do it properly, but I don't want to wait. Brierly, I know I'm not much to look at right now, but the healer said it shouldn't take long before I'm back on my feet. Will you marry me when that day comes?"

"You really meant it?" Her smile returned, a pleasant blush coloring her cheeks.

"Of course."

She took a step closer, her expression sober again. "You should know that I might not be able to bear children."

Garrick grimaced as he raised his head, and his words came slowly at first. "Although I'd like children, there's nothing I want more than you. You've no idea how much I regretted not telling you how I felt before I left. At the time I didn't see any way for it to work—me on one world, you on another. But living without you for the past few years convinced me I have to try. If Archidus needs me here every year for the council, I don't see why I can't just stay. There are three other Keepers living here. Why not me too? So, could you love me, Brierly?"

Tears filled her eyes as she took the chair next to Garrick. "I've not been able to banish you from my dreams ever since that night in Shuyle, when you and Marcus cornered me in the alley. You held your hand over my mouth so I wouldn't scream. Your voice, so kind and gentle, whispered in my ear that you wouldn't hurt me. Even before I discovered Marcus was with you, I knew you were different from all of the other men I had known. Then in Saddle Pass you worked tirelessly to keep me warm—to save me. When I realized you would give your life for mine, I knew I loved you more than anything. Reaching Algonia was bittersweet for me. I would have been content to travel my life away with you. Never before or since have I been happier than I was then. So yes, I will marry you, Garrick the Guardian. And I'll count myself lucky to have gotten the better end of the deal."

Garrick winced as he grinned. "You can think what you like, my dear, but I'll be counting myself lucky to have someone as perfect as you."

Brierly touched his cheek. "My darling, you are too kind, and your words are more than I deserve." Garrick reached his left hand behind Brierly's head and pulled her mouth to his.

—◈—

Our third day in Capstown was nearing an end. The final case of the day was that of Garrick and Brierly's assailant. As it turned out, the man who Marcus had captured was the third son of the lord of Capstown. He was known to be a rowdy drunkard, prone to getting into trouble.

Shahzad, acting as the voice of the council, lifted his head. "The Keepers' Council will hear the case of Marcus Landseer, commander of the guard, against Brandt Capson. The charges are the murder of the elder Marcus Landseer, the attempted murder of a Keeper, and the assault of Commander Landseer's sister."

Marcus stepped forward, along with the accused, Brandt Capson. Behind them, the lord of Capstown and his men, probably the equivalent of Algonian lawyers, stepped forward as well.

"Brandt Capson, how do you plead?" Shahzad asked.

"Not guilty," said one of the lawyers.

"Commander Landseer, how do you substantiate your charges?"

"Witnesses, your honor," Marcus replied.

"How will your witnesses testify?" Shahzad continued. "Verbally or via inquest?"

Without hesitation Marcus said, "Inquest, your honor."

"Very well." Shahzad turned to the defendant. "Brandt Capson, how do you choose to substantiate your defense?"

Capson fidgeted in his chains as soon as Marcus said "inquest." And it was no wonder he was nervous. He was guilty. I'd seen his hands on Brierly. I'd heard his disparaging remarks, as had dozens of other people at the banquet. His lawyers replied, "Verbally."

"I'll see the witnesses now," Shahzad said.

"I submit myself first," Marcus declared, "and then I'll call on the Protector, and last, the Guardian. If the council deems that information inadequate to substantiate the charges, I'll supply an additional witness."

"Step forward," Shahzad instructed.

Marcus walked to the table and extended his arm. Shahzad took his wrist and studied his eyes. After several minutes, Shahzad dropped Marcus's wrist and nodded to Wickliff. The old elf took hold of Marcus's arm in the same manner.

Shahzad motioned me forward. I followed the same procedure as Marcus. Shahzad's hand was strong and warm around my wrist. I looked into his dark brown eyes and waited. I felt him enter my thoughts and forced myself to think about the night Garrick had been attacked.

Memories flashed by. I was at the feast with Ellie. I worried why Garrick was late. I watched him arrive with Brierly. Again I felt the anger at what Brandt Capson had said to her. I saw Garrick beat him up. Then I saw Ellie and myself together that night and quickly tried to think of something else. One side of Shahzad's mouth turned up in a smile.

I moved on to the memory of Garrick appearing outside my tent. I remembered the rush of the wind past my ears as Marcus and I raced our horses to the cottage. Brierly's panicked scream. Running through the woods and finding the three men attacking her. Brandt Capson pushing her into the dirt and running into the woods. Brierly and I finding her father and realizing he was dead.

The last memory Shahzad viewed was that of Garrick's battered body in my tent.

Shahzad dropped my wrist and nodded. I moved in front of Wickliff, and the process was repeated. As he released my arm, Wickliff looked past my shoulder, and I turned to see Garrick hobbling into the pavilion. His leg was healing quickly, but his arm was still in a sling and completely useless. His face, a bruised and bloody mess two days ago, was now a kaleidoscope of yellow and purple splotches.

Garrick approached Shahzad, who took his left wrist. Everyone in the room waited silently as Shahzad probed Garrick's mind. By the expression on his face, he found what he was looking for, as well as something that amused him. He released Garrick's arm when he finished. Wickliff viewed Garrick's memories and then nodded to Shahzad to continue.

Shahzad turned to the defense. "What have you to say to the charges?"

Brandt Capson and his father's lawyers rambled on, placing all the blame on the two men Marcus had already killed, and a fourth man I'd never seen. When they finished, Shahzad took a deep breath and faced the council. "Following my inquest, I find the defendant inarguably involved in the attempted murder of Garrick the Guardian, a Keeper. The defendant commanded the other men to kill the Keeper. I find the defendant inarguably guilty of assaulting Commander Landseer's sister. Although I know the defendant was near the scene of the murder of the elder Marcus Landseer, the evidence against him is inadequate to convict on the charge of murder. Is the second inquisitionist in agreement with my findings?"

Wickliff rested his elbows on the table and directed his gaze to the defense. "I find the accused, Brandt Capson, inarguably guilty on the charge of assaulting a woman and attempting to murder a Keeper. I also find insubstantial evidence on the charge of the murder of an innocent citizen."

Shahzad nodded. "Will the witnesses and the defense please step outside while the council deliberates?"

Everyone who wasn't part of the Keepers' Council or an advisor exited the pavilion. Being witnesses in this case, Garrick and I were asked to leave as well. After ten minutes, the guards motioned to us all and we stepped back inside. Garrick, Marcus, and I stood next to Brandt Capson before Shahzad and the council.

Shahzad cleared his throat. "Based on the evidence presented, the council finds Brandt Capson guilty of assault and the attempted murder of a Keeper. The evidence is insufficient to render judgment on the charge of murder at this time. But in Algonia the attempted murder of a Keeper carries the penalty of death by hanging. The sentence is to be carried out at first light tomorrow. The defendant will be allowed familial visitation under supervision of an armed guard until that time. The fourth man, referred to by the defense as Cutter, was inadvertently taken to the far western border of Shuyle by the Keeper's counter. Although I think it unlikely, should he manage to return, he is also guilty of the attempted murder of a Keeper and will be dealt with in the same manner."

Shahzad raised the mallet and hit the gong, signaling the end of the proceedings. Marcus's soldiers took Brandt Capson into custody and dragged him from the pavilion amid a slew of complaints from both him and his father. Brierly hadn't wanted to face her attackers, so Ellie had stayed with her. Thankfully, the council had reached a verdict without needing her testimony.

Although I knew Brandt Capson was guilty, it was hard to see the look of distress on the face of his father. Nothing could change the fact that Lord Capson would lose a son tomorrow.

Garrick and I exited the tent, followed by the other council members. Throughout the day, dark storm clouds had gathered on the Algonian horizon. The premature darkening of the night sky mirrored my somber mood.

I wasn't the only one who felt it. Garrick raised his eyes to the clouds and said, "The heavens match my mood. It's sobering to ponder the chain of events I set into motion. If I'd skipped the feast that night and had dinner at Brierly's cottage like she asked, none of this would be happening." Garrick shook his head and sighed. "She never wanted to come with me. She was scared—rightly so. She knew better, and yet I made her go. I thought I could protect her, but I was wrong. Her father's dead and now Capson will hang when the sun rises. I know he did wrong, but I can't help but think of his family. Does he have a wife? Children?"

"I have no idea," I said. "But I feel the same. Justice and mercy—only God can balance the two."

"I hope we did the right thing."

"You can't blame yourself. You had every right to be at that dinner, and so did Brierly. It was Marcus's father who was killed, and Marcus brought the charges before the council. Capson made his own decisions. He chose his actions. You've got to let it go, Garrick."

The first raindrops fell on our cheeks as he nodded.

THIRTEEN

Mayfair

As the evening wore on, talk of a rebellion brewed among the townspeople. They weren't pleased with the consequences of the trial, or with the fact that Marcus had killed two of their men and another was now missing. Extra soldiers were put on duty, and I even took a turn standing guard during the second watch. None of us left the safety of our camp that night. If it came to blows, Marcus's squadron, which I had initially considered excessive in size, suddenly didn't seem large enough.

Brandt Capson's sentence was carried out at the crack of dawn. Garrick, Ellie, Brierly, and I declined to attend. If I were to witness a hanging, I feared I'd never get the image out of my mind. Better to simply avoid it. The memory of our massacre on Saddle Pass still haunted me. I didn't need to add fuel to the fire of my PTSD. I had finally reconciled myself to living with the bad memories I already had, and I didn't want to add any new ones.

Once the council completed our business, we packed up camp and departed, anxious to get as far from the turbulent town of Capstown as possible. Still not well enough to ride, Garrick traveled in a carriage with Brierly. We made camp that evening near a creek in a pristine part of the forest. Marcus approached Garrick and me as we sat around the fire after dinner.

"Garrick, is it true what Brierly has told me concerning you?"

At Marcus's stern expression and demanding tone of voice, Garrick shifted his eyes to the orange blaze and tossed in another log. He rubbed the palm of his hand across his pant leg.

I had never seen Garrick nervous before, and I smiled at his obvious discomfort. He kicked at a rock, shifted his weight on the log, and then raised his eyes to meet Marcus's stare. "It is true. I asked your sister to marry me and she agreed."

"Before my father died, did you obtain his permission for her hand in marriage?"

"No, I didn't have a chance to."

"Algonian law requires a man to ask a girl's father, or if the father is gone, her next of kin, for her hand in marriage prior to proposing. I know you didn't speak to me, and if you didn't speak to my father then you are in violation of the law."

The panic stricken look on Garrick's face would have rivaled that of any boy caught red-handed stealing a kiss. He shook his head and swallowed. "What is the punishment for violating the law?"

Marcus folded his arms and narrowed his eyes. "The bride and groom are separated—required to reside in separate towns for fifty days. Absolutely no visiting is allowed. And the groom must pay a fine of twenty Algonian gold coins. After paying the penalty and serving your time of separation, you may have another chance to ask the next of kin for her hand in marriage."

Garrick raised his hand. "Now hang on, Marcus. You can't be serious. You know I had no idea."

The commander didn't flinch. "Ignorance is no excuse. The law is the law in Algonia. You should have learned that by now."

Garrick sat speechless.

Marcus scowled at him. Beads of sweat gathered on Garrick's forehead, glistening in the orange glow. The crackle of the fire was the only sound until the commander burst into laughter. "Ha! I really had you going there, my friend."

Garrick lunged at him with his good arm. "Get outta here, Marcus. You scared me half to death."

Marcus's eyes twinkled as he stepped closer and offered his hand. "Congratulations! Why didn't you tell me sooner?"

Garrick exhaled and smiled as they shook hands. "I was waiting until I got better. You know—in case you didn't like the idea and I had to fight you for her."

Marcus straightened up and gripped the pommel of his sword. "You never would have won."

"Don't be so sure. With motivation like your sister, I don't think you could have stopped me."

Marcus slapped Garrick on his back as he walked by. "In that case, I'm glad I didn't have to try. I'm pleased for you both. I'd better get back to work."

It took three days to reach the town of Mayfair. Garrick's shoulder was mending and he now had some use of it. His leg and bruises had completely healed. During this time, he and Brierly were nearly inseparable.

Heather had included a cream-colored gown in Ellie's wardrobe. She and Brierly spent their evenings altering it to fit Brierly. Despite all his teasing, Marcus was as excited for the wedding as everyone else. He and Garrick shared a close bond, forged during the months they had worked together to get into Shuyle and rescue me. I doubted he could have found a better man to give his sister to than Garrick.

Marcus visited the church in Mayfair and made arrangements with the friar to perform the wedding ceremony the next evening. In this town, no one knew of Brierly or her past. She was simply known as the Guardian's bride and was therefore treated as royalty. Women looked at her in awe, and men sent her admiring glances.

When the time arrived, Garrick and I stood at the front of the church, dressed in our finest Algonian breeches and cloaks, embroidered with shimmering threads. As was the custom in this world, our swords never left our sides, not even for a wedding.

Two musicians played a quaint melody while Marcus led Brierly up the aisle to her place next to Garrick. Marcus smiled at his little sister and stepped back.

We all turned our attention to the cheerful friar with his shiny, balding head. He cleared his throat and looked over the packed congregation. "Dearly beloved, we are gathered together in the sight of God to join together this man and this woman in holy matrimony, which is an honorable estate, instituted of God, and into which holy estate these two persons present come now to be joined. Therefore, if any man can show just cause why they may not lawfully be joined together, by God's law, or the Laws of the Realm, let him now speak, or else hereafter forever hold his peace."

The church was silent for a moment before the friar continued. He smiled at Garrick and Brierly. "I require and charge you both, as ye will answer at the dreadful day of judgment when the secrets of all hearts shall be disclosed, that if either of you know of any impediment why ye may not be lawfully joined together in matrimony, that ye confess it. For be well assured, that so many as be coupled together other than God's word doth allow are not joined together by God, neither is their matrimony lawful."

He paused briefly. "Garrick Eastman, wilt thou have this woman to be thy wedded wife, to live together after God's ordinance in the holy estate of matrimony? Wilt thou love her, comfort her, honor, and keep her, in sickness and in health, and forsaking all others, keep thee only unto her, so long as ye both shall live?"

Garrick smiled at Brierly. "I will."

The friar nodded and then turned his head. "Brierly Landseer, wilt thou have this man to be thy wedded husband, to live together after God's ordinance in the holy estate of matrimony? Wilt thou obey him, and serve him, love, honor, and keep him in sickness and in health, and, forsaking all others, keep thee only unto him, so long as ye both shall live?"

Brierly smiled up at Garrick, her eyes glistening. "I will."

The friar led the way to the altar behind him. Marcus took Brierly's hand and placed it in the friar's before stepping away. The friar then placed Brierly's hand in Garrick's right hand. "Say after me: I, Garrick Eastman, take thee, Brierly Landseer, to be my wedded wife, to have and to hold from this day forward, for better for worse, for richer for poorer, for fairer or fouler, in sickness and in health, to love and to cherish, till death do us part, according to God's holy ordinance, and thereunto I plight thee my troth."

After Garrick repeated the vows, the friar turned to Brierly, who said hers. Then the friar held out his hand and whispered, "The ring?"

Garrick fished in his pocket and pulled out the ring he and Brierly had bought that morning. He set it on the friar's Bible, as instructed.

The friar nodded his approval and continued with the ceremony. "Bless this ring, O merciful Lord, that those who wear it, that give and receive it, may be ever faithful to one another, remain in your peace, and live and grow old together in your love, under their own vine and fig tree, and seeing their children's children. Amen." He took the ring and placed it in Garrick's hand.

Garrick took Brierly's hand in his. "With this ring I thee wed." He looked at her hand and slid the ring onto her thumb. "And with my body I thee honor." He moved the ring to her index finger. "And with all my worldly goods I thee endow." Finally, he slid it onto her ring finger and gazed into her eyes again. "In the name of the Father, and of the Son, and of the Holy Spirit. Amen."

The friar spoke to the crowd. "Those whom God hath joined together let no man put asunder. Forasmuch as Garrick Eastman and Brierly Landseer have consented together in holy wedlock, and have witnessed the same before God and this company, and thereto have given and pledged their troth each to the other, and have declared the same by giving and receiving of a ring and by joining of hands, I pronounce therefore that they be man and wife together, in the name of the Father, and of the Son, and of the Holy Spirit. Amen."

Garrick didn't bother to wait for the friar to say "You may kiss the bride." Whether that was a part of the wedding ceremony in Algonia or not, Garrick made it part of his as he pulled Brierly into his arms and thoroughly kissed her.

He was grinning as he led her down the aisle and into the light of a brilliant sunset. We boarded our carriages and drove the short distance to the town square. Tonight our feast with the local dignitaries would double as Garrick and Brierly's wedding dinner.

The bride and groom were given a place of honor at the head of the table. The contrast between the people of Mayfair and the people of Capstown was drastic. These good people were mostly dairymen and farmers. They were kind and down-to-earth, and we instantly felt a kinship with them.

It was late by the time we left the feast. Garrick and Brierly laughed and talked as they walked in front of Ellie and me. Garrick veered off to his tent, sweeping Brierly into his arms. She squealed. "Garrick, put me down. You'll hurt your shoulder."

"I have to carry you across the threshold."

Brierly giggled. "It's a tent."

He ducked through the tent flap. "I know, someday I'll give you a big old house, but right now this is all I have."

Ellie wrapped her arm around me. "They certainly seem happy. Don't they?"

I pulled her closer and kissed her forehead. "Like we are?"

She smiled. "Yes."

FOURTEEN

Ally

Garrick swam next to me as I floated in the warm, slow-moving current of the river, my eyes closed against the afternoon sun. "You do realize we're both having our honeymoons in Algonia, don't you?" I said.

He splashed water in my face. "What kind of dumb question is that? Of course I realize I'm having my honeymoon. The fact that Brierly climbed into my bed last night was impossible to miss."

I wiped my eyes but caught a glimpse of his grin. "No, I mean isn't it mind-boggling that we're here? Especially considering where we started out. Last year we were racing down the Shuylian border trying to catch up with Legard so we could rescue Ellie and Davy."

"Yeah, little brother, I guess you're right. It is pretty amazing."

I raised my head and started treading water. "What are you going to do with Brierly when we get back to the capital city?"

Garrick lay still, floating in the current next to me. "I don't think what I'm doing with my wife is any of your concern," he answered with a chuckle.

I pushed his head under the water and he came up coughing and spitting. "You know I'm not talking about that. What are you going to tell Archidus? Do you want to stay here, or are you going to try to bring Brierly home with you?"

Garrick now treaded water in front of me. "Honestly, I've just been enjoying the honeymoon. I haven't thought that far ahead yet." He shrugged his shoulders. "I'll talk to Brierly—see what she wants to do—and then go from there."

I nodded. "I hope the Master lets you both go back and forth. I won't like it if you're stuck here. It's nice being able to find you if I need something."

"I'd like that too. We'd better head toward camp before someone gets worried."

Garrick and I swam to shore. We were in the desert high country, not far from the southern border of Algonia, and the temperature had to be over a hundred degrees. The only relief from the heat came from the river or the dark of night. We hobbled across the rocks in our bare feet to our clothes and got dressed. There were two more stops on the tour before we returned to the capital city, and we had already been on the road for over a month. It had felt like a long trip, and I welcomed the thought of going home soon.

⁎

The sweat trickling down my spine had me dreaming of another swim. Our group had set up camp near the trees lining the river's edge. The town was similarly situated farther downriver, taking advantage of the water to run their mills and irrigate their crops. White and black sheep polka-dotted the hillsides in the distance. The wool market was big here, and throughout the day shepherds could be seen leading their flocks to and from the river.

Shahzad rang the gong. "That concludes our session covering the Southern Province in the town of Riverdale. The council and company will depart at dawn." The scribe Perry gathered up his papers, pausing to mop his brow with a handkerchief.

I slid my stool back and stood. "Garrick, you up for another swim?"

"I wish. Brierly wants to go into town and get something for her brother. It's his birthday tomorrow."

The air in the tent had become stifling, even with the flaps tied back, so I was grateful for the slight breeze as we walked out into the open. "I'll see you at dinner."

After we parted ways, I found Ellie sitting in our tent with her dress pulled up above her knees, her hair damp with sweat. "What have you been up to?" I asked.

"Brierly and I visited the orphanage in town, and they were so behind in their cleaning, we couldn't help but pitch in. I haven't worked that hard in a coon's age. I'd fancy a cold shower after the day I've had."

I smiled. "How about a swim in the river?"

"Is it private enough for a bath?"

"Probably."

"It won't be too deep for me, will it? You know I can't swim."

I dug in my trunk for a clean shirt and an Algonian towel. "You can touch the bottom. Come on. It'll be fun."

Once Ellie gathered what she needed for a bath, we walked upriver, away from our camp and the village. I found a secluded place surrounded by trees, just beyond where Garrick and I swam the day before. I stripped down to the Algonian equivalent of boxers and waded in to check the depth. The water gradually grew deeper yet I could still stand on the sandy bottom, making the spot perfect for a bath. "Come on in," I yelled.

Ellie set her towel and soap on a log near the water and panned the area before stepping out of her dress. Wearing her chemise, she hurried into the water.

I dunked my head and came up shaking like a dog. "Throw me the soap." I smiled as I moved toward her.

"What if you drop it?"

I cupped my hands. "I won't." A moment later the soap flew through the air in my direction. It was more slippery than I expected, and I nearly fumbled it. Ellie giggled as she watched me work up a lather. When I sank out of sight to rinse, I swam underwater to her. I grabbed her around the waist and pulled her to my chest as I surfaced. She screamed, her elbow catching the side of my head as she tried to get away. Laughing, I shook my head again, spraying water in her face.

"Relax," I said, then kissed her. I glanced down, admiring the way the wet fabric clung to her every curve. "I love you."

"Uh-huh. I love you too, but I'll thank you to give me the soap so I can scrub. For aught we know this is a popular bathing spot, and I won't take kindly to getting caught in my underthings."

Grinning, I held the soap in front of me. "Do you want help?"

She snatched the soap away. "I can manage on my own just fine, thank you."

I chuckled. "Then I'll watch."

She splashed water in my direction. "You'll do no such thing." Pointing downriver toward the camp, she said, "Go practice that swimming you are so fond of. And please stand guard for me. I hear you and Garrick have had a lot of practice lately, and I don't fancy anyone interrupting my bath."

I stood and bowed dramatically. "Yes, my lady. Your wish, as always, is my command." I turned and dove underwater to swim out into the current. After a few freestyle strokes, I looked back to catch one last glimpse of Ellie before I reached the bend in the river.

I began a lazy backstroke toward shore, closing my eyes as the sun warmed my face. When I turned to check my progress, I had gone farther downriver than I intended. The current was deceptively strong, and I swam for all I was worth toward the shore. My feet touched solid ground and I scrambled out of the river, watching each barefooted step I took. *Smart one, Harper. Way to think ahead.* Dumping my clothes and boots in a pile and swimming away without my counter hadn't been the brightest idea. Obviously, I had been a little distracted.

I picked my way over the rocky ground, heading toward the bend in the river and the grove of trees where I'd left Ellie. Movement near the brush caught my eye. I stood still and scanned the area. Nothing. I tried jogging and winced when a sharp stone jabbed my heel. A flash of gray moved through the branches.

My pulse raced. I tried again to run and nearly cursed out loud. My gaze darted between the ground and the foliage lining the river. I wanted to yell Ellie's name to see if she was okay, but if someone was here, the last thing I wanted to do was draw attention to her.

Another flash of gray moved in the brush, closer than before. I glanced at the ground ahead, planning out my route, and then looked up. I sucked in a quick breath and stopped in my tracks. Appearing out of nowhere, someone in a tattered gray cloak materialized fifty feet in front of me. The large hood covered enough of his head that I couldn't see his face, but he was tall and built.

Like Legard.

The sun had nearly dried me, but I broke out in a sweat at the mere thought of my old nemesis. I felt as vulnerable as if I were still chained in Arbon's dungeon—unarmed, no counter, barefooted, and nearly naked. I didn't see how it could get any worse until I remembered Ellie.

I turned toward the river as the gray-cloaked figure lifted his hood and let it fall onto his shoulders. Blond hair caught the glint of the sun as his ice-blue eyes connected with mine.

Legard.

He walked a straight line toward me, and I didn't see how I could protect my wife except to lead him away from her. I splashed into the river, ignoring the rocks underfoot. As I was about to dive under, I felt a hand on my shoulder. I met Legard's gaze and fought to free myself, but his grip, although firm, didn't hurt like it had when he'd grabbed me near the Borderlands.

He transported me back to shore and released me. I raised my fist, but at the quirk of his eyebrows, I lowered my hand and sighed. Without my counter, there was nothing I could do to escape him. "What do you want?" I asked.

He smiled. "I wish to talk."

"Go ahead. Nothing's stopping you."

I thought Legard might retaliate after my smart-aleck remark, but his expression remained calm. "I have need of an advocate—an ally," he said. "Will you help me?"

I couldn't believe what I was hearing. Probably some trick to get me to lower my guard so he could steal my counter and finish the job he'd started more than a year ago. "We're enemies, Legard. You tried to kill me. There's no way I'm buying this crap."

"At that time, I sought only to extend you mercy. While in the dungeon, tell me you didn't at least once wish I had succeeded?"

That's true. I actually cursed you for failing.

"For most," Legard continued, "death is a welcome companion when compared to torture. And the girl you are so fond of—I took my time searching for her, but I would have caught her eventually. Lord Arbon would have done things to her you cannot imagine. You see, we know the protective instincts instilled in the Keepers of Protector and Guardian won't allow them to give up their counters regardless of any physical pain. They will always die first. Arbon knew his best chance at breaking you was to find someone you cared about more than yourself."

Ellie stepped onto the path, toweling off her wet hair as she walked. Legard had his back to her, and I fought to keep my facial expression neutral when what I wanted to do was yell at her to run. "Nice story, but why are you telling me this?"

"As I said, I need an advocate—someone to represent me before the council. Once I was a foolish boy and made a grave mistake. That decision cost me hundreds of years of my life, and the love and loyalty of my family and friends. I wish to petition the council for the right to earn back my citizenship."

Ellie noticed us and stopped walking. Although I focused my attention on Legard, my peripheral vision caught her movement as she retreated into the trees.

I raised my eyebrows. "You want to be Algonian?"

My old enemy smiled, and for once he didn't look mean, just tired. "Yes, Protector, I wish to rejoin my people. Algonia has always held my heart, although my actions were contrary." Almost as if he had been looking in a rearview mirror, he turned around the moment Ellie stepped back into the open. She held my sword in front of her.

"I shan't detain you any longer," Legard said. "I would not want to further upset your lovely lady when she apparently has need of your company. I shall return in a few days to continue our conversation."

Legard took three steps, his long stride devouring the ground, and then he vanished. Ellie broke into a run and didn't stop until she launched herself into my arms. I took my sword from her. With trembling fingers, she pressed my counter into the palm of my hand. "Darling, that was Legard," she gasped. "Why did he leave like that? Never mind, we can talk later. Please take me back at once."

I may have been in shock, because my mind was blank except for the urge to get my boots on my aching feet. I flipped open my counter, checked the coordinates, and pressed Go. When Ellie and I appeared in the grove near the riverbank, I stooped to gather up my clothes.

"Chase, say something. What did he want?"

I pulled my shirt over my head and stepped into my breeches. "He wants my help getting his Algonian citizenship back."

Ellie shook her head. "That's absurd. I imagine after all he's done, if the council gets hold of him, he'll be hanged for sure. Might it not be a trap? You don't believe him, do you?"

With my sword in its sheath, I sat on a log to brush the dirt from my feet and then looked up at her. "I'm not sure what I believe anymore, but I know we haven't seen the last of him."

FIFTEEN

Debate

We reappeared at our camp in front of two soldiers, who quickly changed direction to avoid bumping into us. "Excuse me, sir," one said. The other dipped his head to Ellie. "Good day, my lady."

She curtsied in return. I scanned the area for Garrick, then laced my fingers through Ellie's and led her to his tent.

"Garrick," I called through the canvas. No one answered.

Ellie and I turned at the sound of horses approaching. When Marcus and three of his soldiers reached us, he reined in his horse. "Protector, Lady Ellie." He nodded to each of us. "If you seek the Guardian, he and my sister are in town visiting the shops." Marcus smiled. "Although they were quite secretive as to why."

I grabbed my counter. "Thanks. We'll look for them there." The soldiers nudged their horses into a trot just before I pressed Go.

Several people glanced at Ellie and me after we materialized out of nowhere in the center of town. But it didn't raise eyebrows, since elves and sorcerers regularly did this sort of thing around here.

As we walked past a bakery, the smell of fresh bread made my mouth water. The display window in the potter's shop featured colorful plates, bowls, and vases. The silversmith had locking cases to display his fancy wares—everything from spoons to jewelry, all polished to a high shine.

Ellie tugged on my arm. "There they are."

Across the street, inside the door of the Durstman Woolen Goods, stood Garrick and Brierly. We waited as a wagon with a span of four horses trotted past, and then we crossed the road. Ellie waved to Brierly, who then pointed us out to Garrick. They were talking to an older woman with curly gray hair tucked under a white bonnet.

Brierly lifted a wool blanket off a stack and smiled at Ellie. "Won't this be perfect for Marcus? Feel how soft and thick it is, and look, it's in the Algonian colors—the same as our flag."

The wool was a brilliant royal blue with a gold-and-black plaid. I touched the blanket after Ellie, who said, "Oh yes, this is quite lovely. I'll guarantee he likes it."

"Last time Marcus visited me, he complained more than once about shivering in his tent at night," Brierly said.

Garrick handed two small silver coins to the woman and thanked her. "I can wrap it in a wee bit of muslin for ya," she said.

Brierly nodded. "Thank you. That would be nice."

A minute later Garrick stepped out of the shop, the muslin package tucked under one arm, Brierly's hand resting on his other. "Little brother, how was the swim?"

My concern over Legard didn't allow me to even crack a smile. "Good, but I need to talk with you." I glanced around. There were too many people within hearing distance. "In private."

Garrick frowned. "Let me escort my wife back to camp, and then we can talk."

"She can hear what I have to say. I just don't want all these other people overhearing."

We followed the street at a brisk walk. When the path back to our camp neared the river, Garrick pointed to a shady spot in the distance. "How about over there? Looks private enough."

We seated ourselves on some boulders and fallen tree trunks. "Legard found me," I said. "While Ellie was bathing, I swam downriver. When I was walking back, he watched me from the woods. The next thing I knew he was standing in front of me, asking for my help. He wants me to be his advocate to the council. He wants an ally. He wants to earn back his Algonian citizenship, and he's going to find me in a couple of days for my answer."

Garrick scowled, his hand tightening around the pommel of his sword. "Tell him to go back to Shuyle where he belongs. He made his bed. Now he can lie in it."

"He said something about making a mistake and it costing him hundreds of years," I explained. "What do you think he meant by that?"

Garrick shook his head. "Nothing. Legard is a liar and a murderer. We're talking about Arbon's main Sniffer. He's trying to deceive you, Harper."

"What should I do when he comes back?"

"Run him through with your sword. That's why you have it."

I slid my hands through my hair. "He could have killed me today, but he didn't. I don't know what to think."

"He nearly killed both of us the last time we were here. I'm not about to forget that, and neither should you. This needs to be reported to Wickliff and Shahzad. They'll know what to do."

—✤—

An hour later I stood in front of Shahzad and Wickliff, retelling the story. They both listened intently until I finished. "Well," I said, "what do you think I should do when he comes back?"

"I tend to agree with the Guardian," Wickliff replied. "His list of deceptions is as long as the length of his life, and I don't trust his motives. But your sword is no match for his magic. You need an escort whose skills match his."

Shahzad nodded. "I agree. But are you not curious as to why none of our Gatekeepers sensed Legard's presence in our lands? And neither did Archidus. We should have been warned as soon as he crossed our border."

Wickliff rested his chin on his knuckles. "Archidus has had his sights on Legard long enough that I too am surprised he failed to notice his presence in Algonia."

I looked at Wickliff. "You're the only one I know who can stand up to Legard."

"Propulsion's Keeper has the skills to protect you as well. One of us will be at your side at all times."

After forty-eight hours, I was ready to ditch my bodyguards. Don't get me wrong—I liked Wickliff and Castile, but I wanted some alone time. What I had to decide was if I wanted the privacy bad enough to risk a run-in with Legard.

We had left the beautiful town of Riverdale and now journeyed toward the coast region—the Shipping Province and the Elf Province. Our company traveled northeast, following the winding dirt roads that crossed the eastern mountain range. Pine trees towered above us, providing welcome shade from the blistering summer sun. Everyone knew each other after all the time we'd spent together, and a general feeling of camaraderie existed throughout the group.

My grumbling stomach reminded me that dinner time was getting close. Within the hour we stopped in a clearing skirted by the river we'd already crossed several times that day. As I helped set up the tents, I noticed the sound of rushing water in the distance, but the foliage kept me from seeing anything. "The water sure is loud," I said.

"Aye, might be a bit of rapids, or a waterfall," said the soldier next to me. He dropped the empty canvas bag and smiled. "Someone shorted us a couple of tent stakes. I'll fetch more and return shortly."

I dropped the hammer and rope and walked toward the woods, knowing Ellie would love to see a waterfall. The river appeared to turn after it came out of the woods, so I figured I could get a glimpse of what lay ahead without going far.

I pushed dead branches out of my way as I entered the forest. The sunlight filtering through the trees glistened off the water's clear surface, and occasionally I saw what looked like a brown trout dart away from the riverbank. The roar of rushing water increased and a woodpecker beat out a staccato rhythm on a dead tree trunk, quickly drowning out the sounds of camp.

As the terrain rose sharply in front of me, I felt sure there would be a waterfall. I was about to turn around and come back later with Ellie, and maybe Garrick and Brierly, when I noticed a bush covered in orange. It moved as if breathing. Curious, I wrapped my hand around the pommel of my sword and moved closer. Recognition dawned and I smiled.

Suddenly, Legard materialized in front of me. "Good day, Keeper." Startled, I drew my sword and swung at him. Behind the Sniffer, the bush erupted as a thousand monarch butterflies took to the sky. Legard raised his hand and I cringed, expecting to fly through the air and land in a paralyzed heap. But I felt nothing, except my sword swinging through empty air.

He reappeared to my left. I stepped back and turned, my sword poised for action. I cursed the stupid butterflies and the insatiable curiosity that had brought me out here alone and unprotected. "What do you want?"

Legard took a step in my direction, smiling. "I do not wish you harm. Please allow me to speak with you."

The "please" caught my attention, along with his hopeful expression. Plenty of men had tried to hurt me over the years, and none had that look in his eyes. I lowered my sword. "Go ahead."

"Have you considered my request?"

"I have."

"And?"

"No one trusts you. They think you're lying. That it might be a trap."

"It is not. I desire to come before the council and beg forgiveness. Once I have explained my error, I am hopeful they will see fit to pardon me." He shook his head and frowned. "I was so young—a naïve and foolish lad, willing to do his friend's bidding without pausing to think for himself."

At the remorse showing plainly on his face, I put away my sword, deciding to trust him for the moment. "If you want my help, explain it to me."

He exhaled, seeming relieved. "Yes, Keeper, I will. For it is a story that begs to be told, and my tongue has been tied for far too long. Hundreds of years ago, when this world was new and the counters were first forged, Arbon and I were friends—nearly inseparable. He was bold and daring, someone we all admired. Although not of an age to be considered an adult, I was very powerful and my skills were advanced beyond my years. So were Arbon's. He thought he would be named Master Keeper, and he vowed I would be his second in command.

"We swore fealty to one another. Whatever our future held, we would stand side by side. We thought we were invincible. One night at a party, he pulled me into an alcove of the castle and drew a dagger from his belt. The blade glowed red. Arbon ran the tip across the palm of his hand and whispered an incantation. The music in the hall kept me from clearly hearing his words. When I asked, he said we were brothers in all but blood. 'Join hands with me, brother,' he said.

"I'll admit the wine had flowed freely that night. I clasped his hand, thinking to humor him and be done with it, since I had promised the next dance to someone special. He smiled and told me to repeat what he said." Legard's shoulders slumped as he paused. "The words were in an ancient language I didn't speak, but to my everlasting horror, I repeated them. When the last phrase left my mouth, my hand burned as if I was holding a hot branding iron. I tried to pull away, but I couldn't. Arbon laughed and said, 'Now we are eternal blood brothers.' Without realizing what I'd done, I'd sworn a blood oath to Arbon. In effect, I'd surrendered my agency to him and made myself his slave.

"His fight was never my fight. I tried to escape but tasted only the sting of his lash, never the freedom I desired. The last time I talked with you, Protector, you accused me of being your enemy— of trying to kill you. But I knew what lay in store for you when I handed you over to him that day, and I sought to give you what I wish someone could have given me—freedom from a life controlled by Arbon's brutality.

"A blood oath can only be broken by death. So back on the old world, when you told me Arbon was dead, I had to see for myself. I did not wish to fight you or the Guardian that day, and if my master had truly perished, then I was free. Free of his thoughts, his pressure and coercion. I would once again be able to act and choose for myself.

"I have spent the last year charting my course home. I have family in the Elf Province, and if I had Algonian citizenship, I would be under that jurisdiction. I desire you to present me before the council and stand as my advocate. I wish for your protection."

I laughed at that, although I shouldn't have. He seemed so serious and worried, it was probably rude of me. "You don't need my protection. You could kill me with one of those magic electric pulses as easy as I could swat a fly."

"That may be true, but at first sight the council could very well sentence me to death for the crimes Arbon forced upon me. If one member believes in me and opposes the others, it will buy me the time I need to plead my case and perhaps petition Master Archidus."

The barking of hounds sounded in the distance. *The soldiers must be looking for me.*

Legard stepped closer and offered his hand. "Protector, you can believe me."

I probably shouldn't have, but I took a chance and shook his hand. As was the custom in Algonia, he wrapped his fingers around my wrist and squeezed. I hesitated a moment and then returned his smile, realizing he was either not the person I'd thought him to be, or he was an exceptional liar.

SIXTEEN

Elf Province

Legard disappeared the moment he released my hand. I walked back toward the camp, pausing to rub the heads of the two large hounds when they found me. They circled me, the tone of their barking changing slightly. The faithful dogs had been with our group since Algonia. Several of the soldiers seemed to claim them, so maybe they were army dogs. A moment later, Marcus, Castile, and a group of armed soldiers broke through the thick foliage.

By the scowl on Marcus's face I knew he was angry, but he gave a slight bow and calmly said, "Keeper, it is good you are well. We feared for your safety."

I smiled. Being a Keeper had its perks. It put me in the "almost royalty" class, and only Master Archidus seemed to be allowed to reprimand us. "I'm sorry, but there's no need to worry. I'm not in danger anymore. Come on, let's go back to camp."

I led Ellie, Garrick, and Brierly along the same path I'd taken the day before. A few of the large monarch butterflies remained, clinging to the tree trunks or floating through the air in front of us. We found the falls and sat to admire the water cascading over the bluish-gray rocks. Ellie leaned her head against my shoulder. "Chase, this is lovely."

I agreed with her and turned to Garrick. "I should tell you that I talked with Legard again." I raised my hand when he opened his mouth. "Let me finish. He was tricked into making a blood oath with Arbon when he was young. He was probably drunk and not thinking clearly. Arbon used a spell in some ancient language, and Legard didn't know what he was agreeing to. He lost his free will and became a slave to Arbon. I believe Legard just wants to come home, and I've agreed to be his advocate before the council. He's going to bring his case to us in the Elf Province."

I expected a lecture from Garrick, but I got a quiet comment from Brierly. "That would explain his odd behavior around the castle."

I raised my eyebrows. "What do you mean?"

"He could be uncharacteristically kind at times," she said. "But if Lord Arbon expressed displeasure with anyone, Legard always followed suit. Once he even stopped what he was doing to carry a heavy basket of grapes down to the winepress for me. He was quite the gentleman, but I never saw him smile. He rarely sought pleasure or leisure for himself, and seemed to be in a state of constant discontent."

"If he was kind to my wife, I'll listen to what he has to say," Garrick declared.

The Shipping Province reminded me a little of Boston harbor in 1863, except the town wasn't nearly as populated, and everything smelled like fish. We ate seafood every night we were there, too. They shipped goods inland via the river and between the other towns located up and down the coast, as well as selling smoked salmon and salted fish of all varieties to the other provinces.

Although the thought of bringing Legard before the council once we arrived in the Elf Province stressed me out, I was happy when we left the stink of the Shipping Province behind. At best, I figured the other Keepers would think I was stupid and maybe crazy. Worst-case scenario, Wickliff and Castile would take Legard out before either one of us got a chance to say a word. Whatever happened, I just hoped I didn't get caught in the crossfire.

The woods near the Elf Province felt magical. Exotic-looking birds kept up a chorus of songs above us, and if I lined up all the different butterflies I'd seen in the past two days, they'd make a rainbow. After Garrick spotted a buck off the trail, Marcus sent two soldiers out to hunt. Thanks to their efforts, we dined on fresh, roasted venison and wild pork for the next few days.

Intricately carved wooden mile markers staked the ground at regular intervals, signaling our progress. As we neared the first elf settlement, Ellie raised her hand to shield her eyes from the sun and said, "What a whimsical little house that is."

I looked past my horse's ears to where a yellow cottage with green trim and a dark orange roof sat nestled in a flower garden. My mom would have loved the curly willow chairs and table on the porch. The roofline sloped and curved around each window. After all the barn construction I'd done, this looked like a builder's nightmare. But Ellie was right—definitely whimsical, and it fit the woman who stepped out the front door.

A silver clip held her long blond ringlets away from her face. She wore a blue dress tied at the waist with a green belt. She raised a hand and called out a greeting. A small girl with a mop of red curls and pointy elf ears ran out the door and hugged her mother's leg. She stuck her thumb in her mouth when I smiled at her and waved.

No two houses were alike in this province. Each one was unique in style and color. When I asked Creation's Keeper about it, she explained that every elf is born with magic. But that magic manifests itself in different ways. Some are seers, some warriors, some manipulate the elements, but many are exceptionally skilled in the arts—creative, inventive, and healing arts.

No wonder the town looked so decked out. Even the cobblestone streets had designs etched into random stones—an oak leaf here, a sunflower there, the moon, or the sun. Ellie oohed and ahhed next to me, pointing from one side of the street to the other. The stuff displayed in the elves' shop windows was way nicer than anything we'd seen in the other villages.

We camped in a meadow on the south end of town and prepared for the welcome feast. When a maid came to do Ellie's hair, I stepped out to see what everybody else was up to. Marcus stood next to his horse, speaking with Garrick. The six soldiers who would accompany us were mounted and ready. Their horses stood in a circle, most with a back foot cocked, resting while the men talked and made jokes. Our carriages, footmen, and drivers waited. Shahzad, Wickliff, and Castile were visiting with two elves I'd never seen before.

I stepped next to Garrick and Marcus. "Hey, what's going on?"

Garrick tipped his head toward his tent. "Waiting on the ladies."

Marcus smiled. "As usual. On the morrow, some of my men want to visit Caverdale, the sword smith, for a bit of sport. Maybe a friendly wager. Would the two of you care to join us?"

"I'm always up for a little sport," Garrick said. "How about it, little brother?"

"Sure. Count me in," I said.

Suddenly, Garrick raised his eyebrows, let out a low whistle, and grinned. I followed his gaze. Brierly walked toward us in a dark-green gown, her auburn hair streaked with burnished-copper highlights in the setting sun. She had always been pretty, but since marrying Garrick something had changed. She held her head a little higher and was quicker to smile. Where she'd been timid before, she now exuded confidence. The whole combination made her stunning.

With a scowl, Marcus elbowed Garrick in the ribs and raised his fist. "It is fortunate you're her husband. A look like that from anyone else and I'd plant this in his face."

Garrick's eyes never left his new bride. "So would I, my friend. If you'll excuse me." He left us and offered Brierly his arm.

When they approached, I smiled, happy for both of them. Marcus gave a slight bow and said, "You're looking well, Sister."

She curtsied. "Thank you. But I hear tale you've made threatening remarks to my husband."

Marcus finally cracked a grin, the tanned skin around his eyes crinkling.

Within minutes, Ellie and the rest of the ladies emerged from their tents, and we climbed into the carriages. I draped an arm across my wife's shoulders and tickled her ear with my nose. "Hey, beautiful." Her maid had gone all out on the hair, and I didn't think I'd ever seen anything like it. "Nice hairdo," I whispered.

She turned her head and smiled. "Jenny said the elf people are quite fanciful and elegant. She wanted me to fit in, and she made me promise to take note of their styles tonight."

"Who's Jenny?"

"Why, the maid, of course."

I leaned back and nodded. "Of course." Ellie had a way of getting to know everyone, from the humblest servant to the king.

When I stepped into the great hall located in the center of town, I had to agree with Jenny. Everything was over the top. My boots clicked across the polished marble floor as my eye followed the carved columns stretching to the high ceiling. Colorful tapestries hanging from the walls depicted scenes from Algonia. An ice sculpture of a unicorn head spewed red liquid from its mouth into an oversized punch bowl. The centerpiece of each table was another ice sculpture, reminding me of the pictures my mom had taken when she and Dad took a week-long cruise in the Caribbean a few years ago.

The food we ate was as artistically beautiful as it was delicious. After Ellie pointed out a few of the elf women, I began to notice their elaborate attire and hairstyles. Most had long hair, woven, twisted, or braided with strands of gold or silver intertwined. Their gowns were works of art as well, but the elves were kind, gentle people. I didn't meet one snob in the whole group. Several of the older elves wore cloaks, like Wickliff's but more elaborate. All the younger ones dressed similar to Garrick and me, with breeches and fancy suit coats. Nearly every man wore a sword at his hip.

When the bells in the clock tower struck eleven, the evening came to an end. Servants darted in and out of the room like bees at their hive, clearing dishes and hauling the melting ice sculptures outside. We took our time leaving, mostly because we were waiting on Creation's Keeper and her husband, who had many close friends and relatives in attendance.

———◈———

Soft candlelight filled our tent. Ellie pulled the final pin from her hair and massaged her scalp before shaking her head. "Wasn't that meal simply divine? I'll guarantee I've never seen anything like that in all my living days."

I had stretched out on the bed to watch her, my hands clasped behind my neck. "Yeah, it was good."

She looked at me and laughed. "Good? It was a work of art and nothing less."

I rolled up on my elbow and put a little foreign accent into my voice. "Yes, my darling, every morsel of food tasted divine and it was a work of art to rival Rembrandt, or Da Vinci, or whoever those famous guys were."

Ellie chuckled, then snuffed out the candles and dropped her robe on the chair. An hour later, she lay sound asleep on my shoulder. The rampant thoughts bouncing around in my brain kept me from resting. Legard had been on my mind all day. He had said this was home and where he wanted to make his plea to the council, but we hadn't gone over any of the details. Was it my job to talk with the scribe and get Legard on the schedule? Or did he think he would just waltz in and announce his innocence? I didn't think he'd make it very far without a confrontation, if that was his plan. I needed to talk with him, and I knew of only one way to get his attention.

SEVENTEEN

Cecilia

I kissed Ellie's forehead and slid my arm out from under her. "I'll be back in a minute," I whispered. She mumbled as she rolled over and kept sleeping.

After I dressed, I opened my counter, shifted the pinpoint of light to the east coast, and pressed Go. I imagined the street near the great hall. I appeared to find the area dark and quiet, with no candle or lamplight emanating from any of the houses.

"See if you can smell this, Legard," I whispered. I started walking, pressing Go every few seconds as I imagined myself fifty feet or so farther down the road. Before long, I reached the edge of town. I transported myself back to the hall and went in another direction, disappearing and then reappearing down the street.

"Keeper," said a voice behind me as my thumb touched Go.

I spun around as I reappeared. Nothing. A chuckle sounded behind me. I wheeled back around and found myself face to face with Legard. For the first time he didn't have his cloak. He wore breeches, boots, and a white shirt that hung open to his chest. He totally had bed head. "Did I wake you?" I asked.

He scrunched up his nose. "Actually, yes. Why are you tossing around your counter signature, like you're throwing out rotten eggs?"

I pocketed my counter. "Trying to find you. It worked, huh?"

He looked over his shoulder. "Yes, but I'm not the only one around here who can smell that, you know." He reached his hand toward my shoulder. "May I?"

I wasn't sure what he was asking, but he was being so polite that I said, "Sure."

He touched me and we both disappeared. Wherever he took me was darker than the moonlit street. "Allow me to light a candle," he said. I heard him snap his fingers, and instantly a dozen or more candles flickered to life around the room. He walked to the window and drew the curtains closed, then motioned to a chair. "Would you care to be seated?"

I sat down. "Where are we?"

He settled himself in the chair across from me. "This is my mother's home, down the street from where I found you. I had opened the window upstairs to enjoy the scent of lilacs on the night breeze, but no sooner had sleep welcomed me than the Protector's stench drew me from my dreams." Legard's relaxed smile softened his words, and I knew he was teasing me. In fact, I had a feeling he was actually happy to see me.

"Well, it's good to know your nose isn't out of practice."

He laughed.

"So, what's the plan?" I asked. "Have you talked to the scribe to get your name on our schedule?"

"No, I had hoped to persuade you to do that for me. I'd also like your help getting into the hall. Without your protection, I fear Wickliff will strike before giving me a chance to speak."

I nodded, thinking Wickliff might not be the only one striking first and asking questions later. "I'll put your name on the schedule. But if you don't want me popping in and out on the street, how should I contact you?"

"Across from the great hall there is an apothecary shop—Cecilia's Herbal and Magical Remedies. Leave a message with her and I will get it. When it is my scheduled time, would you please come to the apothecary and provide me an escort and an introduction before the council?"

I smiled, feeling a little awed by the fact that I was now plotting to help the man I'd feared almost as much as Lord Arbon. "Sounds good. I'll talk with the scribe tomorrow and leave a note with Cecilia in the afternoon."

"One more thing. It may not be wise to use my name."

I nodded. "Anything else?"

Smiling, he stood and offered me his hand. I let him pull me to my feet. "That is all, and thank you, Keeper. I will forever be in your debt."

"Don't thank me yet. I haven't done anything."

He held my hand for a moment before releasing it. "In that you are wrong. You listened and you believed, when others would have scorned me."

I smiled. "In that case, you're welcome. Can I use my counter to leave, or will that stink up your mom's house too much?"

"You may use your counter. I'll open the windows after you are gone."

The next morning, I stood in line with the elves bringing cases before the council. There were fewer petitions than in the other provinces. After what I'd seen last night, that didn't surprise me. The elves were intelligent, kind, and considerate.

I stepped up to the scribe's table and cleared my throat. Perry lowered his feathered quill. "How may I assist you, Keeper?"

I pointed at his schedule book. "I need to schedule a time for a friend of mine—an elf friend."

Perry dipped his quill into the ink. "Name?"

"Just put 'Anonymous.' I'll introduce him before the council."

The scribe raised his eyebrows but did as I said. "And this request is regarding?"

"A petition for Algonian citizenship."

Perry scratched the words onto the parchment. I could tell I had his full attention as he looked up at me. "A Shuylian friend, eh?"

"Maybe." I touched the book where he had written my request. "What time do you think we'll hear his petition?"

"Tomorrow, in the morning."

"Thank you. Can I please borrow your pen and a scrap of paper?"

Perry handed me his quill and a piece of parchment the size of an index card. I put the quill to the parchment and began to write the note to Legard. A blob of ink landed where I intended to write a "T," and then the ink faded to nothing before I finished the second "O" in tomorrow. I dipped the quill again, covering the tip with dark ink.

The scribe leaned forward, "May I be of assistance? You've too much ink to form proper letters."

I held out the quill pen, and he quickly rescued it from what I'm sure he considered my abusive hand. With care he wiped the excess ink on a soft cloth. He rolled the quill between his fingers as he dipped it in the inkwell. "You wish to inform your friend of the time?"

I nodded. "Yeah."

He wrote: "The Keepers' Council will hear your petition for Algonian citizenship on the morrow, before the noon hour."

Perry looked up. "Does that meet with your satisfaction?"

"It's perfect. Thanks." Before I could pick up the paper he sprinkled sand on the ink, and I waited while he shook it off. "What's that for?" I asked.

Perry smiled as he handed me the parchment. "The sand absorbs the excess ink. Have you not done much writing, sir?"

I touched the letters on the parchment, and a few grains of moist, dark sand stuck to my finger. "I've done a lot of writing, but never with a feather."

Garrick and I had it pretty easy in the Elf Province. Everyone showed up, and we didn't have to go chasing down any criminals with our counters. Although, if the elves around here were anything like Wickliff and Legard, we wouldn't have been able to force them to do anything they didn't want to.

As the day drew to a close, I was anxious to deliver my message to the apothecary shop and then go see Ellie. In the other provinces, we had heard cases in a large tent set up near our camp, and I frequently saw her during the day. But here we met in their great hall. The chairs were more comfortable than the stools in our tent, and the elves kept us supplied with drinks and food. But I hadn't seen my wife since early that morning.

Before leaving, I glanced at Perry's schedule book. Our anonymous case for Algonian citizenship was next up on the roster. I walked a step ahead of Garrick and Marcus as we exited the hall. "Where are you going?" Garrick asked.

I had angled left toward Cecilia's shop while my friends had all headed right. "The apothecary. I'll be back at camp in a minute. I've got an errand to run." My brother looked a bit baffled as I turned away from him and jogged across the street, dodging between two horse-drawn carriages.

A bell over the door jingled as I stepped inside Cecilia's shop. My eyes adjusted to the dimness, and I wandered down an aisle of corked vials. Some were large, some small, and I'd never seen so many different colors of glass. I smiled when I noticed some blue vials with the words "Skin Restorative" etched into the wooden sign below them. I picked one up and shook it.

"Sir, may I be of assistance?"

I spun around, finding myself face to face with an elf girl. Her hair was as black as the ink on my scrap of parchment and as curly as Ellie's. Her pale skin and dark-red lips reminded me of my sister's favorite Disney princess. I returned the vial to the shelf and took a step back. "Are you Cecilia?"

She laughed. "Oh no, I'm Atarah."

I nodded. "Is she here?"

"Certainly. She will be with you momentarily." The girl left without making a sound as she moved across the wooden floor.

I turned back to the vials, reading their names—Hair-Curling Potion, Sleeping Tonic, Relaxation Potion, Stomach Remedy, Liquid Energy, Strength Builder, and Love Serum. A door creaked and I looked up.

The woman walking toward me had to be nearly six feet tall. A golden hair clip held most of her dark hair back from her face, leaving a few loose curls near her temple. She had full lips that turned up in a slight smile. Her eyes were soft and kind. She looked close to my mom's age, but with elves that probably meant she was hundreds of years old and was aging way better than my mom. Like nearly every other elf I'd met, she was beautiful, confident, and graceful. "I am Cecilia. Atarah said you wished to speak with me."

"Is she your daughter?" I asked.

The woman shook her head, sadness clouding her features. "No. I never married."

I picked up the pink vial holding the love serum and smiled at her. "You never found anyone to use your potion on, huh? Or is love too strong an emotion to be controlled by magic?"

"I lost my love to something a love serum could never change. And, yes, in some, love can be too strong an emotion to be controlled by magic. Now what can I do for you? Are you in need of a potion? Perhaps there is a girl you wish to pursue?"

I returned the vial to the shelf and offered her the parchment. "No, but a friend of mine said I could leave a message with you. We have an appointment with the Keepers' Council first thing tomorrow morning. Do you know who I'm talking about?"

She smiled, her eyes twinkling as she took the paper. "Oh yes. I'll make sure he gets this."

I had never said my friend was a man, so I figured she must know Legard. "Thanks. Tell him I'll meet him here."

EIGHTEEN

Caverdale

"Ellie, are you going to let Harper come with us to Caverdale's?" Garrick said.

She looked up at me. "What's Caverdale's?"

"He's a famous sword smith. Marcus, Garrick, and a bunch of the guys are headed over there. You can come if you want."

Ellie smiled at Garrick's wife. "We'll leave the swordplay to you boys. Brierly and I can keep ourselves entertained."

Caverdale's shop rivaled the armory at Master Archidus' castle. Sparkling weapons and armor covered the walls from floor to ceiling. Torches cast flickering light across the wooden floor. Most of the elves I'd seen were built like runners. Caverdale, on the other hand, was built like a football player—tall and muscular with a barrel chest—and he had the forearms and biceps of a blacksmith.

Once we introduced ourselves, Garrick described his sword, which was back in Illinois, saying he thought Caverdale had made it.

The sword smith's hearty laugh filled the room. "Of course I forged it. I never forget a blade. I sold that one to Theobald, Archidus' master of weapons, in the 1960s. I'm honored to hear it is wielded by one of the Keepers."

Caverdale gave us a tour, explaining how he forged a typical sword. Some of his swords gave off a faint glow when picked up.

There was an orange-tinted blade and a blue one. When I asked why they glowed, he winked and gave a vague answer—magic. I figured that must be one of his patented trade secrets. Each sword I picked up seemed to fit my hand and felt like an extension of my arm, the same as mine did, and I had to agree with the general opinion that he was a master sword smith. I described the sword Master Archidus had given me, and Caverdale claimed to have forged it as well.

After the sword smith passed out chain mail, we formed into teams for a sparring match with blunt-tipped swords. We moved outside, and with a snap of his fingers, Caverdale brought twenty torches to life around a circular dirt ring. I stood with the three soldiers who had also drawn short sticks, across from Marcus, Garrick, and two other soldiers. We listened to Caverdale explain the rules and then donned our helmets, "At the ready, men," he yelled. "Attack!"

Mayhem reigned for the next hour during our mock battle. I had better form and speed from my fencing days, but Garrick and Marcus both swung their swords like they were batting home-runs, and all the soldiers had a lot of fighting time under their belts from the ongoing wars with Shuyle. We earned points by forcing our opponents out of bounds or disarming them. With eight of us in the ring, someone was always sneaking around behind me, but nobody called any fouls.

When we'd exhausted ourselves, Marcus raised his sword. "We're done, men."

Garrick asked who won, but Caverdale said he'd lost track of the points once both teams got in the double digits. Marcus stepped behind me and undid the clasp on my chain mail. "How was the apothecary?" he asked.

"Fine."

He chuckled. "You need a little help with your wife? Maybe a love potion?"

I wiggled my shoulders, letting the armor slide down my arms. "Knock it off, Marcus. It's nothing like that."

"I hear tell the elves make a good love potion," said Trenton, one of the soldiers. "Though I've not tried it on any of the lasses."

I undid the clasp on Trenton's chain mail. "I don't need any love potion. I'm happily married. And it's none of your business anyway." I heard Trenton and Marcus laughing as I walked toward Caverdale's shop to return my helmet and chain mail.

Every one of us walked with a limp from the bruises to our legs, and I had my arm wrapped around my sore rib cage. The old broken-rib injury had flared up with a vengeance after getting slammed by Marcus. "I'm going to be black and blue tomorrow," I said. "Ellie's not going to be happy about this."

Garrick laughed. "No she won't, little brother."

"What is that red spot on your cheek?" Ellie asked.

I blew out the two candles nearest me. "I can't see any spots."

"And how would you see anything on your face without a mirror in front of you?"

I pulled my shirt over my head and carefully lowered myself onto a stool to take off my boots. My wife walked closer, carrying a candle, and I clamped my mouth shut to keep from laughing. Round two of the reprimand should start any moment. When I bent to tug off my boot, I sucked in a sharp breath as a stab of pain went through my chest from my bruised ribs.

"You're moving like an old man. Were you attacked?"

"Aw, it's nothing. We were just messing around."

"We? Was it Garrick? Were you two sparring again?"

I smiled up at her as she ran her fingers across my cheekbone. "Yeah, with him and Marcus, and Joel, and Trenton."

Ellie set the candle on the table as she raised her eyebrows. "You were fighting all four of them?"

"Well, yeah, but I had Camden, Billy, and Jack on my team."

"Who, pray tell, are Camden, Billy, Jack, Joel, and Trenton?"

I held my hand out to her and chuckled. "Baby, they're soldiers. Now come on. Let's go to bed. I'm dead tired."

She threw up her hands and shook her head. "Do you have some kind of death wish that makes you want to go around fighting a bunch of soldiers? Really, Chase, sometimes I think you'll send *me* to an early grave with all the worry you put me through."

I pulled her onto my lap and touched my lips to her neck. "I love you, you know that?"

The next morning, I left early, not taking time for breakfast. With all my stress about how things might go when I brought Legard before the council, I wasn't hungry anyway. Ellie was still sleeping when I disappeared from my tent. I thought of the front door to the apothecary as I pressed Go.

A moment later I raised my hand and knocked. Cecilia opened the door. "Come in."

I followed her to the living quarters in the back of the shop. A small fire crackled in the hearth, and a teapot started whistling above the flames. "Please have a seat." She wrapped a towel around the kettle and moved it to the table. "I'll let Legard know you are here."

I pulled out a chair and grunted as I seated myself. Cecilia peered at me closely. "You appear injured. Would you like something? Here in the elf district we stock every possible remedy."

"Like what?"

"Describe what ails you."

"Just some bruises. A bunch of us guys were sparring with swords over at Caverdale's last night."

She laughed. "I'm surprised I wasn't called to mend something more serious. It wouldn't be the first time I received a summons from Caverdale late at night. That man enjoys his sport like no other. I have just the thing for you." She spun on her heel and left the room.

Legard appeared across the table from me and picked up the teapot. "Good morning, Keeper. Would you care for some tea?"

Seeing Legard doing something as domestic as pouring tea was a little surreal, and it took a moment for me to get my mouth in gear. "Uh, no thanks," I said.

He took a sip of tea before pulling a towel off a basket of rolls and handing me one. I ripped it in half with my teeth and chewed.

Cecilia came back with two orange vials. "Do you have other bruises besides the one on your face?"

"I've got some on my arms and legs," I said, deciding not to mention the big one I got on my butt when I fell on a rock after Marcus pushed me out of bounds. She handed me the larger vial.

"Is this a refilling vial?" I asked.

"No, but would you like one?"

Before I could answer she snatched it away and left the room. I finished my roll and grabbed another. They were dark and sweet.

"Here you are," Cecilia said as she walked toward me. "A refilling vial of bruise repair serum. After application, you should begin to feel and see results within an hour. I can help you apply it, or you may step into the back room if you wish to do it yourself."

I smiled. "I think I can do it myself." I went into the room she indicated and treated my bruises. Once I corked the vial, I shook it. Sure enough, it was full again. I couldn't wait to see Ellie to point out how uninjured I actually was after last night's adventure.

I held up the vial as I walked back into the kitchen. "Do you want this back?"

"Keep it," Cecilia said. "In your line of work it might be useful to have around."

"Thanks." I pocketed the vial and turned to Legard. "You ready?"

He finished his tea and stepped in front of Cecilia. He held her hand and rubbed his thumb across her knuckles, pausing to look down when he touched the ring on her finger. I caught a glimpse of his brief smile before he leaned forward and whispered in her ear. As he pulled away, he unbuckled the belt holding his sword and wrapped the leather around the sword's sheath, before placing it in her hands. "I won't need this where I'm going. Please keep it for me."

She touched his cheek and said, "Godspeed, and may we both live long enough to be together again."

He nodded before turning and walking out of her kitchen. Clutching the sword to her chest, Cecilia pulled her tear-filled gaze away from the empty doorway and looked at me. "Please watch over him."

"I will," I said.

Legard stood waiting inside the apothecary shop, facing the door. When I reached for the knob, he grabbed my arm. "If it doesn't go well today, I'd rather not be seen walking out of this door. Cecilia should not be made to suffer for associating with me."

I pulled my hand back and reached for my counter. "Okay, should I meet you inside the hall?"

"You'll need to take me in. To ensure the safety of the Keepers, someone will have put a shield over the hall to prevent anyone who isn't a Keeper from transporting into the council meeting."

I vaguely remembered hearing something about that during our training at the castle, and I wondered what else I might have tuned out while I was dreaming of my honeymoon. "Oh yeah." I clicked the counter open and placed my hand on Legard's shoulder.

He faced me and placed a hand on my shoulder as well. "Keeper, take care. If I'm attacked, there is no need for you to fall victim as well. You've already done more for me than I deserve, and for that I am grateful."

I looked deep into his eyes and felt my throat constrict. He had set aside his sword and would walk into what might turn out to be a lion's den. I had a feeling he did not intend on fighting, and whether I was right or not, I decided then and there that I'd do whatever it took to keep him alive. This wasn't the same man that had hunted me. He had changed, and I figured he deserved a second chance. I wondered why Legard had sought my help, out of the seven Keepers. That question would have to wait. We'd be late if we didn't get moving.

NINETEEN

The Tether

I imagined the entrance to the elves' hall. There would be four soldiers standing guard outside, and Marcus would be inside with Garrick and a couple more soldiers. Wickliff and the other Keepers should be gathering around the table, getting ready to hear the first case of the day. By now they might even be wondering where I was.

I pressed Go. Legard and I materialized inside the hall. I left my hand on his shoulder and took a step forward, nudging him so he kept pace with me. The buzz of conversation around the room died as people noticed us. The sound of swords sliding from scabbards behind me caught my attention. I spun around, raising my hand in warning. Marcus and his men held their weapons at the ready and were advancing on us. "Stand down, you guys." I said. "He's with me."

Marcus stopped but didn't lower his weapon. We continued toward the table. Castile and Shahzad rose to their feet, and their eyes never leaving the elf walking next to me, their hands twitching at their sides.

Wickliff raised his staff, and I felt Legard flinch.

I took a protective stance in front of my former nemesis and held up both hands as if to deflect the tornado of magical energy brewing in front of me. "Wait," I said. "Please hear us out. Legard comes in peace and unarmed—other than the magic stuff he can do, but he's not gonna do any of that. He just wants to talk. Lord Arbon was using him. He didn't even want to do any of that crap he did."

I panned the room, taking in the guarded expressions. Quiet hung in the room until Garrick said, "I vote we hear what Legard has to say. Everyone deserves a chance to explain himself."

Wickliff partially lowered his staff. "How is it you entered Algonia, Legard?"

"I simply walked across the border."

The old elf shook his head. "But you are on our watch list as an enemy. Someone should have sensed your presence at once."

"Uncle, the gatekeepers look for trouble and malice. I come in peace. I mean no harm, and my heart is loyal to Algonia."

Again silence stretched out between us, until Shahzad spoke. "The Keepers' Council is hereby brought to order and will address the petition for Algonian citizenship by Legard, formerly second in command of the Shuylian nation, but apparently without a country at the moment. Due to the history involved and the dangerous nature of this situation, I propose the plaintiff submit to tethering by another elf of equal skill, before we begin."

Legard stepped in front of me, lowered his head, and held his hands out in front of him. "I acquiesce."

"Wickliff, if you would please . . ." Shahzad said.

The old elf raised his staff and whispered a phrase. A bolt of light the same color as the one inside my counter shot out of his staff and circled his nephew's wrists and ankles with transparent blue manacles and a chain that looked more like a hologram than real metal. A thick cable of light linked Legard's wrists to Wickliff's staff. The whole thing glowed. Legard grunted and fell to his knees as if a huge weight had dropped onto his shoulders. He took a deep breath and raised his eyes to meet his uncle's.

I'd learned during previous discussions with Wickliff that elves and other magicals are only able to give birth once in their lifetime.

When I'd questioned the old elf on how Legard could possibly be his nephew, Wickliff said he was born with a twin sister named Wilmeeka, who later became Legard's mother.

"The council will please be seated," Shahzad announced.

I frowned as I watched the tether's effect on Legard. "Protector," Shahzad said, pulling my attention away from the elf, "if you will please take your seat we shall begin."

I moved to the other side of the table and sat next to Garrick. Wickliff remained standing with his staff trained on Legard. The older elf seemed to be in a serious mood, although not visibly straining from the magic he was using on his prisoner.

"How do you wish to plead your case? Verbally or via inquest?" Shahzad asked.

Legard met his gaze. "Inquest, and I request permission for the entire council to witness my testimony."

"I see no harm in that. Your request is granted. Step forward."

Legard climbed to his feet and shuffled to the table. He lifted his chained hands and Shahzad grasped one of his wrists. Kalipsia, Creation's Keeper, and Castile, Propulsion's Keeper, touched Shahzad's arm. Castile placed his other hand on Raoul and motioned for him to do the same to Illusion's Keeper. Kalipsia touched Garrick's wrist, who then reached over and grabbed mine. Shahzad closed his eyes, and a moment later a vision began playing out in my mind.

The hall of Archidus' castle stretched before me. I heard music and laughing. The air held a haze of smoke from the fires burning in the double hearths. We entered the great hall on the ground floor. A party, like something that could have happened in a Camelot movie, was in full swing. There was dancing in the center, with groups of people talking and eating along the walls. I recognized much younger versions of Archidus and Legard talking with each other. They looked about the age of juniors in high school and were clearly friends. Legard smiled, then elbowed Archidus and pointed to the entrance. A group of girls in fancy dresses had just walked in. One elf girl, who looked an awful lot like Azalit, caught my attention. She must have been the one Legard pointed out to Archidus, because he handed Legard his wine glass and crossed the room to her. Archidus bowed and then held out his hand. She smiled and placed her hand in his, and they joined the crowd of dancers.

Archidus looked away from his dance partner to Legard, who then raised the wine glass in salute and tossed the liquid down his throat. The elf placed the empty glass on a servant's tray, then drained his own glass in one long swallow. He wiped the back of his hand across his lips, straightened his tunic, and took the same path as Archidus had toward the group of girls.

One of the girls smiled at Legard before dropping her gaze. She had dark hair and stood taller than the others, and as I looked closer I recognized Cecilia. All the girls turned and started flirting with Legard. I guess for a guy, he was pretty good-looking. He had the build of a basketball player—tall, broad shouldered, and athletic. His blond hair was cut short, and his blue eyes had a mischievous sparkle when he smiled.

He reached past the other girls and offered his hand to Cecilia, who looked like she was the shy one of the bunch. When she took his hand, he shot her what my sister would have termed a winning smile. They never made it onto the dance floor, though.

My pulse quickened at the sight of Arbon sliding up next to Legard and wrapping his arm around the elf's shoulder. "I need a moment of your time, my friend."

Legard frowned. "Can it not wait?"

Arbon beckoned to a servant with a wave of his hand and gave Cecilia a goblet of wine. "Here, my lady. This song is nearly at an end. I'll have him back to you before the next set begins."

Legard raised her hand to his lips. "Wait for me?"

Cecilia smiled, blushing. "Of course."

Completely focused on the girl in front of him, Legard didn't seem to notice the wicked twist of Arbon's mouth or the evil glint in his eye. By the time Legard turned his full attention to his friend, Arbon's face was a mask of indifference.

As the two friends walked away, Arbon snatched a couple more glasses of wine. "I've had too many of these already," Legard said when Arbon handed him one. "Had to work up my courage to talk with Cecilia, and now you pull me away from her?"

"Drink up. It'll do you good. But you've no need of courage where that girl's concerned. I think she'd do anything for you, and if I don't take care, I'll lose you to a woman."

Legard put the goblet to his lips and drank the wine. "You'll never lose me. I may love a woman, but we will always stand together. Soon you will be named Master Keeper, and Archidus and I will be at your side, as always."

Arbon laughed. "My little brother . . . more like underfoot as usual. My friend, *you* are more a brother to me than he who shares my father's blood, but I fear it will not always be so. People change."

Legard had followed him down the hall and into a small room. He gripped Arbon's shoulder and smiled. "I'll never change. Your nerves are getting the better of you. This is a momentous week in your life and in Algonian history, and I assure you nothing will change between us. What need I do to prove it?"

Arbon's sigh was followed by a charming smile. "You are right, Legard. Perhaps it is just the jitters as I await the announcement of the Master Keeper. But to ease my mind, will you swear fealty to me and become my brother in blood as well as in purpose?"

"Anything. But hurry. I've promised the next dance to Cecilia, and I've left my heart in her hands. I'm anxious to claim both."

Arbon drew a dagger from his belt. Some of Caverdale's swords glowed, but none of them had a blood-red gleam like this blade. With the flick of his wrist Arbon slit his hand. Drops of crimson hit the stone floor as he handed the blade to Legard.

"Don't you think you're overindulging your nerves just a wee bit?" the elf said with the dagger poised above his palm. He winced as the blade separated his flesh.

Arbon grabbed Legard's hand and squeezed. "Not at all. Say this, my friend, and then I will leave you to your dancing." The words that followed were unrecognizable, at least to me. Legard paused when it was his turn, his eyebrows knit together in confusion. Arbon squeezed his hand tighter. "Speak it, my friend. The next dance is about to begin."

Legard glanced over his shoulder and then quickly repeated the phrase to Arbon. As the last word left his mouth, his body jerked. He yanked his hand away. The blood ran black from the cut. With a look of fear, he raised he eyes to Arbon. "What have you done?"

Arbon laughed as he sheathed the dagger. "'Tis not what I have done. 'Tis what you have done. You swore a blood oath to me. Now we are brothers in blood, and I have my assurance that you shall always stand by my side. Go, enjoy your dance. I will have need of you on the morrow."

Moments later, Legard stood alone in the small room, cradling his hand. He fell to his knees and cried, "What have I done?" When he got up, he staggered as if dizzy or drunk. He took three steps and disappeared, transporting himself to the entrance of the dance hall. He leaned against the doorframe as he looked for Cecilia. She stood where he'd left her, a crowd of people separating them, her eyes searching the room while her thumb absentmindedly rubbed the spot on her knuckles his lips had touched. Legard pulled himself out of sight and lowered his head, staring at his hand as he disappeared.

The vision blurred and then shifted to a new scene. Legard, sitting astride a palomino, galloped across a rolling plain toward a group of horsemen. He intercepted the group, jerking his horse to a stop in front of Arbon. Legard jumped to the ground and grabbed a fist full of Arbon's robe. "What have you done with my cousin?" Legard yelled as he pulled Arbon to the ground.

Arbon threw up his hand and blew Legard twenty feet through the air. "Never speak to me like that again!" Legard writhed on the ground in pain as Arbon approached. "She served her purpose well enough, and now we have no need of her. You will mount your horse and fall in with the others, but spare me your complaints. These men and I have a country to plan, and I can't think with you badgering me."

Legard looked up. "She's dead, isn't she?" When Arbon didn't deny it, the elf said, "You were supposed to propose marriage. You deceived me. You've changed. I won't follow you. This isn't what we planned, and I want no part of it."

Arbon laughed. "You've no choice in the matter, my friend. You are mine. Only death can break the bonds of a blood oath—you know that. You will do as I say, or suffer the consequences. I'd rather not spend my time in your head, but if necessary that is where I'll be, making certain you do your duty to your king and country."

"I'll die first."

Arbon shook his head. "I won't permit you to take your own life, and if you allow someone else to attempt it, I *will* be in your head and force you to take theirs. Do not underestimate me." Arbon strode back and mounted his horse. He circled his hand in the air above his head and galloped away, followed by his chief sorcerers.

Once again the vision blurred as it shifted to another memory in Legard's head. I heard the crack of a whip, and I flinched. Legard stood in the same dungeon cell I once occupied. The corners of the stones along the wall were crisp, not worn smooth by age as they had been when I'd lived there. He was strung up to the hook on the wall, like I had been. But his shackles and chains were magic, like those currently tethering him to Wickliff.

The lash cracked across Legard's back, drawing blood. My heart raced. Beads of sweat sprang to my forehead. I yanked my arm away from Garrick, breaking the connection and freeing myself from the vision.

Legard's shoulders sagged and his face was twisted in pain as he stood before the council, reliving his past. Garrick pulled away from Kalipsia and looked at me. "You okay?" he whispered.

Taking great gulps of air, I shook my head. "I can't watch that."

Garrick nodded. "I'll reach out my hand when it's over." He wrapped his hand around Kalipsia's arm and merged back into the vision. It wasn't long before Garrick's other hand slid across the table. I took a deep breath and grabbed his wrist.

My sight blurred. When it cleared, I saw Legard bloodied and bruised, curled in a ball in the center of the cell. Blood dripped from his wounds onto the white stone floor, making a stark contrast. How many prisoners had darkened that floor with their blood to get it as black as it was when I got there?

TWENTY

Petition

The vision Shahzad was pulling from Legard's memory shifted to another room in Lord Arbon's castle. Of the three men present, there was one I didn't recognize. He turned and left, slamming the door behind him. Arbon picked up a glass and took a long swallow. "Kill him. I won't tolerate insubordination by one of my chief sorcerers. We must present a united front if we are to succeed."

A slightly older version of Legard stepped forward. "But milord, he meant no harm. A difference of opinion is all. Vesipius is young and hot-tempered but will follow your orders in the end. You need not fear."

Arbon's face reddened. "Do not presume to tell me what will or will not threaten my crown. But in one thing you are right—there is no need to fear, because by your hand he will be a dead man before the morrow."

"Milord, please. I cannot, for he is one of us. And a friend."

"He will be an example. I won't have my leadership questioned in this manner again, by anyone. Now catch him quickly, before he leaves the castle."

Legard hesitated. "Do it yourself. You know it will please you, and I haven't the stomach for the cruelty you desire."

Arbon shook his head. "So be it, but he will die at your hand."

A terrible internal struggle took place, and a feeling of darkness settled over me as Legard left the room. He vanished, then reappeared outside in the castle's courtyard. Their target was about to mount a horse when Legard called out to him. But the tone of voice was Arbon's, not Legard's. Vesipius turned, a curious expression on his face.

I felt Legard fighting not to raise his hand, but Arbon's presence in his mind was overpowering, and he blasted the man with a magic pulse. The other sorcerer fought back initially, but Legard's power was too great, and the man soon crumpled to the ground, lifeless. Servants, soldiers, and peasants stood watching. The clatter of shod hooves rang as the nervous horse danced around his fallen owner.

When Legard turned away from his crime, we heard his voice, not in the vision but as a narration. "Keepers, I admit to doing things unconscionable, yet they were never done willingly. Enslaved to Arbon, I had no choice. In all my years of searching, I never found a way to break the blood oath he'd tricked me into swearing. His death set me free. I come before you to plead for mercy and petition for Algonian citizenship. I wish for peace and a place among my people."

The vision ended, and the Keepers opened their eyes to face Legard. A somber stillness filled the room. I felt bad for the guy. Although he'd told me what happened, it was nothing compared to seeing and feeling it. Legard shifted his weight, looking dead tired.

Shahzad cleared his throat. "This case is unusual. Any thoughts?"

Still holding Legard prisoner by magic chains, Wickliff said, "I have yet to witness your testimony, but my daughter was delivered to her death by your hand. That will not easily be forgiven or forgotten, by me or our people."

Shahzad stood. "Castile, maintain the tether while I give Wickliff the testimony."

Castile took the staff, and Wickliff and Shahzad clasped wrists. I tried to weigh what judgment would be fair to both Legard and Algonia, but couldn't come up with a clear answer.

Several minutes later, Wickliff took back his staff, and Shahzad again asked for the council's input. Garrick said, "I'm all for second chances, but you killed my neighbor on the old world, Legard. He was an innocent man and no threat to you. Someone should be accountable for that."

Legard shook his head. "I know of the man you make reference to. It was not I that brought about his death, but an accident. I can show you what I saw if you wish."

Shahzad fed us the information from Legard, and another vision began to play out in my mind. This time the setting was familiar—Garrick's Ohio property. The sun had dipped below the horizon. Legard, wearing his traditional Sniffer's cloak, was snooping around the cabin. He walked across the snow-packed ground to the barn. A mournful moo greeted him, and a series of snorts from Garrick's pigs followed. Legard tossed a pitchfork full of hay to the cow and was looking for something to feed the pigs when a man carrying an ax burst through the door and yelled at him.

Legard fled, jumping the fence into the cow's stall. He tried to unfasten the latch on the door to the outside, but it stuck. He began to disappear as a scream sounded behind him. He reappeared and spun around. The cow scuttled to the side. Garrick's neighbor lay sprawled on the straw, with the blade of an ax buried in his chest. The cuff of the man's pant leg was hooked on a nail head and must have tripped him.

Legard removed the ax and pressed on the wound to stop the flow of blood. But the man's shirtfront and coat were drenched by the time Legard carried him out the door. He took him to the closest house with a light in the window, lowered him onto the porch, and banged on the door. Then Legard transported himself to the shadows, where he watched until someone opened the door.

The vision ended and Legard said, "That man had seen me there before, and I presumed he planned on protecting your interests. My intent was to escape him, not bring harm. I have never killed on the old world."

Garrick gave a satisfied nod. Shahzad turned to the others. "Are there any other questions?"

"I request we postpone a decision on this case until the morrow," Kalipsia said. "I, for one, must ponder the circumstances and the effect of our decision on all involved. I won't cast my vote lightly."

Castile and Raoul spoke their agreement.

"I agree as well," said Shahzad. "With a majority of the council in favor of deferring the decision, we shall reconvene on the morrow."

"What of the prisoner?" asked Wickliff.

"Leave him in the tether, but anchor it to something," Shahzad replied.

Wickliff scanned the hall and settled his eyes on one of the great pillars. His mouth moved as he tilted his staff and sent the chain flying across the room and around the pillar. The council members rose and began to leave. Other than two soldiers instructed by Marcus to guard Legard, I was soon the only one left in the room. Legard looked like he was about to collapse. I dragged my chair across the floor. "Do you want to sit?"

The elf half smiled as he took a seat. "Thank you, Keeper."

I ran my fingers through my hair. "That could have gone a little better."

"Ah, but it could have gone far worse," Legard said.

"I guess you're right. Did Wickliff do something to you? Other than the chains, of course."

"By agreeing to be tethered, I consented to fuel the tether with my own energy. I will grow weaker the longer I am shackled."

"Can't you break free, especially if your own energy powers the tether?"

"Probably not, but I won't try. I sanctioned the tether and am honor bound to remain within its grasp."

I paced in front of him. "Will you be okay until tomorrow?"

The door opened behind me. "Halt. No one is allowed in here tonight," Joel said.

I turned to see the soldiers blocking a woman from entering. She pulled back the hood of her blue cloak. "Please, I won't stay long. I brought food for the prisoner. Surely you don't mean to starve him?"

As I walked closer, Trenton said, "You can leave the food, but we can't allow you to cross the threshold."

"Guys, can I talk to her for a minute?" I said.

Both soldiers stepped back.

"How is he?" Cecilia asked.

"He's okay. Tired, but okay. The council will think about his petition tonight and vote on it tomorrow morning."

She seemed nervous, her fingers twisting around the handle of the basket she carried. "Will you give him this?" She pushed the basket toward me.

"Sure." The soldiers escorted her out and closed the door, while I carried the basket back to Legard. "Your girlfriend brought you a present." A slow smile spread across his face, but he said nothing. "So it's true? You still like her, don't you?"

He didn't answer the question, but his expression betrayed the truth as he raised his chained hands to point at the basket. "What do we have to eat? I feel the need to replenish my energy."

I pulled another chair over and sat opposite him, then began rummaging through the food. "Looks like some of those awesome rolls we ate this morning. A couple of apples. Some grapes. And surprise, surprise, magic jerky. This should keep you full for hours. At least it does me when I eat it. Would you look at this?" I pulled out a flask, full to the brim with a thick brown liquid, and glanced at the soldiers. They were talking with each other, but I lowered my voice anyway. "How much do you wanna bet this is liquid energy?"

Legard held out his hands. "Quickly, hand it over." His Adam's apple bobbed up and down as he swallowed. He lowered the flask and shuddered before wiping the back of his hand across his mouth.

I took the flask and replaced the cork for him. "Feel better?"

He grinned. "That woman is very wise. I shall rest much easier tonight."

TWENTY-ONE

Verdict

The next morning I slammed down some breakfast, kissed my wife goodbye, and disappeared with my counter. I didn't want to freak out the soldiers on guard duty, so I reappeared outside the great hall. Word of Legard's hearing must have spread overnight, because clusters of elves stood talking along the street in front of where he was being held. I listened for a moment but couldn't gauge the feeling of the crowd. The elves, as usual, wore serene, peaceful expressions and spoke in quiet voices. Judging by the fact Marcus had tripled the guard since the night before and two of them were sorcerers, I figured the elves' calmness didn't mean they weren't working up a riot. If they didn't like our decision, I doubted we had enough magical firepower to stop them from turning into a lynch mob.

I entered the hall and found Legard on the chair where I'd left him. "How you doin' this morning?" I asked.

The elf turned his head, smiling. "I am well, Keeper. And you?"

"I'm good." I pointed behind me toward the door. "There's quite a crowd out there. Will you be in danger if they don't accept the council's verdict?"

Legard shrugged his broad shoulders. "That I cannot say. At one time I was well-liked among my people. But my actions have been nothing but traitorous, so they may well seek retribution."

"Hopefully you'll get lucky and they'll welcome back the prodigal son with open arms."

"One can hope."

I picked up Cecilia's basket. The food was gone, and only an inch of liquid energy remained in the flask. "Are you hungry?"

Legard shook his head. "I finished the food this morning. There was enough for two meals."

The other council members trickled into the room. Legard stood, and I dragged the two chairs back behind the table. When he nodded toward the basket, I picked it up and put it by my seat.

Garrick slapped me on the back as he took his place. Once everyone was seated, Shahzad said, "Are there any questions before we take a vote?"

Raoul cleared his throat. "Last night while perusing the scrolls containing the Laws of the Realm, I read that while the council can grant citizenship, it can only recommend an individual be considered for pardon. Only the king may grant a pardon. Based on the facts of this case and the sentiments expressed by the plaintiff, a pardon is needed. Regardless of our decision, I recommend this matter be brought to Archidus."

Shahzad, Wickliff, and Castile whispered among themselves. When they pulled back, Shahzad said, "Thank you. What you have said is correct, and your recommendation will be followed. Now, are we ready to vote?"

"Aye," Castile said.

The other council members muttered their agreement.

Shahzad turned to me. "Protector, your vote."

I stood. "Legard is not the same man who hunted me at Lord Arbon's command. I believe Legard told us the truth. He made a dumb mistake, but what he did after he took the oath wasn't his fault. Under the circumstances, I think we should forgive him and let him live here with his people. So my vote is yes on Algonian citizenship, and that we should recommend he be pardoned."

Shahzad nodded and turned to Garrick. "Guardian."

Garrick stood. "As I said before, I believe in second chances, and all things considered, I vote yes on both counts."

After Garrick took his seat, Shahzad called on Kalipsia. She stood and smiled at Legard. "Although I was but a child at the time, I knew both Arbon and Courtenay, Creation's original Keeper. None of us who knew them could have seen what lay in store. Arbon was a master of deception, and you were unfortunate enough to be the one he set his designs on. If not for your exceptional strength and skill, you would never have been a target. I see you as a great asset to Algonia in the future. I vote yes on both counts as well."

"Wickliff," Shahzad said.

The old elf stood. "As an advisor to the council, I carry no official vote, although I've cast them aplenty during our journey. I did not sleep last night as thoughts of bygone days swirled through my mind. As much as I wish to see Legard punished for his part in my daughter's death and the subsequent destruction of so many men on the battlefield, I find myself honor-bound to agree with Kalipsia. I know the power a blood oath can hold over another. You could not, at the age you spoke the oath, have known the full breadth of what you were doing. My recommendation to the council is also yes on both counts."

Legard sighed, clearly relieved at his uncle's comments.

Shahzad stood. "Lord Arbon is not the only Shuylian leader renowned for his skill in the art of deception. I am wary of the testimony we have heard and wish to have it substantiated by a seer. That will happen when Legard is brought before the king. If what we have seen is the truth, my vote will be yes on both counts as well. But I refuse to cast an official vote until then." He sat and turned. "Castile."

Propulsion's Keeper stood. "Because Legard is the former second in command of the Shuylian army, I feel we should demand some measure of accountability. I cannot recommend a pardon without appropriate compensation being requited to Algonia. On the matter of citizenship, I vote yes. Although I could not find the reference, I believe I read somewhere that once an Algonian citizen, one is always subject to the Laws of the Realm, the same as any other citizen."

Shahzad looked over to Raoul and nodded. Wisdom's Keeper stood and stated, "I agree with all that has been said before me. I vote yes on the matter of citizenship. I find merit in what Castile has requested, but feel Master Archidus is the one who should determine the conditions of a pardon, if granted. I do, however, recommend that it be considered. I feel Legard's remorse is genuine."

"Mei-Lien," Shahzad said.

Illusion's Keeper stood. "I am not of this world, but I think what I have learned on my world applies here as well. At all times there must be a balance between justice and mercy. While there should be mercy extended, it should not come at the expense of justice. I vote yes on citizenship, and agree with Castile on the matter of a pardon. Legard should make recompense for the wrongs done to Algonia."

Shahzad stood. "The vote is unanimous. Legard you are hereby recognized as an Algonian citizen, but as such you have committed acts of treason against our nation. You shall be detained until such time as you can be brought before the king to petition him for a pardon. The council is dismissed and shall reconvene on the first day of the next Algonian New Year in Cadré Unair." Shahzad brought the mallet down on the gong, signaling the end of the proceedings.

Most of the council members left the building. Wickliff, however, sat looking at Legard, and I watched both of them.

Legard spoke first. "I am sorry, Uncle. Please forgive me. Had I known what Arbon intended for Courtenay, I never would have helped him."

Wickliff nodded. "You might mean those words, but under a blood oath you never had control of your actions or your life. Last night, I decided I could never forgive you for the loss of my beloved daughter."

Legard's shoulders sagged and his gaze dropped to the ground. "I understand. You need not say more."

Wickliff stood, pushed his chair under the table, and picked up his staff. I figured he'd leave the room immediately, but the old elf moved closer and wrapped his arms around his nephew. Then he pulled back, his staff in one hand and the other resting on Legard's shoulder and said, "The decision has not sat well with me. I knew what must be done, yet I fought against it in my heart. I see now that holding onto the anger and pain does me a great disservice and robs you of what is rightfully yours. So, I extend my full forgiveness. Welcome home, Nephew."

Tears welled up in Legard's eyes as he leaned into his uncle's embrace. "Thank you. I never meant to bring shame upon our family."

Wickliff patted his nephew's back. "I know."

TWENTY-TWO

Spies

I hated to see Legard shackled, especially with the magical tether that drained his energy as fast as water from a hole in a bucket. I suggested we use our counters to get us all back to Archidus so he could review Legard's case sooner rather than later, but Shahzad insisted we travel overland and keep the caravan together. Before we left the Elf Province, Cecilia delivered a supply of liquid energy, and I assured her Legard would appreciate her thoughtfulness. As she turned to leave, I told her I would do my best to make sure he came back to her.

She smiled. "I'd like that. Very much."

On the second day of our journey, a messenger overtook us on the road, riding at a hard gallop. He handed a sealed parchment to Shahzad. We halted while he broke the blue wax seal and read the letter. After Shahzad thanked the messenger, he pulled his horse out of line and motioned to the other Keepers. The rest of the caravan continued down the road. I told Ellie I'd catch up in a minute and followed Shahzad, with Garrick by my side.

"What was that all about?" Garrick asked.

Shahzad handed over the parchment. Garrick read it, frowned, and passed it to me. Castile and Raoul stopped their horses next to ours as well. I looked down at the letter.

A message dictated by Master Archidus, the King of Algonia, to all members of the Keepers' Council:

Make all haste back to the fortress city and use the utmost caution in your travels. Our spies found evidence that Lord Dolosus has contracted with Legard to hunt down the Keepers. Beware he may be following the council.

Signed,
Archidus, King of Algonia

"That's a bunch of bull," I said, handing the letter to Castile. "Wickliff has Legard in chains. He's no threat. We've all heard what he plans to do with his life, and it isn't hunt down Keepers."

"Unless Legard had his poker face on," Garrick said. "Maybe he duped you, little brother. Maybe he duped us all."

Raoul read the letter and passed it back to Castile, who said, "I will make Wickliff aware of the danger."

That night when we stopped, I started across the camp to where Wickliff had tethered Legard. Each night Wickliff transferred the tether from his staff to something virtually immovable, so he could rest. He had explained that with an elf of less skill the tether could be attached to a tree or large boulder, but with Legard it had to be sunk deep into the ground. Evidently, once an elf has given assent to be tethered, he is honor bound to stay, although there is no magic preventing an escape attempt, and according to the old elf, some have done it.

A bottle of Cecilia's liquid energy swung next to my side. "Hey, Wickliff. Hey, Legard. How are you guys?" I said once they came into view.

Wickliff raised his staff so it banged against my chest, stopping me. I tried to push the staff away, but it wouldn't budge. "What's this for?" I asked.

"Give it to me."

I raised the flask. "This?"

"I can no longer allow you to supplement his energy. It is too dangerous. For all of us."

"You're his uncle. You'd believe a letter over what he says?"

"I am now withholding judgment until I know what Archidus sees. You would be wise to do the same. There is no place in this business for carelessness."

Doubt crept back into my mind. I had tried to ignore the warning from the Master Keeper, believing I knew the real Legard. But what if I didn't?

I raised the bottle. "It will take us days to get back to the castle. Without this he'll be exhausted by then. That's torture."

"That may be true, but it will be safer for us that way. Now give it here."

I stepped back. "I thought we were better than the Shuylians."

Quicker than you'd think possible for someone of his age, Wickliff dipped his staff toward my hand. A flash of blue light yanked the bottle out of my grasp and sent it sailing through the air into his free hand. With a scowl, he said, "Return to the camp and leave the prisoner to me."

Through all of this Legard had remained silent. He looked tired, like he had each night before I delivered the liquid energy. I spun around and marched past Castile, who had watched the whole thing.

—⬥—

If I had been a cartoon character, steam would have poured out of my ears as I paced the ten-foot width of the tent I shared with Ellie. "Do you think Wickliff would wake up if I crept over there in the middle of the night?"

"Darling, let it go," Ellie said. "I don't understand why you're so angry. Legard isn't going to die. We've only a couple more days until we reach the castle."

"But did you see him today? He nearly fell from his horse, and he can't even walk a straight line. What's he going to be like tomorrow?"

"I'm sorry, Chase, but I don't see what you or anyone else can do for him. Archidus is his only hope. No one except you dares to believe Legard now."

I grabbed a fistful of my hair and sat next to her, then propped my elbows on my knees. "I really thought he'd changed, Ellie. One minute I still believe in him, and the next I'm second guessing myself."

"Please come to bed. We will be rising early to leave."

I grabbed my sword and buckled it around my waist as I walked to the tent flap. "I'll be back in a minute. I've got a question for Legard."

"But Chase—"

I threw aside the canvas and hurried through camp. The cooking fires had dwindled to mounds of dark coals speckled with orange embers. The night guards stood at their posts, some resting on their spears. When I neared Legard, I ducked behind a tent and scanned the area. The pale-blue glow of the tether combined with the light of a full moon allowed me to see he was alone. With all of Wickliff's magical senses, however, I'd be lucky to get even a minute to talk.

I pulled out my counter and pressed Go, transporting myself next to Legard. He jumped when I appeared. I crouched in front of him, our faces a foot apart. "Did you lie to me?"

He shook his head. "All that I said is truth."

"Then why is there a letter from Archidus' spies saying you're here to capture the Keepers?"

"It is true that Lord Dolosus approached me. He is plotting a revolution and requested my assistance."

I glanced over Legard's shoulder but saw no sign of Wickliff. "Who is this Lord Dolosus, anyway? And why on earth didn't you tell me this sooner?"

"He is Arbon's son. He claims to be the rightful heir to the Shuylian throne, although some would disagree."

"Did you tell him you'd hunt down the Keepers?"

Legard tipped his head to the left, then the right. "I may have implied that."

"So when were you going to sink your talons into my shoulder and yank me back to that dungeon? Before or after I helped you get your pardon from Archidus?"

"I never intend on sinking my talons into you again. You have my word."

I grabbed a fistful of Legard's shirt. "Then you'd better start explaining why you were hanging out with Arbon's son talking about hunting down Keepers, because right now I'm the only one who even hopes you told us the truth back in the Elf Province. And I'm starting to regret trusting you."

"Since Shuyle fell, I have been followed by Lord Dolosus—" Legard stopped talking, his eyes darting upward.

I was yanked to my feet by a firm grip on my arm and came face to face with Wickliff. "You should not be here, Protector."

I knew my face mirrored his scowl. "I just wanted to talk to him for a minute."

The old elf pushed me away. "Return to your tent."

I took a step back as I pulled out my counter and pressed Go.

The light of dawn filtered through the curtains. I rolled over to watch Ellie sleeping. It was nice to have a roof over our heads instead of a tent. Our caravan had traveled late into the night to reach the capital city. Wickliff had been in a bad mood the whole trip, and I hadn't talked with him since the night he sent me back to my tent. But as he had turned toward the dungeons with Legard, he said, "Keeper, you can rest easy now. The cells here are secure, and he will be released from the tether for the night."

"Good. It's about time," I replied.

After that, the rest of us went straight to bed. Today I expected Master Archidus to send for us, wanting a full report of what had transpired on our tour of the country. I hoped we'd get to sit in when he made his decision regarding Legard.

A light knock sounded. Ellie didn't stir, so I rolled out of bed and opened the door a crack. "Hi, Garrick," I whispered when I saw him.

"I couldn't sleep at all last night," he said. "I've got to talk to Archidus about Brierly before this whole thing with Legard starts up, but I'd rather not be alone. You're good at making him see things your way. I could use your help." Garrick had grown increasingly uneasy as we approached the capital city, and he'd admitted to being worried about the Master Keeper's reaction to his marriage.

I yawned as I nodded, "Sure, Garrick. Let me get dressed."

"Hurry. I want to catch him first thing."

Soon we marched through the castle corridors to Archidus' meeting hall. Two armed guards raised their eyebrows, probably surprised at our early appearance. "We'd like to see Master Archidus," Garrick explained, "as soon as he's available."

"Wait here and I'll give him your message," said one of the men before turning to enter the hall.

I shoved my hands in my pockets and rested against the wall, while Garrick paced the floor between the other guard and me. When the door opened, the first guard stepped out and said, "You may wait at the table if you would like. He will see you shortly."

We wandered around the vacant hall and looked at the coat of arms above the fireplace. I ran my hand over the large table, the hard wood scratched and darkened by years of use. The velvet on the high-backed chairs was worn on the edges—something I hadn't noticed before. The brilliant stained-glass windows glowed as the morning sun lit each pane of glass, splashing an array of colors across the stone floor.

My head jerked up at the sound of a door opening. Archidus limped to his chair, saying, "The old bones are a little stiff in the morning. Welcome back, Keepers. I trust you had a successful journey?"

"We did, sir," I answered, while Garrick nodded.

"You wanted to see me on a personal matter, I take it."

My friend stepped forward. "Yes, sir, I do."

Archidus smiled, maybe because of Garrick's obvious discomfort, or maybe he had already taken a peek into my friend's head. "And what is it you'd like to ask me?"

"I—" Garrick shook his head and pulled out the chair next to Archidus. "Maybe you should just read my mind. It'll be a lot easier that way. I'm not sure I can adequately put what I feel into words."

Archidus chuckled. "Easier? For whom?"

"Uh . . . for me, I guess, but I didn't think—"

The Master Keeper laughed and waved off Garrick's concern. "No matter, it's a small expenditure of energy, and I usually find it entertaining to experience what someone else is thinking. Relax your mind and show me what it is that's got us all up so early this morning."

Garrick took a deep breath and closed his eyes. Archidus rested his hand on Garrick's wrist and closed his eyes as well. The Master smiled at times as if enjoying what he saw. When his brow furrowed, I wondered if he had experienced the memory of Garrick's beating, or if he was upset about the Guardian's marriage.

Archidus opened his eyes and folded his hands in front of him. "So, Guardian, you've taken an Algonian bride. I suppose for you it was a successful journey then."

Garrick smiled. "Yes, sir, it was."

"So the question we face now is what to do with this lovely bride of yours. Do we send her to the old world with you, have you stay here with her, or split you two up?"

"I can't leave her, Master. I love her, and I'll do whatever I have to so we can be together."

"Can they come back to the old world?" I asked. "And can Garrick have permission to use his counter with her, like I do with

Ellie? Brierly knows the history of the Keepers. She can be trusted with the secret."

Archidus laced his fingers together on the table and smiled at me. "Protector, you were supposed to be the exception, not the standard by which I operate. But I perceive your bond with the Guardian, and his with you, goes beyond that of mere friends. Having lost my brother in more ways than one, I sympathize with your plight.

"I will make a compromise with both of you. You may each return to the old world with your wives. For the time being, they will be allowed to accompany you if you use your counters. However, when the day comes that you have children, I insist you commit yourselves to the time and place of your choice, and your children must stay there. Children should not be required to conceal the secrets we adults do. Next year, I will summon you both to the Keepers' Council. If you desire, your wives may accompany you when you return. Guardian, since your wife was born in a later era than you, bring her by this evening and I will reset her internal clock to match yours. The two of you will age in tandem, regardless of where you settle."

Garrick blinked his eyes, his gratitude evident. "Thank you, sir. I don't know how I'll ever repay you."

"You already have." He motioned to me. "You retrieved my Keeper from the dungeons of Shuyle. Your wife's brother put a stop to Arbon's madness. And now, for the first time in centuries, my country is on the brink of peace. What more could a king ask from a man?"

A single tear trickled down Garrick's cheek. He stood and clasped wrists with the king. "Both of you enjoy your morning," Archidus said. "I will call for the council members to make their official report at noon, and I hear we have the matter of Legard to address. It is well you captured him."

I frowned. "We didn't capture him. He turned himself in. I don't think he meant to commit any of those crimes. Arbon had him under a blood oath and forced him to turn against you and Algonia. Your spies don't know the whole story."

Archidus watched me, his fingers like a steeple under his chin. "Wickliff mentioned you had developed a certain fondness for your former nemesis. To be honest, I doubted him. But I see now he is correct. Be assured, Protector, I intend to uncover Legard's secrets. We will discover where his true loyalties lie soon enough."

TWENTY-THREE

Price of a Pardon

Garrick slapped me on the back as we headed down the hall to our rooms. "Thanks for your help, little brother. You always could get Archidus to see things your way. I knew you wouldn't let me down."

"You're welcome. Hopefully I don't let Legard down, either."

Garrick put his hand out, stopping both of us. "You really think he's innocent, don't you?"

"I do. I can't explain why—just a feeling, I guess."

"Archidus will work it out. He's fair, so good or bad, Legard will get what he deserves."

"I hope he deserves a little mercy. For Cecilia's sake, I'd like to see him make it back to the Elf Province a free man."

The council members and Wickliff met in Archidus' hall at noon. We listened as Shahzad reported on our visit to each province. Occasionally, someone else on the council would comment, but I just listened. I'd have plenty to say during Legard's case.

Once we finished the council business, Archidus stood to say, "We'll take a short break and meet back here at half past the hour." He left the room, and a servant offered drinks to the rest of us.

Two sorcerers brought Legard through the door and seated him next to Archidus' chair. His tether was doubly anchored. Legard caught my eye and gave a hint of a smile.

When Archidus returned, he stopped in front of Legard. "It has been a long time."

"It has, and I wish to apologize to you and your country."

The Master sat and said, "The Protector mentioned a blood oath to my brother. Tell me from the beginning what transpired to turn you and my brother against me."

In detail, Legard told the story, starting with the ball in the castle where Arbon tricked him. Legard talked for over an hour, and I kept wondering why Archidus didn't just read his mind. It would have been a lot faster. Plus, anybody can tell a good story. Although I wanted to raise my hand and suggest it, I kept my mouth shut. I had to trust that Archidus knew what he was doing.

When Legard finished his story, Archidus reached out his hand. "May I?"

"Of course. View what you like. I will do whatever is necessary to earn back my place among my people."

Archidus motioned to Wickliff, who rose and went to his side. "There is a box in my quarters. I will show you how to retrieve it." Archidus touched the old elf, passing along the information.

The Master Keeper took Legard's wrist. For the next half hour we sat in silence, watching Archidus' facial expressions as he probed the Sniffer's mind. Wickliff returned, carrying a small box made of dark-colored wood and held together with black hinges. The elf set the box on the table in front of the king.

When Archidus finished, he looked around the room. "Do any of you have evidence or testimony relating to this case?"

The other Keepers shook their heads. Despite my doubts, I followed my gut and said, "I do."

"Proceed," Archidus replied.

I took a deep breath, trying to organize my thoughts. "Legard is not the same man—uh . . . elf, I mean—that he was before Arbon died. There have been a few guys who have wanted to kill me, including Legard. Each one had a certain look in his eye before he tried. When Legard found me in the woods a few weeks ago, he seemed totally different from the last time I'd seen him. I saw kindness and respect in his eyes, and since then his actions have shown me the same. He's changed, and I think he should be forgiven. Plus, Brierly, who was a slave in Arbon's castle, says that when Legard wasn't under orders from Arbon, he was kind and considerate—a gentleman, even. It just doesn't seem fair that Legard should suffer the rest of his life for what Arbon forced him to do."

"Thank you, Protector. I will take your recommendation into consideration." Archidus pulled the box onto his lap and looked at Legard. "You say you will do whatever is necessary to regain your citizenship?"

Legard nodded.

Archidus opened the box and drew out the same dagger I'd seen in the vision from Legard. My pulse accelerated as Archidus pulled the glowing blade across the palm of his hand. Crimson blood dripped onto the table as he spoke. "There are no inconsistencies between your testimony and what I viewed in your memory, but I've never met anyone more skilled in the arts of deception than you and my late brother. If I grant you a pardon, I know of only one way to ensure your loyalty. Swear a blood oath to the throne of Algonia, and I will grant your wish."

Archidus flipped the knife and presented it handle first to Legard. Other than a twitch in his cheek muscle, the elf didn't move. He looked at the blade and then up at the king. "Milord, I will swear fealty to you. I will pledge my allegiance to Algonia and whoever sits on her throne. I will offer my services in the defense of her borders and her freedoms, but what you ask I cannot give. It is the one thing I now value more than life itself—my free will. If that is the price of a pardon, I beg you to take my life. And do so quickly." He held the king's gaze, his shoulders sagging as if he waited for death. My gaze darted between the two men.

"Very well. If that is what you wish." Archidus placed the knife in the box and closed the lid. "Wickliff, if you don't mind." The old elf stood and took the box out of the room. Tension filled the air like smoke. A servant stepped forward and offered the king a white rag, then wiped the blood from the table with another.

Archidus wrapped his hand and leaned back in his seat. "If you had accepted my offer, I would know you had not learned from your mistake. A man's actions should be dictated by his own honor and his conscience and nothing else.

"However, I do have another cause for concern. My spies saw you meeting with Lord Dolosus. You disappeared with him for a day, after which you were seen heading in our direction. Lord Dolosus then informed his chief sorcerers that you were working for him, hunting the Keepers, and would return with a counter within the month. What have you to say to that?"

Legard shifted in his seat. "They are correct in what they saw and in what they reported to you."

A low buzz filled the room as several Keepers whispered to one another.

Legard continued. "I did meet with Lord Dolosus, and I did agree to find the Keepers. But I assure you, my purpose in finding them was to gain an audience with you and plead my case. For obvious reasons, Lord Dolosus wasn't privy to that information. Had he known, he would have hunted me down before allowing me to turn against him. He is jealous like his father."

"What you say is consistent with what I saw in your mind," Archidus replied. "And although I have some reservations, I will concur with the council in returning your Algonian citizenship. We were friends once, and I look back on those days with fond memories. In my heart, I wish to pardon you, but the crimes against our nation are numerous, many of which you were a party to. There must be recompense for the damage."

The council members sat perched on the edge of their seats as stark silence filled the room. Legard leaned forward. "Would Lord Dolosus be a fair price for a pardon?"

Again, the silence stretched on as the king held Legard's gaze. "Yes," he finally answered, "especially considering what you have shown me. Dolosus plots a revolution and has his father's thirst for power. He will bring nothing but misery to both the Algonians and our brothers, the Shuylians."

"Although I most likely won't have a choice," Legard said, "would you prefer him dead or alive?"

"Alive, if possible, but he will not come willingly, so I will leave it to the Fates."

"I need a way to get close to him—a bargaining chip."

"What have you in mind?"

"Two counters and fifteen or so of your best men who can disarm a troop of Shuylian soldiers and take their places. In a fortnight, Lord Dolosus sends a small troop of cavalry to meet me at the Dragon's Lair. He seems to think I must be escorted to him, but he underestimates me. I know how to find him and have no need of his soldiers or his escort."

"And what of my Keepers?" Archidus said. "He won't be fooled by the counters for long with their Keepers still alive."

"A simple lumens spell should get me close enough. By the time he realizes the counters are still attached, it will be too late. He will be within my grasp."

Archidus smiled. "I hear my commander Marcus Landseer makes a convincing Shuylian soldier."

Garrick raised his hand. "Give me a few days to grow my beard, and I'm not half bad myself."

"Legard can use my counter," I said. "I can do the Shuylian soldier thing."

Archidus sat still, glancing between Garrick and me. "This is a dangerous game we play. But with Shuyle's current leadership working in tandem with my own, and our countries on the brink of peace, I desire to exterminate, once and for all, this last threat. There is one man who stands in our way, stirring up contention and spreading rumors among the Shuylians. Given time, I see he will succeed in turning their hearts to violence. Our countries will again be plunged into war. Legard, give me your word that your allegiance is and will always be in the future to Algonia, and I will give you my commander and two of my Keepers. The commander will find the rest of the men you need."

Legard fisted his right hand and placed it over his heart, then bowed his head. "You have my word and my fealty, sire."

Archidus turned to Wickliff, who had returned to his place at the end of the table. "Will you accompany Legard and ensure he fulfills his end of our bargain?"

Wickliff nodded. "I will do as you wish."

The king flicked his fingers toward the two sorcerers. "Release him. Upon the safe return of my counters and their Keepers, as well as the elimination of the threat Lord Dolosus presents to our nation, I shall issue a proclamation throughout the country, declaring your citizenship and your pardon."

The restraints fell off Legard, and he said quickly, "My thanks, milord."

A half smile turned the king's mouth. "Forgive me for not allowing you free rein of my castle at this time, but I will provide you a room more comfortable than my dungeon, with guards stationed outside your door. They will accompany you if you wish to move about the grounds."

The elf stood and bowed. "Thank you. That is more than I dared hope for. I look forward to proving my loyalty."

TWENTY-FOUR

Castle Life

Garrick matched me stride for stride as we left the meeting hall. "Tell me, brother," he said, "whatever possessed me to volunteer to put on the Shuylian clothes and go back there?"

"I don't know, but we can't trust anyone else to do it. I get the feeling the Algonians around here are hoping to punish Legard. It's like they want him to fail."

"They have a longer history with him, so I suppose we can't blame them for wanting revenge." We stopped in front of Garrick's door, and he grinned at me. "Wish me luck telling my wife."

Brierly opened the door. "Tell me what?"

Garrick put his hand on her lower back and kissed her cheek before ushering her inside. "So, dear, you remember that case with Legard—"

Their door closed and I took a deep breath, knowing I needed just as much luck or more.

When I explained the situation to Ellie, she spun around from the mirror, drilling me with her gaze. "You did *what*?" I was thankful all she had within her grasp was hairpins, because she threw one at me. "You do have some kind of death wish."

"No, I don't. How bad can it be? We have Legard on our side now. We'll get in, get out, and I'll be home before you know it."

Her cheeks were flushed, and I couldn't remember ever seeing her this angry. "Pray tell, is that not the logic you used in persuading Archidus to let you come rescue Davy and me? I'm sure you thought you'd get in, get me, and get out. But I lost you for over a year. Know that I cannot go through that again, Chase—I just can't."

I crossed the room to her, and even though she tried to push me away, I succeeded in pulling her to my chest and pressing my lips to her forehead. "Please don't be mad. I promise I'll be okay. This is something I have to do. We'll have Wickliff there. And Marcus will get us a group of the best soldiers. We'll have plenty of protection. Plus, Garrick's going. I can't let him go by himself. I'm his wingman."

"His what? Oh, never mind." Ellie wiggled away and walked across the room. "I'm not mad at you, although I am angry. Maybe Legard is the one I am displeased with. He continues to sabotage my every chance at a peaceful existence. Will he never let me be?"

I couldn't help it. I laughed. But now she had something substantial in her grasp—the brass candleholder. She spun around and sent it soaring toward me.

I didn't relish the thought of explaining a broken mirror to Master Archidus, so instead of ducking, I caught the candleholder before it hit my head. My finger jammed and I shook my hand to clear the numbness. "Ellie, I'm sorry. Let me do this to help Legard. Then he can go back to that elf girl he loves, and he'll never bother you again. I promise you'll get your peaceful existence after that. Plus, you like a little excitement now and again, don't you? You'd probably get bored if life was *too* peaceful."

She took a big breath and let it out slowly. "How long will you be gone? And what of me during that time?"

"I'll find out. Garrick and I will work out all the details in the next few days. You can hang out with Brierly while we're gone. You like her, right?"

"Of course I like her. That will be the only pleasant part of this whole nonsense."

—◆—

This would be the last night in the castle for most of the council members. After we had finished the case with Legard, Archidus invited everyone to a feast the following evening to celebrate the successful completion of our Keepers' Council tour. Garrick and I had endured the silent treatment from our wives during dinner the night before, and I hoped tonight would be an improvement.

I spent the day with Marcus, Garrick, and some of the soldiers who would accompany Legard. We planned the expedition, ran through training exercises, and got fitted for Shuylian uniforms. The Algonians had taken so many prisoners of war that there were stacks of used clothing in one of the buildings near the training fields.

I parted ways with Garrick and went to my room but found it empty. With a couple of hours until dinner I assumed Ellie was taking a walk or something, so I lay on the bed and got some sleep.

Sometime later, my wife threw open the door. "Chase, we're going to be late!"

I peeled open my eyelids and saw her dart across the room. She was dressed in servant's attire, her hair tucked under a bonnet and her dress covered in flour. I sat up and smiled at her. "I'm going to be late? Look at you, Cinderella. This isn't a costume party, you know. Why are you dressed like that?"

Ellie pulled the bonnet off her head and shook her hair out. She untied her apron and tossed it on the chair, then grinned as she pulled a piece of parchment from her pocket. "I got it."

"Got what?" I asked, relieved to find her in a good mood.

She pulled her dress over her head and walked to the washbasin, where she scrubbed and dried her arms and face. "The recipe for the star rolls. Remember, they're my favorite?"

"Yeah, I remember."

Her maid, Heather had hung a shimmering, royal-blue gown next to Ellie's wedding dress. Ellie pulled the blue gown off the hanger and stepped into it. "Well, not only did I succeed in getting the recipe, I made a batch with the baker this afternoon. I'll have you know it was no small task getting into the kitchen. The thought of a castle guest setting foot in there was absolutely unacceptable to the cook. I finally convinced Heather to loan me her daughter's clothes and plead my case. Once I looked like one of them, I had better luck." Ellie twisted her hair into a bun on top of her head, talking all the while. "It was a delight working with them. After the rolls, we made lemon custards for the feast tonight. I can't wait to try one—they smelled divine. I am so hungry." She added a few sparkling pins to her hair. "There. If you'll button up my gown, I'll be ready."

She turned to look at me. "Darling, why aren't you dressing?"

I jumped to my feet and walked to her. "Too busy watching you, I guess." She turned her back to me. I buttoned her dress halfway up and then couldn't resist the urge to kiss her shoulder.

"Chase, we're late. Keep going."

I wrapped my hands around her stomach and kissed my way across her neck. She pulled my hands off her. "Chase, I meant keep going with the buttons, not the kissing. Or do I need to ring for Heather to do me up?"

I let out a dissatisfied sigh. "No, I can handle it."

The tables were pushed aside after dinner to make room for dancing. Ellie beamed. She loved a good party, especially the kind with fancy dresses and ballroom dancing. Archidus' court musicians tuned their instruments and started to play. Five of us were rookies when it came to Algonian dancing—the four Keepers from the old world, and Ellie. We watched from the sidelines until Brierly pulled Garrick onto the dance floor. "Follow me, Garrick. It's not difficult."

"That's easy for you to say," he grumbled.

Ellie tapped her toe in time with the music. "I think I know it," she said a few minutes later.

"Know what?"

She took my hands in hers and backed onto the dance floor, dragging me with her. "The dance steps. Come on, darling, let's try it."

I shook my head. "I don't know, Ellie."

"We are among friends. Look, Garrick is dancing."

I chuckled. "Yeah, and he's butchering it."

"What does it matter? Look at them. They're having an enjoyable time. They're smiling."

"I can have fun and smile from the sidelines."

"But it will be more fun out there." She tugged me forward. I could see there was no getting out of this. Plus, I figured I owed her big time for letting me go with Legard.

"All right," I said, "but no laughing."

We got into position and followed the other couples around the floor. The dance went into a sequence that required a brief change of partners. Ellie moved into the arms of the man to my left. Archidus' daughter, Azalit, raised her hand to mine and we began the steps. "You look well," she said. "The potion did, in fact, repair your face. And your back? How is that?"

"It's fine. Not as good as my face, but that was a great potion you gave me. Does the refilling vial last forever?"

"As long as the cork stays intact, the potion will be effective. And yes, it will last forever."

The sequence ended and it was time to change partners. "It's good to see you again," I said to Azalit.

Illusion's Keeper took my hand, and the two of us fumbled through the dance steps, bumping into Creation's Keeper and her partner. We apologized and shifted back into our places. Their graceful movements made us look like a couple of drunkards.

I was relieved when Ellie danced her way back into my arms. As the next song began, I tried to edge my way out of the center of the dance floor, but she resisted, placing her hand on my chest. "Chase, this music is in three-four time. We could waltz."

I smiled back at her. "We could? That was my thought exactly," I said sarcastically. Regardless, I squared up my shoulders and waltzed her around the dance floor. Garrick took one look at us and pulled Brierly out of the Algonian dance line for a quick lesson in the waltz. They were soon waltzing along behind us.

The Algonians watched us curiously, but no one complained. The waltz involved more contact between partners than any other dance I'd seen them do, and I chuckled at the thought that perhaps they might consider our waltzing a bit risqué. We danced until the clock in the tower struck twelve. When the final gong sounded, the musicians began packing away their instruments.

"I guess this place shuts down at midnight," I said as we moved with the current of the crowd toward the exit.

TWENTY-FIVE

Shuylians

The morning I was to leave for Shuyle, a footman brought a Shuylian uniform, sword, and thick-soled black boots to my room. With Ellie still asleep, I stepped into the hall to talk with him. He passed me the stack of clothing and then pulled a small potion vial out of his pocket. "Sir, for your beard."

I touched the one-day stubble on my chin. "For my beard?"

"Beards are the preferred style in the Shuylian army. The commander ordered a hair-growth potion for all the men."

I rolled the green vial across my palm. "How do I use it?"

"Spread a thin layer over the face. I can assist you, if you'd like."

"No thanks. I got it."

After the footman left, I eased the door closed and glanced at my sleeping wife. I dribbled a few drops of the potion onto my fingers and massaged it onto my jaw, then set the vial on the mirror table and dressed.

The bedcovers rustled as I fitted the sword to my belt. "Good morning, beautiful," I said.

Ellie opened her eyes, then lifted her eyebrows and giggled.

"What's so funny?" I said.

She pointed at me as her giggle progressed to a full-out laugh. I spun around and looked in the mirror.

"Wherever did you get all that hair on your chin?" she asked.

The face staring back at me could have belonged to a mountain man who hadn't seen a razor all winter. I rubbed both my cheeks and turned my head slightly, noticing my beard had more brown in it than it had a year ago. I turned around. "What, you don't like my beard?" I said, feigning injured pride.

"Darling, I didn't mean that. Where did it come from? The face I kissed last night was as smooth as a child's, and now—"

I picked up the vial off the table. "Catch." She lifted her hands and I tossed it to her. "Put that in my bag and let's take it home with us. It might come in handy when I'm fifty and balding."

Ellie turned the vial and read aloud, "'Hair Growth Potion.' Well, I can plainly see it's effective."

I looked back at the mirror, thankful I hadn't used more than a couple of drops. "This is a freak of nature. It'll drive me crazy having whiskers this long." I pulled out my dagger and tugged the hair tight before sawing at it.

Ellie rolled out of bed. "Chase, I've got scissors. Put the knife away before you cut yourself." She walked to the chair near the fireplace and returned with a pair of small brass scissors. They didn't have the usual handles, so you had to squeeze them to get the blades to cut.

"Where did those come from?" I asked.

Ellie pulled me down onto the stool. "Heather let me use them for a needlepoint I'm working on."

I watched in the mirror as my wife trimmed my beard. When she finished, I thanked her and stood. I kissed her soundly, relishing the feel of her leaning into me, and the little sigh she always gave when I stopped kissing her. I took a deep breath, hoping Legard would keep his promise and return me unharmed to Algonia.

Ellie looked up at me, her eyes glistening with unshed tears. "Take care, my darling, and know that I love you always."

"I love you too. And I will be back for you." Before I had to see her cry, I turned and walked out the door.

I met Garrick coming down the hall. "Hey, brother, where's your beard? Didn't you get some of that potion?"

He smiled and pulled a vial from his pocket. "Almost forgot."

Before I could warn him, he dumped the potion in the palm of his hand and splashed it across his face like water. The extra liquid ran down the back of his hand.

"Dude, that's way too much. You're supposed to use only a drop or two."

Garrick tucked the empty vial back in his pocket, ignoring me until I started laughing. With the beard he was already growing, there might be a spot for him on *Duck Dynasty.* He lifted his hands. "What in tarnation?"

Where the potion had spilled on the back of his hands and wrists, the hairs were three inches and growing. I laughed so hard I had to grab my sides. "I told you, only a drop or two. Not the whole bottle."

"What's Marcus trying to do—scare the Shuylians by making us look like Sasquatch?"

"You think that's bad, you should see your face."

Garrick tugged at the beard covering his throat. "Confound it."

The other imposter Shuylians sat on their horses waiting for Garrick and me on the practice green. They all sported beards— none as long as Garrick's, though. Marcus looked at his friend and raised his fist to his mouth to hide a smile. I grabbed my horse's reins and remarked, "It's okay, Marcus. Go ahead and say it. He looks ridiculous."

The commander lowered his hand and let out a deep chuckle. "Aye, Guardian, you do look as if you've taken the disguise a bit too far. With a beard like that, you'll be lookin' more like an oversized dwarf than a Shuylian."

Garrick scowled and yanked his reins away from Marcus. "Are we riding out of here, or sitting around talking like a bunch of ladies at a church social?"

Marcus raised one hand and turned his horse with the other. "You heard the Guardian. Move out, men."

Legard and Wickliff were talking off to the side of the group as we left the practice green and headed for Shuyle, and our date with Lord Dolosus.

—◆—

We rode through Algonia and across the Borderlands, forgoing the use of magic to transport us. The date Legard and Lord Dolosus had set was still over two weeks away, plus no one wanted to expend the energy to move all of our weapons, supplies, and horses. Three days into the journey, I realized most of the men Marcus had chosen were magicals. There were a few elves in the bunch, their distinctive ears disguised beneath long hair and helmets. I also noted several sorcerers and a few half-magical soldiers, including Barhydt, who I knew from a previous expedition. I was happy to see some familiar human faces as well—Segur and Aiton.

The evening before we reached the Dragon's Lair, Wickliff tucked a bundle of Shuylian clothes beneath his arm and went off by himself to work some magic. While we waited for dinner, Barhydt conjured a flaming fireball and tossed it in the air. He added another and then another until he was juggling three of them. After the cook whistled, signaling dinner was ready, Barhydt stood and dropped them onto the bed of coals beneath the kettle.

When Wickliff came back and lowered himself onto a boulder, his gray beard was a light brown, and he looked at least forty years younger. He took the plate of food the cook held out to him, and I thought he could have passed for Legard's brother.

"That's a good look for you, Uncle," Legard said, barely cracking a smile.

Everyone within hearing distance chuckled. The strained relationship between Wickliff and Legard had shifted. No longer did Wickliff guard his nephew. They talked and rode as companions and possibly even friends. More than once they had laughed together over some private joke.

"Youth is a good look for anyone," the old elf said. "Enjoy yours while it comes naturally, Legard. The illusion of youth goes no deeper than the skin. My old bones still ache inside."

Leitner, one of the elf soldiers, said, "Not everyone can cast that spell. Yours is very convincing, old man. You could snare a wife with that."

Full-blown laughter erupted through the camp. Wickliff shook his head and waved Leitner away. "An old man like me has no need of a wife. I'll leave the women to you young bucks."

Before we rode out, Legard addressed the group. "I expect a small squadron of cavalry and possibly a sorcerer or two to meet us at the Dragon's Lair. I'd prefer to take these men alive, as I want no more blood on my hands. Wickliff, Leitner, Nebus, and I will seek out and engage any magicals. The rest of you circle and disarm the remaining soldiers."

We all nodded our understanding of the plan. Marcus had led the expedition until that point, but now that we were in Shuylian territory he pulled back and motioned for Legard to take the lead. We fell into formation, our cook and his packhorses bringing up the rear.

By midday, the countryside resembled what I remembered of the Dragon's Lair, with charred boulders and stubby grass covering the barren hillsides. The bright sun nearly blinded me. I raised my hand to shield my eyes and scanned the blue sky on the horizon. A small flock of crows circled ahead of us. Legard must have seen them too, because he raised his arm, signaling a stop.

He pointed to the birds. "They have arrived ahead of us. Maintain a tight formation and be ready, but appear at ease." Legard squeezed his heels against his horse's side and trotted toward the crows and the Shuylian militia we expected to find beneath them.

When we neared the Dragon's Lair, I saw several hobbled horses, their heads lowered as they looked for feed. Two guards raised their spears in salute when Legard passed. Three large tents had been erected, and the ashes of a cook fire still smoldered within a ring of blackened rocks. Several soldiers gathered around the tents upon our approach. A large man, clearly the leader of the group, flipped back the canvas of one tent and stepped out into the open. "Legard, what is this? I expected you to travel alone."

"You expected wrong, Cassius. One can't be too careful with so many Algonians on this side of the border. These men are loyal, and Lord Dolosus will no doubt welcome reinforcements."

Cassius nodded. "You have a counter, I presume?"

"Our lord will be doubly pleased, as I have two."

Their leader grinned and stepped closer. "Let me see them."

Legard shook his head. "My orders were exact. They are to be taken directly to Lord Dolosus. Gather your men. I wish to address our group before I break for the midday meal."

Cassius turned to the soldier at his right. "Call the men to attention."

Legard dismounted and quietly turned to Marcus. "Have the men secure our horses and return quickly."

Marcus gave the order. I stepped to the ground, and Segur held out his hand to take my horse's reins. Half of the soldiers fanned out behind Legard, while the other half led the horses away from what might soon become a battlefield.

The Shuylian soldiers gathered around Cassius, most of them armed. Legard raised his hand for silence, and every soldier obeyed instantly. "My Shuylian brothers, we stand on the brink of revolution. A revolution that will no doubt plunge our country back into war with our Algonian neighbors. Their army patrols our villages. Their beliefs pollute our government. The odds against us are great, and we must use the most cunning of means to achieve our purposes. Our success hinges on our ability to deceive—to mislead our enemy—since we haven't the brute strength to take them in open battle. Nothing must stand between us and victory."

A cheer went up from the Shuylians. Legard again raised his hand for silence.

A flicker of doubt crossed my mind, and I could tell the Algonians around me felt the same. The lies rolled off Legard's tongue as convincingly as the truth had, and for a minute I wondered which was which. *Did he deceive us all?* Was his purpose to sacrifice us as part of his "most cunning of means"? Sweat beaded on my forehead and trickled down my spine as I shifted my feet. Next to me, Marcus gripped his sword with white knuckles. To my right, Leitner clenched his fists, causing a blue spark of magic to drop onto the ground at his feet.

"If any of you wish to step down and rejoin those countrymen who are content to live under Algonian rule, I invite you to come forward. No punishment will be meted out. I demand only your oath of silence, sealed with your blood, and you will be free to go home."

Cassius stepped closer, shaking his head. "What is this? Lord Dolosus will not approve. We have need of every man."

Legard shot the leader a stern glance. "Every man needs be wholly committed to our cause or we will fail. I demand loyalty above all else." Legard turned back to the soldiers. "Men, now is your chance to choose sides. I give you my word that no harm will come to you."

One man stepped forward and cleared his throat. "I have a wife and a new son. I apologize, but now my heart belongs to them, not the revolution."

Another soldier followed. "My family would be better served following the path to peace. My son is of soldiering age. If we go to war I may find myself opposite my son on the battlefield. I'll be no good to you then."

Legard nodded as if accepting his excuse. A third soldier moved silently out of line and joined the other two, his head bowed. The remaining Shuylians whispered among themselves as they glanced between Legard and their leader, a few of them fingering their swords and scowling at the defectors. The expression on Cassius's face darkened. What Legard was doing reminded me of the time

Adam and I shot a wasps' nest with our BB guns, sending the insects into a frenzy. Every soldier, both Algonian and Shuylian, seemed agitated. My eyes darted between Legard and Cassius.

"Cowards! All of you," Cassius said, raising his hand as if to strike the backs of the three retreating soldiers.

But Legard flicked his wrist, sending a pulse of energy through the air. It hit Cassius in the chest, nearly knocking him off his feet. Leitner threw up both hands and sent a shower of magical sparks and blue smoke into the crowd of Shuylians. Men doubled over, coughing as they gasped for air. I drew my sword but hung back, fearful of the toxic fumes and neon blue sparks swirling in front of me.

The three Shuylians who had opted out of the revolution stood off to the side, their eyes wide. While Cassius and Legard duked it out with their magic skills, Marcus and the rest of our soldiers rushed into the cloud of smoke. Once we saw the fumes didn't affect them, Garrick and I leaped forward into the fray and confiscated every sword, dagger, battle-ax, and spear. Anyone who resisted us was blown to the ground by a crippling pulse of magic from Wickliff. Segur handed out lengths of rope, and we secured the prisoners.

Legard put Cassius in a magical tether and anchored it to a large boulder. The former Sniffer smiled as he scanned the battlefield. "Are there any injured?"

We looked around and shook our heads.

"Well done then." Legard turned to the three men standing. "You chose wisely, and I commend you. But I still require your oath of secrecy. Our country has seen enough war. It is time for peace with Algonia. Once we were a united people, and it is time to be so again." He turned to Marcus. "Do we have anyone other than Wickliff or myself who can extract the oath?"

Marcus raised his hand and pointed to one of the sorcerers. "Nebus, see to the oaths and send these men on their way."

Nebus drew his dagger as he moved toward the men. I hoped all he had planned was another version of the blood oath and not something more deadly.

TWENTY-SIX

Twisted Faeries Springs

The three soldiers who willingly surrendered to Algonian rule rode south on their horses with white bandages tied around their hands. The men had taken an oath of loyalty to Algonia and vowed to protect the secrecy of our mission. Before they left, they thanked Legard for their freedom. He sent them away with the charge to keep the peace and obey the Laws of the Realm.

Nebus took control of the tether binding Cassius and disappeared with him. I supposed they were on the fast track to Master Archidus' dungeon. Wickliff closed his eyes and wiggled his shoulders. His body shuddered as he transformed into his old self. Then he loosened the clasp on the Shuylian pants and said, "Excuse me while I change. With age I seem to have grown out in places that used to be in."

Our cooks prepared the midday meal and we ate in shifts, taking turns guarding the Shuylians. Nebus returned, looking like he'd been gone overnight without any sleep, instead of the hour it actually took. Since Cassius didn't willingly submit to the tether, the energy to maintain it had been generated by Nebus.

Marcus stripped the prisoners of anything metal—their chain mail, helmets, and other armor—then divided them into three groups. Wickliff, Legard, and Leitner each disappeared with a group. Marcus had made arrangements for the regiment stationed in one of the Algonian border villages to transport our prisoners back to Cadré Unair. They were taking the captives to that village.

We inventoried the Shuylian armor and uniforms, taking what we needed to pass ourselves off as the same group we'd captured. Later that night I asked, "Won't Lord Dolosus realize we are not the men he sent out?"

Legard shook his head. "Dolosus is his father's son in every way. Arbon would not have lowered himself to the level of mere soldiers. He never knew their names or their faces, and neither will his heir. But Lord Dolosus does have an eye for horseflesh, so we will ride their horses. And of course, we will carry their weapons and wear their armor, which bears the Shuylian insignia."

We packed up their camp the next morning and headed north, riding the Shuylian horses in the opposite direction I'd gone the last time I'd been at the Dragon's Lair. We wouldn't be entering Shuyle via the Valley of Tierran because it was still occupied by Algonian soldiers. Lord Dolosus would expect his men to use the northern route, Saddle Pass, one I was all too familiar with. I'd never forget the harrowing days I spent coming up the pass and then taking the outpost from the six Shuylian soldiers on guard there. Memories of the time I spent with Marcus, Garrick, and Brierly—the never-ending snow, the icy air burning my throat, the hunger pains—still frequented my nightmares.

Late in the afternoon on the second day of our journey north, Legard reined his horse to a stop and pointed out a narrow horse trail. It veered off the main road and led up the forested hillside. "Uncle, have you caught a whiff of these men we're traveling with? They stink like a pack of dogs. There are hot springs, the Twisted Faeries, less than a mile up that trail. We could all use a visit."

Marcus rode up the line of soldiers. "Why the delay?"

"Legard thinks we need a bath," I said.

Wickliff turned his horse toward the trail. "I, for one, am in favor of a bath."

I nudged my horse into a walk and started after Wickliff. "I'll second that." Under the beating sun, I had sweat through the same shirt for the last five days, and I smelled worse than the practice gym during a wrestling meet.

Garrick, who hadn't heard any of this conversation, trotted his horse closer. "Where you going, little brother?"

"Swimming. Legard says there are some hot springs up here."

"Count me in," he said.

Legard and Garrick rode up the trail after Wickliff and me, but when I looked over my shoulder at the road below, Marcus hung back, scowling. His dutiful soldiers waited for his order. Some of their horses stamped the ground or shook their heads impatiently.

Could Marcus be worried this was a trap? Would Legard lead us this far, sacrificing those other soldiers, just to get us to this obscure trail on the edge of the Shuylian mountainside? Marcus had recruited Algonia's best soldiers for this trip. Was Legard's plan to lure these magicals into a snare? Getting them out of the picture would certainly beef up Lord Dolosus' chances.

I had marveled at the ease with which Legard had rallied the Shuylian soldiers. His words—about using the most cunning means to achieve their purposes, and about their success hinging on their ability to deceive—had bothered me since the day he'd said them. Were we being deceived even now?

"Leitner, Nebus, and Barhydt, follow me," Marcus called out. "The rest of you be on guard and keep a tight formation." The commander trotted his horse up the steep incline.

Our horses were soon laboring to breathe as they climbed. We must have gone nearly a mile before Wickliff reined his horse to a stop. The trail forked ahead of him. The gurgle of water sounded in the trees far below the trail. From behind me, Legard said, "Uncle, go left."

I took a sip from my water flask and shuddered at the hint of sulfur that clung to my tongue after I swallowed. Our last two water holes had been sub-par and reminded me of the stuff I had been given in the dungeon. For what felt like the hundredth time, I wiped the sweat off my forehead so it wouldn't run into my eyes. Although riding in the shade of these trees sure beat the road we had traveled the past few days, the air still felt like a sauna.

The sound of gurgling water grew louder. When we emerged from the forest, two waterfalls cascaded down the rocky cliff face on the opposite side of the clearing. The multicolored rocks swirled and twisted behind the water—blue, gray, and black stones woven together into a geological masterpiece. Steam rose off the surface of one of the pools.

Garrick dismounted and began to unsaddle his horse. "I say we camp here for the night."

I scanned the vacant meadow and rocky outcroppings, then pulled off my helmet and hooked it onto my saddle. "Sounds good to me, but you'd better check with the commander before you unpack anything."

Garrick grinned as he dropped his saddle to the ground and then hobbled his horse. "Leave Marcus to me. He'll issue the order once I'm through with him."

My horse jerked on the reins as he tried to lower his head to the grass, and I decided to pull out my hobbles and turn him loose to graze as well. Behind me I heard Garrick yell, "Marcus, watch this!" I turned in time to see Garrick take a running leap off of a cliff ten feet above the water. He pulled up his knees and landed a cannonball. Several seconds later he surfaced, shaking his head like a dog.

I stripped off my armor and weapons as I walked toward the pools, then stacked them next to Garrick's. The rocks in the cliff face were staggered like steps, and I climbed up to the ledge. "Watch this one, bro!"

Garrick had pulled his shirt off and stood near the edge of the pool scrubbing it. Once he turned in my direction, I vaulted over the edge and did a front flip.

Legard walked toward the pool. "Keepers, watch this."

Both of us looked at him, but he vanished. Then he whistled above us. "Up here." He had reappeared on the ledge.

I raised my hand to shield my eyes from the sun. As soon as Legard and I made eye contact, he disappeared again. I scanned the water. No splash—nothing. Then someone grabbed my ankles and pulled my feet out from under me so fast that I sucked in a mouthful of water as I sank. I kicked my feet free, coughing as I resurfaced. Legard came up next to me, laughing.

I slapped the water with my palm, sending a spray into that gloating grin of his. "Knock it off!" I said. When I lunged for him, he simply transported himself a safe distance away. "All right, you and your little elf tricks win."

Legard now stood where the water was waist deep. He bowed in my direction. When he straightened up, his expression appeared completely serious. "Keeper, please accept my most sincere apology. That was uncalled for, and it shan't happen again."

"Dude, you don't need to apologize. If I could pull a stunt like that, I'd be doing it all the time." Even as I spoke, I thought to myself, *Hey, with my counter, I could do that.* My hand slipped to my pocket and I sprung the latch. Without taking my eyes off of him, I moved my thumb to the Go button. "Really, it's fine. I think—"

I pressed the button, reappeared behind Legard, and sprang forward to tackle him. We fell with a splash into the water, but he disappeared right out of my arms. I stood and wiped my eyes as I looked for him. He sat on a large boulder, coughing up water.

"You've got to admit you had that coming," I said.

He smiled. "Yes, I agree. But now that you've polluted my air with the Protector's stench, the least you could do is bathe properly. Catch." He tossed me the bar of soap that magically materialized in the palm of his hand.

I pulled off my clothes and scrubbed them with the lemon-scented soap. After I'd cleaned myself, I held the soap out to Legard, who transported himself next to me and took it from my hand. When he turned to drape his shirt over the rock, I caught sight of his back. Scars like the ones I'd had after my time in Arbon's dungeon crisscrossed his flesh. I moved closer. "You should see an elf healer. They have this skin restorative potion that can fix your back. I used it and it worked great."

Legard looked sad as he faced me. "I am pleased the potion worked for you. But for me these scars are everlasting. Arbon made sure of that. After he killed my cousin, I tried to escape. I thought it better to die trying to reclaim my freedom than to live another day enslaved by someone as foul-minded as Arbon had become. He found me, of course, and I was the first to occupy the cell you briefly called home. I spent the better part of a year locked in there.

"When I finally resigned myself to my detestable fate, I gained a small measure of freedom. At that time there was only one elf healer in Shuyle, and she did an excellent job. My skin bore no trace of the abuse once she finished. I was quite pleased with the results. Lord Arbon, however, was not. He flew into a rage. He wanted my scars to be a constant reminder of where my loyalties should lie. Again I found myself subject to the lash of his whip. Only this time he added a curse, guaranteeing the scars could never be removed. My skin festered and bled for months. The pain was so great I began to think I might actually perish from my wounds. I wanted to die in the worst way, since that would have been the closest I could come to revenge—accidentally dying by Arbon's hand. It would have served him right. As you can see, I didn't get my wish. I had hoped now that he was gone I might be healed, but Cecilia has tried in vain."

Unable to think of anything to say, I climbed out of the pool to dry my clothes.

I swam in all four pools at Twisted Faeries Springs. The first, which smelled faintly of sulfur, was so hot it was nearly unbearable. The steaming water bubbled out of a crack between two black rocks, filling the small pool and then flowing into a larger pool where a waterfall churned the water like jets in a hot tub. The temperature of this pool was as comfortable as bath water. The water overflowed into the largest pool—the swimming hole Garrick had first jumped into. On a hot day like this, the cool water was perfect. The last pool was ice-cold and fed by both a spring and the other waterfall. The crystal-clear water bubbling out of the blue-gray rocks tasted sweeter than any bottled water.

Everyone bathed and strung his clothes across the rocks to dry in the late-afternoon sun. We set up camp wearing nothing but our underwear and boots. I gazed across the open space toward the forest as I pulled the rope tight on our tent. This would not be a good time for a Shuylian ambush. I was thankful Marcus and a few of his men had walked the perimeter of the clearing and inspected the surrounding woods before he issued the order to make camp.

TWENTY-SEVEN

Arbon's Heir

Both Shuylian outposts in Saddle Pass had been abandoned. We camped at the one on the summit, and I was anxious to get moving again. The place brought back unwanted memories—too many men had met their deaths there.

As we rode down the Shuylian side of the mountain, I looked for familiar landmarks. Instead of snow-capped peaks, jagged cliffs rose above us. Wildflowers of all colors dotted the sparse grass along the trail. Summer had transformed the treacherous pass into a calendar-worthy picture of perfection.

Late that evening, Marcus pointed ahead of him. "Keepers, look there."

I followed the angle of his arm and saw the rocky ledge protruding from the cliffs—the meager shelter where we had waited out the blizzard.

Garrick grinned. "Over yonder in those trees, I kissed my wife for the first time."

I swiveled my head to the side. "When?"

"The first night we stopped here. While we gathered firewood."

Marcus turned in his saddle and scowled back at his brother-in-law. "I thought I made it clear at the time that I didn't take kindly to anyone touching my sister."

Garrick shrugged his shoulders, smiling. "What can I say? She's very beautiful. You shouldn't have left me alone with her."

The commander raised his voice a notch. "I sent you out to collect wood that night. I thought I could trust you with something as simple as that, but as I recall neither of you came back with much of anything. What if we'd frozen to death out here? How would you have felt about disobeying orders for a little kissing then?"

Garrick sighed. "I would have died a happy man."

I wondered what else I hadn't noticed. "If that was the first kiss, when was the second?"

"One of the nights we were stuck here. The old commander was snoring up a storm and your breathing was as regular as the tic-tock of a clock. Sweet Brierly was so cold I moved a little closer to share my body heat, and I might have sneaked a kiss or two before she fell asleep."

The commander seemed to growl under his breath. "I knew you were nothing but a worthless rogue. I don't know what my sister sees in you."

I wasn't the only man chuckling after that exchange.

For the next few days we traveled the backwoods of Shuyle. After we exited the pass, we continued farther north into the forest. Legard led the way, since this was uncharted territory for the Algonian soldiers. Game was plentiful, and each morning and evening Marcus sent out a hunting party. The men usually succeeded, keeping our cooks busy skinning and roasting rabbits, turkeys, and an occasional deer.

At one point, Legard tilted his head and flared his nostrils as if testing the air. He pulled his horse to a stop. "Uncle, do you sense that?"

I turned in time to see Wickliff searching the woods and sky. "I do," he said. "'Tis time for me to turn back the cogs in my clock and assume the guise of my younger self. If you'll excuse me for a moment." The old elf dismounted and gathered his Shuylian uniform from his saddle pack before slipping out of sight into the dense trees.

"The cooks should fall back a mile or so for safety," Legard said to Marcus.

The commander turned and gave the order. Our cooks, accompanied by two soldiers, led a string of packhorses with all of our gear back the way we had come. Wickliff, dressed as a Shuylian soldier and again looking more like Legard's brother than his uncle, rejoined the group. Other than the rattle of chain mail and armor as the men prepared themselves, the woods seemed unusually quiet.

I maneuvered my horse closer to Legard. "You look worried," I said. "What are you thinking?"

"The air is darker than I would have expected."

I looked up at the bright sunshine filtering through the trees. "Slightly shaded perhaps, but I wouldn't call this dark. What did you expect in the middle of a forest?"

"I speak not of the quality of the light, but of the magic in the air. It is dense, cold, and bleak. This is much darker than what Lord Dolosus and his cronies would emit on their own. I fear they may have formed an alliance since we last spoke."

"What kind of alliance?"

Legard pulled his eyes away from the trees and looked into mine. "An alliance with someone familiar with the art of black magic."

"That doesn't sound good."

"No, Keeper. This does not bode well for any of us."

Marcus's horse nudged mine as he moved next to us. "What is the plan?"

Legard glanced at me. "I should carry the counters now."

I motioned for Garrick to come nearer as I dug mine out of my pocket. "Brother, he needs our counters."

After Legard pocketed both of our counters, he said, "I will lead the way into their camp. Through my negotiations with Dolosus, I will position myself where I can touch him. Without a hand on him, it is too risky to engage any of them in battle. I will say what I must, but the rest of you cannot tip them off prior to me securing Dolosus, or we risk losing him. He can transport faster than anyone I have yet encountered. If he disappears, the game is over. We will never catch him. Trust me, this is the only way to achieve our purposes."

Marcus nodded. "What should we do?"

Legard looked over our group. "All magicals should take up the positions closest to me. You humans stay in the background, unless their soldiers attack. Everyone must appear at ease. Dismount. Tie up the horses and begin to unsaddle them. We need to convince them we have arrived home, not stepped into our enemy's lair."

Marcus wheeled his horse toward the back of the group. "Take your positions as directed."

"Protector, ride behind me," Legard said. "I may have need of you before we are finished."

I wasn't sure I liked the sound of that, but I put my horse in line behind him. Wickliff, Leitner, Barhydt, Nebus, and the other magicals followed us. Segur, Aiton, Marcus, Garrick, and the other humans brought up the rear. During the next hour Legard frequently shifted positions in his saddle as he tested the air. I wasn't sure what he was doing, but I assumed that just as Wickliff could sense the dragons getting closer when we traveled the Borderlands, Legard could sense the magic surrounding Lord Dolosus and his sorcerer friends.

The path he took meandered in a haphazard way as if he was feeling his way through the dark toward their camp. Suddenly, Legard's spine stiffened and he stopped his horse. "Hail the camp," he called in a loud voice, "Legard requesting an audience with Lord Dolosus."

Two fierce-looking sorcerers materialized in front of us. They glanced over the line of soldiers and seemed to relax a notch. "Welcome back, Legard. What news do you bear?" one of them said.

"Tell Dolosus I have done all he asked of me. He will want to see what I have to show him."

One of the sorcerers disappeared. The other leaned against his staff and said, "Our lord will no doubt be pleased. Little else has arrived in the way of good tidings as of late, and his mood suffers as a result."

"Aye, so I've noticed. He is his father's son in every way." Legard bent across his horse's neck and spoke quietly. "But tell me. Have we new allies? I sense magic from someone I don't recognize."

"Lady Ravinia is here."

"The witch—Ravinia the Raven-Haired?"

"Aye."

The second sorcerer reappeared and said, "Lord Dolosus sends his greetings. You may continue." The guards stepped aside, and we rode past them.

"Would Ravinia be a wicked witch?" I asked.

Legard turned and put his finger to his lips as I heard Wickliff shush me from behind. *I guess that's a yes.*

The path we followed intersected a dirt road leading to a remote village. The small, thatched-roof houses had overgrown garden plots, and the dogs I saw were thin. Scattered among the houses were large military tents, as well as makeshift paddocks for the army's horses. Shuylian soldiers sat sharpening their axes and swords, cleaning their tack, and talking. Two cooking fires crackled beneath large black kettles, and a delicious smell floated on the breeze. Every eye seemed to follow us as we rode through the enemy stronghold.

Three tents were situated around what looked like an outdoor living room. Woven mats covered the dirt. Plush chairs were situated in a half-circle, and a small table sat off to the side.

A man stepped out of the largest tent. I'd bet money he was Lord Arbon's heir. He had his late father's dark hair, angular nose, and prominent cheekbones. He also must have inherited his father's love of fancy clothes, money, and power. His facial hair was shaved with precision into a goatee. And although I knew he had likely lived a few centuries, he looked to be in his twenties, strongly built and in prime physical condition.

As we drew closer he scanned our group and scowled. "I sent Cassius for you. Why has he not returned?"

Legard dismounted and bowed before Lord Dolosus. "Milord, I have recruited more men, and Quixtar, one of your father's chief sorcerers, has renounced the peace treaty with Algonia and wishes to join us. I sent Cassius for them while I hastened to bring you these." Legard pulled the two counters out of his pocket and held one in each hand.

"Very well. Open them."

Legard sprang the latches. Both counters emitted a bluish light—the simple lumens spell he had mentioned. From where I sat on my horse, I could see the light didn't form a pinpoint on the globe like it usually did, but from a distance that wouldn't be noticeable.

Lord Dolosus smiled. "Bring them here and let me see them."

Legard closed the counters. "First we have a matter of business to attend to. It is no secret we have not always seen eye to eye. You even petitioned your father on one occasion to have me executed. So, milord, surely you can't fault me for asking something of you in return—a guarantee of sorts."

A funnel of black smoke curled up from the ground next to Dolosus. When it reached six feet in height, a black-haired woman stepped out. She had an olive complexion, blood-red lips, and brown eyes outlined with makeup. Her dark-colored dress fit tightly around the kind of body you'd see on a model. In a sinister sort of way she was beautiful, but every instinct I possessed told me to get away.

"I thought I sensed a visitor in the camp," she remarked.

Legard bowed to her. "Lady Ravinia, 'tis good to see you again. What brings you out these days? It's been at least a century since I've had the pleasure of your company."

She laughed as she walked a tight circle around him, sliding her long black fingernails across his cheek and down his neck and arm. "Legard, relax, you lying scoundrel. I'm only here to watch." As she stepped onto the mat and moved toward a chair, she waved her hand and said, "Carry on."

"You bring me two counters," Dolosus said, "but you want something in return. What is it you desire of me?"

"Freedom. I want your guarantee, sworn with a blood oath, that I walk away from here unscathed. I know you desire my oath sealed with blood, guaranteeing my services to you as they were once promised to your father, but I vow I will pledge only fealty to you, no more."

"Give me the counters, and I will give you your blood oath."

Legard walked close enough to touch him, but instead of grabbing Dolosus so we could end this, he handed him a counter. Dolosus opened it, revealing the blue light of the lumens spell, and touched one of the buttons. His eyes narrowed as he pushed it again. "You fool! It is still attached."

Legard smiled. "I am no fool. Give me my oath, and I will give you the Keeper. Then you may do with him as you wish."

"Where is the Keeper?"

My heart skipped a beat when Legard turned and pointed at me.

Lord Dolosus laughed. "No shackles? No chains? And a Shuylian soldier, no less. What kind of fool do you take me for? That man hardly looks like your prisoner—or a Keeper, for that matter."

"The easiest prisoner to keep is the one who believes he isn't," Legard replied with a feral glint in his eye.

I couldn't help myself. I gasped and yanked on my reins. My horse responded by backing up. "You've not seen what they wear on the old world these days," Legard continued. "He's no Shuylian. Better to have him blend in than stand out like a dwarf among elves."

"Bring him to me," Dolosus commanded.

I panicked, driving my heel into my horse's side and doing a one-eighty. My horse slammed into the gray gelding ridden by Barhydt, and I caught a glimpse of the surprised expressions on every Algonian face. Garrick began drawing his sword, but Marcus clamped a hand around his wrist to stop him. A wall of horses and men blocked my escape. It didn't matter, though. I wouldn't have made it far. Before I drew my next breath, a pulse of magic hit me in the back, knocking me to the ground.

As I rolled clear of the horses' hooves, I saw it was Legard who had raised his hand, not Dolosus.

Legard has betrayed us.

The blood running through my veins felt like molten lead. Each beat of my heart sent a throb through my body. I crawled away, but Legard's long legs devoured the distance and his hand sank into my shoulder like a talon. So much for his promise.

Like I weighed nothing more than a rag doll, he dragged me across the ground and hauled me to my knees in front of Lord Dolosus. "No!" I yelled. I punched Legard in the arm, trying to break his hold. But it did no good—I was at his mercy.

Arbon's heir clicked my counter open, and this time Legard didn't work his magic. It remained dark. He pushed the gold device against my cheek and it lit up. I tried to grab it from him, but my body was too weak to move fast enough. Dolosus jerked the counter back and snapped it closed before setting it on the table next to him. He yanked the helmet off my head and then drew a dagger from his belt. Why wasn't Marcus doing something? Would it take my death for him to realize Legard had double-crossed us? With his other hand, Dolosus grabbed a fistful of my hair and exposed my throat.

TWENTY-EIGHT

Death Curse

Lord Dolosus moved the dagger toward my throat. I was dead. Or so I thought until Legard wrapped his hand around the blade, momentarily giving me a stay of execution. "You may have him only after you take the blood oath guaranteeing my safety and freedom."

Dolosus jerked the knife out of Legard's hand, making him wince as it severed his skin.

"And the second counter?" Dolosus said.

Legard held out his hand, blood dripping onto the reed mat at their feet. "It will be yours as well. But first, the oath."

Dolosus gritted his teeth as he pulled the blade across his palm. They gripped hands, but before he could speak the oath, Legard pushed me away and attacked.

The impact nearly buckled Lord Dolosus' knees. He partially faded, like he was trying to transport or disappear but couldn't. The muscles in Legard's hand and forearm strained as he held Dolosus in place.

Hope flickered in my heart as I crawled away. Legard hadn't sacrificed me after all.

Mass mayhem broke out. All of the magicals in our group attacked Lord Dolosus' sorcerers, who rushed forward to rescue their leader. Somebody—maybe Wickliff, from the direction of the blast—hit Ravinia. She screamed as she disappeared in a cloud of black smoke.

Loud cawing overhead drew my attention to the sky. A black bird the size of a large bald eagle trailed smoke as it flew through the treetops.

Since Barhydt was shooting flaming fireballs at it and Leitner was trying to hit it with a beam of smoking blue sparks, I figured the raven must be the wicked witch in disguise. She dove toward our men, spewing black smoke from her mouth. One of Barhydt's fireballs nearly struck her, but she vanished.

Nebus turned his attention to the deadly smoke, trying to corral it so it wouldn't spread. Men staggered and fell to the ground, coughing. Segur yelled for help. His horse had collapsed, pinning him to the ground amid the smoke. Marcus and Garrick pulled their extra shirts from their packs and tied them around their faces before rushing in to help. They dragged Segur clear of the hovering toxin and went back in to help the others.

Weakened from encountering friendly fire by Legard, I slowly drew my sword and watched the battle unfold around me. Once our sorcerers, dressed as regular Shuylian soldiers, joined the fight, the true Shuylians must have realized this wasn't just a spat between old enemies. They took up their arms and moved closer, although they seemed wary of the raven's smoke.

Amid the flurry of blue sparks, smoke, fireballs, and electric pulses shooting back and forth, an anguished cry sounded. I turned to see a Shuylian dragging his sword across Segur's throat. Marcus left Garrick and the man they were rescuing and ran toward his fallen soldier. Before he reached the man, an arrow pierced his chain mail at the seam under his left arm. Marcus fell to earth. My heart broke at the thought of losing him. The clang of swords rang out as the true Shuylians attacked our men.

At the sound of Lord Dolosus' voice, I turned back to the duel. "Legard, even if you succeed in killing me, you will never win, and you will never have your precious freedom."

Legard didn't acknowledge the threat. He continued firing magic into his enemy, total concentration on his face. Dolosus pulled his hand back from the fight, stuck it in his pocket, and drew out a small vial of red liquid. As he fell to his knees under Legard's pressure, he crushed the vial between his fingers. The glass exploded into tiny shards. The liquid, which hung suspended in the air, glowed a dark red.

Legard's eyes widened as he backed away, dragging Dolosus along with him. Although the elf seemed to falter for a moment, he resumed his attack, gritting his teeth as if pouring all of his energy into ending the sorcerer's life. Dolosus returned fire again, sending vibrating pulses into Legard.

The red liquid swirled into the shape of a sharp-toothed snake. It coiled midair and then looked at each man in the vicinity. When it glanced in my direction, a cold shudder ran down my spine. The snake shifted its gaze to Legard and slithered toward him.

I crawled to the table and pulled myself to my feet. My fingers touched something small and metal—my counter! I snatched it up. The snake stopped two feet away from Legard, opened its mouth, and spewed a fiery red stream of light into the elf's chest. Legard yanked back on Dolosus as if trying to break free, but Arbon's heir just laughed as he now held the elf in place. "Did you recognize the vial? It was my father's. Your own blood will be the end of you. Lady Ravinia was kind enough to conjure me a potion from that old vial of blood. A death curse is inescapable. Soon the world will be rid of your traitorous soul."

Legard fell to his knees, eye to eye with Dolosus. I clicked my counter open as I watched the snake. The beam of light had burned through Legard's clothing, and his skin bled. I adjusted the globe as I tightened my grip on my sword and then pressed Go.

I reappeared behind Dolosus and drove my blade into his heart. He flicked his hand in my direction, hitting me with a blast of magic that felt like a wrecking ball on steroids. I flew back across the woven mats and slammed into the circle of chairs. Ears ringing, I gasped for air as I climbed from the wreckage. A sharp pain radiated from my ribs. My head hurt, and when I touched my forehead my fingers came back bloody. *Where is my counter?* Both of my hands were empty. I had skewered Lord Dolosus like a shish kebab, and my sword now protruded out of his chest a good six inches. I scanned the area for my counter, shoving chairs out of my way as I crawled across the mat to grab it.

Nebus, Wickliff, Leitner, Barhydt, and our other sorcerers had most of Lord Dolosus' cronies locked in magical tethers. I couldn't see the raven and wondered if someone had killed the witch or if she had escaped.

Marcus was back on his feet, blood soaking his side and the broken shaft of an arrow protruding through his armor. A Shuylian lay bleeding at his feet. The commander stood with his sword poised for action as he negotiated for peace with a band of armed men.

The red snake hadn't died when I stabbed Dolosus, so I hobbled over to see if Arbon's heir was still alive. My heart raced as I neared the fallen sorcerer, remembering the nasty wound his father had given Marcus after the commander had beheaded him. But with Legard failing fast, I had to do something or it would be too late for him. I yanked my sword free of the sorcerer and rolled him onto his back with my boot. Lifeless eyes stared back at me.

I turned, swinging my sword through the snake. The blade went through the creature as if it was nothing more than a hologram. The snake didn't even flinch. Cautiously, I reached out, but my fingers felt only air. Legard collapsed. I yelled for help and dropped to my knees next to him.

The elf's eyes met mine as he gasped for air. "Tell Cecilia I'm sorry . . . I won't be returning to her as I promised."

Barhydt ran to my side and threw up a magical shield between the snake and Legard. The fiery red beam easily pierced it. I held my sword up, hoping to deflect the deadly beam with the blade, but that failed as well. Curious, I moved my bare hand into the beam's path. It passed through my skin, leaving me unharmed.

Wickliff hurried to his nephew's side, attacking the red snake with pulses of magic as he ran. "What can we do?" I asked him when the snake's attack never faltered.

"I've never seen the likes of this before. Did you hear Dolosus invoke a curse?"

"He said something about a death curse, and Legard's own blood being the end of him."

Legard raised his quivering hand. "Uncle, please forgive me. I tried to make restitution for my mistakes."

The old elf stepped between the snake and his nephew. He dropped to his knees, and they clasped hands. "My dear boy, you are forgiven." Wickliff squinted his eyes and clenched his jaw as if in pain. "Restitution will be paid in full by your faithful service to Algonia in the years to come," he said, his voice cracking.

I didn't understand why he would utter those words when it seemed obvious Legard would die. Wickliff leaned back to remove his breastplate, giving me a clear view of Legard. I gasped. The old elf had blocked the fiery beam by using his body as a shield.

"Wickliff, what are you doing?" I yelled.

A weak and pained smile turned his lips. "Only the passing of one whose blood matches that used to invoke the spell will satisfy a death curse. I am old and my time is near."

Tears sprang to my eyes. "Isn't there something else we can do?"

"This is the only way," Wickliff replied.

I looked up at Barhydt and then to Nebus, who was monitoring the prisoners as he watched the drama unfold. Looking solemn, both of them shook their heads.

"Protector, fetch the liquid energy from my packs," Wickliff said.

I hurried away, moving as fast as my aching, tired body would allow. At least two men and three of our horses lay dead from the effects of the witch's smoke bomb. A few men nursed wounds sustained in the ensuing battle. Segur's lifeless eyes were locked on the blue sky. Garrick and the men least affected by the smoke stood guard over the others, while Marcus, cradling his left arm, continued negotiations with the leader of the Shuylian soldiers. By the time I came back, Wickliff's body had returned to its proper age, and his breathing sounded labored.

I offered him the bottle. He shook his head. "Not for me. For my nephew."

I lifted Legard's head and held the flask to his lips, urging him to drink. He gulped down half of the bottle and closed his eyes. When he opened them again, he motioned to the flask. "You drink some. You need it after what I did to you."

I took a big swig of the liquid energy, trying to keep the stuff from touching my tongue longer than necessary. Still, I shuddered at the aftertaste. Wickliff toppled over, landing on his side.

Legard propped himself up on his elbow and leaned closer to his uncle, tears wetting his cheeks. "Why? A wretch like me deserves to die, not you."

The old elf smiled. "A wretch like you needs a second chance. You still get to die, but not today. Other than your mother, we are the last of our family. You must carry on our line, or it ends."

Legard reached to touch Wickliff, but the old elf's stern rebuke stopped him. "Take him away from me," Wickliff said, looking at me. "I don't want the curse to latch onto my nephew once I am gone. We must give it no reason to think it hasn't claimed its prize with my death."

Tears pooled in Legard's bloodshot eyes, and a sob tore from his chest. "I'm sorry!"

Wickliff's breath rattled in his chest. "Mourn me not. Instead, live for me."

I pulled Legard to his feet, but before I could take him away he looked down and uttered, "Thank you, Uncle. Your sacrifice will not be in vain. I vow never to disappoint you again."

I wiped the back of my hand across my eyes and tried to see through a blur of tears. Barhydt wrapped one of Legard's arms around the back of his neck, and together we dragged him into the woods. I looked over my shoulder and through the trees. Some of our men were gathering around Wickliff and the red snake, which glowed with fury.

The gaping hole in Legard's chest had left his skin blackened. Dark blood soaked his shirtfront and dripped onto the ground as we struggled to put distance between him and the death curse. If the snake was thirsty for blood, what would stop it from getting confused and coming after Legard once it stole Wickliff's life? The blood trail led right to us.

I didn't know if what I was about to do was the right thing or not, but I had to try. "I can take it from here."

"Are you sure?" Barhydt asked. "He's heavy."

I pulled out my counter and sprung the latch. "I'm sure."

"Where will you go?"

"The Elf Province."

Barhydt stepped away. "Godspeed on your journey, Keeper."

TWENTY-NINE

Coming Home

Legard was dead weight, like he had been paralyzed from the waist down. Once Barhydt let go, it was all I could do to keep us both on our feet. With one arm wrapped around the elf, I adjusted the globe and pressed Go, imagining Cecilia's kitchen with her bowl of sweet rolls. I hoped one of the potion vials in her apothecary shop could save Legard.

As the shimmer cleared, my knees buckled and we fell to the floor in the healer's kitchen. I looked around as I pulled Legard's arm off my shoulder and climbed to my feet. "Cecilia?" I yelled.

The door to the shop flew open. The surprise on Cecilia's face when she saw me turned to horror as she caught sight of the bleeding Legard. Quickly, she turned. "Atarah, please attend to the customers and then close the shop for the day. I must excuse myself immediately. A patient in the most dire of need has just arrived."

She closed the door behind her and ran to Legard. Tears filled her eyes as she rolled him onto his back and peeled his shirt away from the wound. "Black magic?"

"Yes. Dolosus had a vial of Legard's blood that some wicked witch named Ravinia made into a death curse."

Cecilia went pale. "Please help me get him into bed."

Once we had Legard settled in another room, I lowered myself into the chair in the corner, wanting nothing more than to sleep off my aches and pains. Atarah came in a few minutes later and asked if she could assist Cecilia. They cleaned Legard's wound with potions and whispered incantations in a strange language. For the next few hours, I drifted in and out of sleep, waking at times to see Cecilia or Atarah sponging Legard's forehead or chest with a damp rag.

When I woke fully, the sun had set, and numerous candles burned around the room. Cecilia sat next to Legard, holding his hand. I stood and stretched before dropping back into the chair, too tired to go anywhere. Beads of sweat covered Legard's flushed body. "Does he have a fever?" I asked.

"He does. I regenerated his blood supply, cleaned the wound, and administered liquid energy, but black magic is resistant to many of our remedies. His road to recovery will be long and hard."

"I'm sorry," I said.

Cecilia looked up at me. "Oh no, I didn't mean it like that. I am grateful he is alive. That is more than I dared hope for. It is a wonder he is here at all. The death curse is inescapable, or so I thought. How did you ever get him away with blood still flowing in his veins? Only death should have satisfied the curse."

A pang of sadness cut through me. "There was a death—Wickliff's. He sacrificed himself."

Cecilia brought her hand up to cover her mouth as tears again sprang to her eyes. "That dear, sweet man. How can I ever repay him?" She looked fondly back at Legard.

I smiled, seeing the bigger picture behind my old friend's sacrifice. "All Wickliff asked was for Legard to carry on the family line. You might be able to help with that someday."

She glanced back at me, blushing. "Perhaps. It is good that Legard has come home, but is he free to pursue a living as an Algonian citizen? Or is he doomed to live out his life in hiding?"

Late into the night we talked. I told her of our meeting with the king and his promise to publicly recognize Legard as an Algonian citizen once the threat of Lord Dolosus' revolution was removed. I assured her Dolosus was dead, so there was no reason Archidus wouldn't keep his word.

I needed to relieve myself, so I walked toward the door. When I let out a groan, Cecilia said, "You're injured as well, and I've not thought to offer you a thing. What ails you, Keeper?"

I gave her a brief rundown of my injuries. By the time I returned, she had placed two potion vials and a flask of liquid energy on the table by my chair. She helped me apply the orange potion to the cut on my head. Then she massaged the potion for bruises into my back, after which I rubbed a generous portion over the purplish bruise forming on my stomach and chest.

"Drink as much of the liquid energy as you'd like," she instructed. "That bottle is for you to keep as a token of my appreciation."

I raised the flask in a toast before bringing it to my lips.

The next morning I woke to the incessant ringing of bells. I rolled out of the small bed Cecilia kept in the room above the apothecary and opened the window. Elves walked the cobblestone street in groups as if summoned by the bells in the church tower. None of them seemed to hurry, so I figured it wasn't an emergency. I pulled on my shirt and boots and buckled my sword around my waist.

Cecilia was cooking eggs when I got downstairs. "What's all the commotion?" I asked her.

"That is the death knell. It announces the passing of one of our kind from this life into the next."

"It isn't Legard, is it?" I turned to see for myself that my old nemesis was still alive and kicking.

Cecilia smiled. "Oh no. He is sleeping comfortably now. I haven't been out to read the announcement yet."

I cracked the door to the bedroom. Sure enough, the color of Legard's skin looked better, and he breathed deeply. Cecilia and I ate breakfast while the bells continued their somber chiming. Soon I stood to clear my plate. "I'll go see what's going on."

"Will you take note of the deceased?" Cecilia asked. "I won't be getting out for a few days."

—⬥—

As I neared the church, a familiar voice called my name. Garrick stepped toward me, smiling. "How you feeling, little brother?"

"I'm good, but what's going on? I didn't expect to see you here."

"Leitner and the other elves brought Wickliff's body home. I tagged along to check on you and get my counter from Legard."

Thanks to Cecilia's potions and the liquid energy, I felt almost as good as I had before Legard let his magic loose on me. "I haven't seen your counter," I told Garrick. "It's probably still in Legard's pocket, and he's asleep. Cecilia said it would take a while for him to heal. Let's go look for it." I turned and started back the way I'd come.

Garrick glanced over at me. "I about had a fit when I saw him shoot you. For a second there, I thought we were all goners. But you look well enough."

"I know what you mean. I was sweating bullets when he said that stuff about the easiest prisoner to keep is the one who doesn't think he is a prisoner. I thought I was a dead man for a minute there. But last night Legard's girlfriend hooked me up with some potions, so I'm doing great."

When we got back to the apothecary shop, I told Cecilia the bells had been ringing for Wickliff. Again I saw sadness in her eyes at the mention of the old elf's passing. She listened to me explain what Garrick was looking for and said, "Ah, yes, I saw that. The counter is on the table next to the bed."

I opened the door. Garrick followed me into the room and pointed at Legard. "Never thought I'd be sorry to see him laid up in bed."

I crossed the room and scanned the small tabletop, cluttered with potion bottles, white cloths, a used glass, and a water pitcher. "Here it is." I picked up the counter.

Garrick took it from me. "Thanks."

We both stood watching Legard until Cecilia came in to change the bandage on his chest. The wound oozed dark puss, and the surrounding skin was discolored.

"When will he wake up?" Garrick asked.

Cecilia used a glass dropper to put three drops of a blue potion into the center of the hole in Legard's chest. As she fashioned a new bandage out of a piece of cloth, she answered, "I hope 'tis soon, although one can never be certain when black magic is involved. It may take one week or twenty."

"He will recover, won't he?" I said.

"He has already improved, so I believe he will wake up, but there are those who never do."

After a moment of strained silence, I nudged Garrick. "Let's go back to the castle and check on the girls, should we?"

We said goodbye and left the room. I pulled out my counter and adjusted the globe. "You want to come with me?"

"Nah." Garrick pulled out his own counter. "There's a funeral for Wickliff tonight at sunset. I'm coming back for that. If you and Ellie want to come, let's meet after dinner."

"Sounds good." I pressed Go and disappeared.

I imagined the room I shared with Ellie in the castle, thinking I would get cleaned up and go find her. It was late morning, so I expected she would be out with Brierly. As I materialized next to the bed, I heard a sob. My wife sat crying at the small table across the room.

"Ellie, what's wrong?" I hurried over and dropped to one knee in front of her.

She jumped at my sudden appearance and quickly wiped her eyes. "Nothing. I didn't hear you come in. When did you return?"

I took her hands in mine. "It isn't nothing if you were crying. Tell me. What happened?"

She smiled, but her eyes looked unhappy. "Really, darling, it is nothing but a little disappointment. I never would have been crying over it if I'd had any idea you were coming back at the moment."

A sick feeling settled in my gut. When she tried to stand, I pulled her down onto the seat. "Well, I am back and I want to know. What disappointed you? Did I do something?" I tried to lighten the mood by grinning and saying, "What, did I miss our two-month anniversary or something?"

Ellie laughed softly, then touched my cheek and kissed me. "Nothing like that. You're perfect. I'd just rather not say, because you'll think it a bunch of feminine foolishness."

I shook my head. "You're wrong. If it's important to you, it's important to me. Just tell me, please."

She took a deep breath and sighed. "If you must know, I suppose I can tell you." She paused. "Last week I thought I might be expecting, and even though I know you aren't excited about the prospect of a baby, I was quite delighted by the idea. But as of this morning, I know I'm not expecting."

She looked like she might cry again, so I pulled her into my arms as I stood. I didn't know what to say at first, because honestly this didn't seem like something worth crying over. But Ellie sure seemed upset about it, and suddenly I wondered if I was ready to be a husband. *What would Garrick say?* Before I figured out the answer, Ellie continued, "I know we talked about waiting to have children, and that's fine. I understand why you want to do that. But with being here for so long, I began to hope nature would take its course and I'd get my baby early. That doesn't seem to be the case, though, and I'm feeling quite melancholy."

"I'm sorry, Ellie." While I cradled her head against my chest, one reason after another popped into my mind as to why we should wait to have a baby. But if Garrick was in my shoes, I didn't think he'd bring up any of those things right now, so I kept my mouth shut.

—◈—

Garrick and I met with Archidus and reported on our journey. When I asked if Legard would get his pardon and his citizenship, Archidus nodded and said, "I will issue the proclamation. He has earned it."

That night after dinner, Ellie and I met Garrick and Brierly before leaving for the Elf Province. Master Archidus, his wife the queen, and Azalit arrived shortly after we did. Wickliff's body lay in an ornate casket in the back of a fancy wagon. People walked by, paying their respects, and many set bouquets of flowers next to the coffin. I met Wickliff's twin sister—Legard's mother, Wilmeeka—who stood next to the wagon accepting condolences.

By the time the funeral procession prepared to leave the church grounds, flowers filled the bottom of the wagon. Six elves lifted the casket lid into place. An old elf shuffled forward and pointed to each corner of the coffin, sending a beam of golden light into the wood. When he stepped away, the top had been fastened with thick brass clips. It didn't look like the lid would come off anytime soon.

Four white horses pulled the wagon up the road. Wilmeeka, along with Master Archidus and the queen, followed directly behind the wagon. The rest of us fell in line. It was maybe a mile to the cemetery. The foliage and flowers surrounding the graves looked perfect, without a single weed in sight. We stopped near a marble headstone engraved with the name Courtenay and one engraved with the name Maribelle. Azalit leaned over and informed me that Maribelle was Wickliff's wife. Figuring he would be buried between his wife and daughter, I was surprised no one had dug the hole yet.

Archidus spoke words of gratitude and praise for Wickliff and the service he had rendered to his country over the course of his life. An elf stepped between Courtenay's and Maribelle's headstones and raised his staff. He pointed to the coffin, which suddenly glowed with light. Then he drove his staff deep into the earth at his feet. The coffin disappeared as a beam of light shot from the staff into the ground and then ricocheted up into the heavens.

He moved aside, and another elf took his place near the gravesite. This one conjured up a headstone with the flick of his wrist. The green marble had ivy and flowers engraved around the edge, with the name Wickliff etched in bold black letters. An image of a younger-looking Wickliff was carved next to his name. The queen blew on the wick of a candle, which sputtered to life. She placed the light in front of the headstone, where the small flame flickered in the evening breeze.

When the queen stepped away, a group of elves began singing in their ancient language. A hauntingly beautiful melody filled the air. Fireflies floated on the breeze, circling the singers and filling the air above the cemetery with dancing lights. When the song ended, everyone quietly left. As I walked away, I looked over my shoulder. The solitary candle burned brightly in front of the headstone, and the image of Wickliff seemed to smile back at me.

THIRTY

Honeymoon

Ellie and I enjoyed our final night in the castle, sleeping in until ten o'clock. After we packed our bags and dressed in our modern clothing, she let out a sigh and closed the wardrobe door. "I'm sad to leave all these beautiful gowns behind."

"They do look nice on you," I said, thinking of how glad I was to be back in shorts. "Maybe you can wear them again next year."

"Next year?"

"I'll have to come back for the Keepers' Council tour, and Archidus said you're invited if you want to come."

"How delightful. I'd certainly enjoy that."

I pulled a T-shirt over my head and stepped into my sneakers. With a bag on each shoulder, I smiled and offered Ellie my hand. "Should we go?" She looked so beautiful in her flowered sundress.

She gathered her wedding gown into her arms, then slid her fingers between mine. "I suppose we should."

We stopped at Garrick's room and knocked. I'd promised not to leave without saying goodbye. He opened the door and said good morning. He wore the tuxedo pants from my wedding, with the sleeves rolled up on the white shirt, and the bow tie hanging loosely around his neck. Brierly appeared amused by the three of us. To her Algonian eyes, I'm sure our outfits looked funny.

"Good morning, you two," I said. "We'll be leaving as soon as we find Archidus."

"Wait and we'll come with you. We're almost ready," Garrick said.

Brierly had condensed her belongings into one military-style pack. Garrick closed the top and pulled the pack onto his shoulders. With care, he draped the suit coat over his arm and smiled at his wife. "Are you ready, my dear?"

She smiled back at him. "As ready as I'll ever be, I suppose."

Until that moment, I hadn't fully appreciated that she was leaving her whole world behind. She might return someday, but there was no guarantee.

"Where's Marcus?" I asked.

"We said goodbye earlier this morning," Garrick said. "His men marched out at first light. If things go as planned, we'll all be meeting here next year for the Keepers' Council."

"Sounds good," I said.

Garrick wrapped his arm around Brierly, and we followed them through the castle. Archidus must have been expecting us, because the guards opened the door to the great hall as we approached.

Archidus and Leitner stood waiting. "I see you are prepared to return," the king said. "My sincere thanks for your hours of dutiful service to my country."

Garrick and I both nodded.

"Once you reach Witches Hollow, I'll send you back to the old world," Archidus continued. "I had Leitner take Wisdom's Keeper and Illusion's Keeper to the Hollow. But Protector, I do believe you know how to get there with your counter."

"I do," I said, remembering the coordinates Shahzad had shown me the day I gave him Davy's counter.

Archidus raised his eyebrows and smiled. "Very well, I'd prefer you didn't traipse about Cadré Unair looking so . . . foreign."

Garrick and I chuckled. Ellie dropped her gaze, most likely embarrassed by the shortness of her skirt and sleeves in comparison with Algonian custom. Brierly nodded in agreement with the king's assessment. I'd bet she was relieved at not having to be seen in public in the new world with people looking as bizarre as we did.

Once our counters were set, Garrick wrapped his arm around Brierly, smiled at Archidus, and saluted. They disappeared.

I nodded and pressed Go. Ellie and I appeared in Witches Hollow just before Garrick and Brierly left. "See you on the old world, little brother," Garrick called out before they vanished.

I returned the counter to my pocket and smiled at Ellie as we too left Algonia behind. Soon, we dropped into the old world, stumbling in the darkness of our hotel room.

A woman's panicked voice sent me fishing in my pocket for my counter.

"What was that? Eric, I heard something," the woman said.

I pulled Ellie toward the bathroom. There was no time to set the counter with someone in our room, so I flipped the latch and pressed Shuffle. We appeared in a beautiful valley surrounded by mountains topped with snow.

"What happened?" Ellie asked.

I set the counter for Hawaii on our wedding day. "Archidus returned us to the right location, but it was the present time, not when we left. After a couple of months, someone else was using our room."

"Oh, I see."

Imagining our hotel room as it was the night we left, I pictured the clock next to the bed reading 10:00 PM. I pressed Go, and we reappeared in our room. The soft glow of the lamp welcomed us. "Home at last," I whispered.

I slid our bags off my shoulder and wrapped my arms around my wife. The wealth of experience I had gained in the short time I'd been gone from this room brought a smile to my face. I lowered my head and kissed her. Ellie interrupted me to ask, "What time is it?"

Without looking at the clock, I answered her. "Ten PM."

She frowned. "Hmm . . . I wish it was morning. I'm not even tired. We'll be up all night, and when the sun rises we'll long for sleep."

With my counter still in the palm of my hand, I flipped the latch. "You make a good point." I rolled the day forward half a notch, knowing every dial on my counter by feel. "I can fix that for you. Your wish is my command." I slid my thumb over the Go button and felt it click.

The air shimmered around us, flooding the room with brilliant Hawaiian sunshine. Ellie smiled. "I assume it's AM now?"

I closed my counter and dropped it in my pocket. "Yup. What do you want to do today?"

"Everything! Show me all there is to see in this amazing place."

I walked toward the swimming pool in my flip-flops and swim trunks, practically dragging Ellie behind me.

"I'm not sure I want to know how to swim," she said. "When I said *everything,* this wasn't quite what I had in mind, you know. I'm perfectly content to live out the remainder of my days with both feet on dry ground."

"I'm sure you are, but what if I take you fishing? What if you fall in a river? It only makes sense to know how to swim—at least a little."

She pulled back. "Then I won't go fishing. You'll have to do that on your own."

I laughed and tightened my hold on her wrist. I contemplated throwing her over my shoulder, but there were too many spectators lounging in their beach chairs on the perfectly groomed grass. "Ellie, trust me, it's not that hard."

"I don't see any need for it, and I really don't care to learn."

I decided to try a new line of reasoning. "You want to be a mother someday, right?"

Without hesitation she said, "Of course. You know I do."

"What are you going to do if your toddler falls in a swimming pool someday and I'm not there?"

She stopped walking, color draining from her face. "That's an awful thing to say."

"I know, but that's one of the reasons I want you to know how to swim. Please, if not for me, will you try for our unborn children?"

She took a deep breath and nodded her head. And she did try, too. Every day we swam in the pool together. By the end of the week she could float, tread water for a few minutes, and swim a short distance. With a life jacket, she braved the ocean. We rented a sea kayak and explored the shoreline.

On another day, we snorkeled along the rock formations. The water was crystal clear, the fish plentiful. Watching the sea life up close fascinated both of us. When we left the water behind and walked through the surf, Ellie turned to me and said, "That was actually quite enjoyable. I may be starting to like the ocean."

Our last night, I took her to a Hawaiian luau with Polynesian dancing. They had roasted a pig in a pit all day, and we feasted on traditional island foods. When it ended, we walked through the moonlight back to our hotel.

"It's beautiful here, Chase. Thank you," Ellie said.

"I never thought I'd say this, but I think I'm ready to get home."

"I never imagined our honeymoon would turn out to be so lengthy."

I laughed and pulled her closer. "I didn't either, but I'm not complaining about that part."

She wrapped both arms around me. "And I never dreamed I could be so happy."

—◈—

I finished packing my bag and set my counter. I had checked us out of our room while Ellie showered. She pulled her hair into a ponytail and tossed her brush into her bag. "I guess I'm ready."

Her skin was bronze from a week in the Hawaii sunshine. "You look nice," I said.

She smiled back as I put a bag on each shoulder. With my counter in one hand and her hand in the other, I pressed Go. The air shimmered around us, and a few seconds later we stood in my bedroom. I dropped the bags on my bed.

"Someone left you a note." Ellie held out a piece of paper.

I took the note from her hand and read it aloud.

Little brother, the tux is hanging in your closet. Thanks for coming to get me for your wedding. It was the best trip yet, for more reasons than one. We're going back to Vandalia. Davy and I have a busy schedule with our business. I can't leave him to manage it on his own right now, especially with their baby coming. Plus, I think for Brierly the transition to 1834 will be easier than 1968. Come see me next Fourth of July—I'll be looking for you. Best of luck to you and Ellie.

Garrick

"That sounds like a good plan," Ellie said. "Vandalia will be a nice place for them to start out."

"I'm glad Garrick found someone. I was worried he'd never get married again after Rose."

My mother poked her head through my doorway. "You're back?"

"Yeah," I said. "We just got here."

"We found your car in the shop. How did you get to the airport?"

I shrugged my shoulders and smiled. "Mom, I didn't use the airport. Magic, remember?"

After everything I'd told her, and everything I'd been through in the past year, it surprised me that she looked shocked. "You never bought plane tickets?"

"Why waste the money when I can get there for free? And there's no risk of a plane crashing."

"Yes, but aren't there risks of magical failure or something?"

"Mom!" I rolled my eyes. "I used to worry about that, but it's never been a problem. Can we talk about something else?"

She sighed. "Okay, how was your trip? Tell me about Hawaii."

In January, Ellie and I moved into a small house off campus. Garrick's wealthy, older self had remembered that his younger self promised us a wedding gift. A realtor showed up with keys to a house and closing documents for us to sign. My mom came down for a week and took Ellie shopping for house stuff. They seemed to have fun painting and decorating.

I kept busy with school and track. Ellie found a job at a daycare center within walking distance. Occasionally I stopped by the old dorm room to get some tutoring on statistics—it seemed to make Robert's day when I asked for his help. Ellie started inviting him over for dinner on Sundays.

Now that I lived off campus, I hadn't seen Jenna—my fall-semester stalker—in a long time. But one day in February, her voice calling my name brought me to a stop.

I turned. She waved as she weaved her way through the crowd of students. I nodded in her direction but kept walking. It wasn't long before she tugged on my arm. "Hey, Chase, wait up. I haven't seen you around in like, forever."

"Yeah, I've been pretty busy."

"There's a party on Friday in the commons room at our dorm. You should come. Bring your roommate—whatever his name is."

"His name's Robert. But he's not my roommate anymore." I held up my left hand to show her my titanium wedding band. "I'm married, remember? I don't go to parties."

She let go of my arm. "You really married her? Wow, I didn't think you'd actually go through with it. Are you happy?"

I smiled. "Without a doubt. See ya around." I turned and rejoined the river of students flowing down the sidewalk.

THIRTY-ONE
Fourth of July

One morning the birds woke me. I had slept in my own bed at my parents' house, with Ellie next to me. My dad's side of the family had a family reunion over the weekend, and Ellie and I decided to stay an extra few days before going home to Eugene. I had a summer job working construction down there, and she was still working at the daycare. The highlight of each day was coming home to her.

I glanced at the calendar on my wall—July 4. The words in Garrick's note flashed before my eyes. *Come see me next Fourth of July—I'll be looking for you.* Over the last six months, Ellie and I had often wondered how Brierly and Garrick were getting along.

"It's the Fourth of July," I whispered. "Do you want to go see Garrick and Brierly?"

Ellie stretched in her sleep and let out a lazy yawn. "Hmm . . . I don't know." I figured she was still half asleep.

I wrapped my arms around her. "Aren't you curious about Brierly? We should go to Vandalia today. Davy and Sylvia's baby will be about a year old by now. You'll want to see it, won't you? And the Gibsons—how old will their kids be in 1835?"

That woke Ellie up. "Chase, are you serious? Do you really want to go to Vandalia today?"

"Yup, do you?"

"Of course. When?"

"Now. Why wait? Let's go before everyone else wakes up."

With my counter, we popped into our house and changed into our frontier clothes. Then I set the counter for Vandalia, Illinois, July 4, 1835, and pressed Go. We appeared at sunrise behind the cabin.

It looked like they had been busy. The garden was in full bloom with rows of corn stalks, tomato plants, and squash. Closest to the house was a long row of sunflowers. We stepped onto the porch and I knocked. Sylvia opened the door. "Ellie, my goodness, what brings you out here so early? I had no idea you were in town."

"Sorry if we woke you, but it's been so long, we were too excited to wait," Ellie said, giving Sylvia a hug.

"That's all right. You didn't wake me. Little Rose always gets us up before the rooster crows."

It was then we noticed the small girl clutching her mother's skirt as she tried to stand. "Rose?" I said.

"She's named after Davy's mother," Sylvia answered.

I went down on one knee. The little girl had dark hair and large brown eyes. "She's cute. She looks like her grandmother Rose."

"How would you know her? That's not possible. She died when Davy was very young. He barely remembers her, and you're even younger than he is."

My face felt hot as I tried to back-pedal. "I saw pictures . . . years ago I saw pictures. And I guess after everything Garrick told me about her I feel like I know her." Then I realized Davy and Garrick were about the same age now, so Sylvia wouldn't understand how Garrick could possibly remember Rose either. Hoping to change the subject before I dug myself in any deeper, I said, "Speaking of Garrick, where is he?"

"He and Davy are getting the wagon ready. They leave tomorrow. Garrick and Brierly have their own place now. It's a quarter mile down the road. Davy's already there. He said I should send you over if I saw you."

"Thanks," I said.

Ellie gave Sylvia another hug. "I'll be back soon. I want to catch up on all your news."

We walked the short distance to where Garrick's cabin was set back off the road. It was a buzz of activity with two loaded wagons in the yard. One was a covered wagon, the white canvas top looking out of place next to the freight wagon. The horses shook their heads and swished their tails at the flies buzzing around them.

"Go on," Ellie urged.

I ran up the driveway as Garrick hauled a wooden trunk down the porch steps. "Hey, Garrick," I yelled.

His head shot up and he blinked against the bright sunlight. "Little brother, that you?"

"What are you doing? It looks like you're moving."

He set the trunk in the wagon. "I am. I'm going back home."

"Why?"

Garrick turned around and looked at his house. As if on cue, Brierly stepped through the doorway with a pile of linens. She was visibly pregnant. He ran to the door and took the load from her arms. "I can get that. You should sit down. I don't want you overdoing it." He kissed her on the forehead.

The glare of the sun kept me hidden in the shadow of the wagon. "Garrick, I'm having a baby, not dying," Brierly said. "I can still do things. I hate sitting around watching you do everything."

I stepped closer to the cabin. "It's useless arguing with that stubborn old mule. You may as well give in and let him pamper you."

Her hand flew to her forehead, shading her eyes. "Chase, is that you?" She came down the steps.

Ellie walked around the wagon to join me, and I said, "Yup, we thought we'd stop in and wish you a happy Fourth of July."

My wife wrapped her arms around Brierly. "Well, look at you! How much longer?"

Brierly set her hand on her bulging stomach. "The midwife thinks three or four weeks."

I fell in step next to Garrick. "You said you're going home. Like Texas A&M, back to your apartment kind of home, or some other home?"

"College Station, Texas." He packed a stack of quilts in the covered wagon.

"What are you doing with all this stuff?"

Garrick stopped walking and smiled. "Making it look like we're moving out west. Since I saw you last, Brierly and I were married again—for the benefit of all the townspeople around here. And now I'm packing my wagon and driving out west, so no one will suspect anything is amiss about us leaving."

His expression grew thoughtful. "Remember what Archidus said about us having children? He said we needed to commit to one time after that." Garrick looked behind him to where Brierly stood talking with Ellie. "I won't stay here. I don't want my wife going through childbirth without the benefits of modern medicine. And I don't want my son or daughter dying of an infection because we don't have access to penicillin. I don't want them to deal with the issues of slavery and women's rights. I want my daughters to be free to do anything they choose with their lives. And I don't want my sons fighting in the Civil War. So I'm going back to 1968, and I'll take my chances in Vietnam."

"All right," I said.

"But I'm going to need your help with something."

"Sure, Garrick, anything."

"Come to Texas with me, and I'll explain when we get there."

Garrick had sold his property, and everything he didn't pack in the covered wagon went into Davy's freight wagon. Davy and Sylvia would use it or sell it.

When the house was empty except for a bedroll for each of us, we visited the Gibsons and then ate supper at Davy and Sylvia's. Ellie had baked the Algonian star rolls that afternoon. Sylvia left the room to feed Rose, and Garrick, Davy, and Brierly agreed the rolls were as good as any they'd tasted in the castle.

At first light, Davy, Ellie, and I hid beneath the canvas top in the wagon, while Garrick drove, with Brierly riding shotgun. On the way out of town, several people stopped Garrick to wish him and Brierly well on their journey. We sat cramped in the back of the wagon until we were clear of the townsfolk. Once the road was empty in both directions we climbed out and walked alongside the wagon.

When we reached the fork in the road, Garrick turned south instead of west. Around noon, he stopped the wagon in a grove of trees, where we were hidden from the view of anyone passing by on the road. Brierly and Ellie found a grassy spot to rest, while Garrick, Davy, and I set to work dismantling the wagon. We removed the food boxes that were attached to the side of the wagon, uncovering the painted letters spelling Eastman & Adams Freight, Co. The wood frame holding the canvas in place was taken off and abandoned in the brush. The white canvas was folded neatly, and everything was concealed under an oilskin tarp, making it look like a typical load of freight.

Davy tied the last knot and turned to Garrick. "Pa, you'll take care of yourself?"

Garrick pulled his son into his arms and held him there. "I will, and you take care my little Rose, you hear?"

"Yes, sir, but you'll visit, won't you? At least every Fourth of July, like you said. You, me, and Harper—we'll all get together in Vandalia next year, right?"

Garrick smiled. "Of course. I'll be here on the Fourth, if not sooner."

The two of them looked at me and I nodded. "I'll be here too."

Davy stepped away from his pa and shook my hand, then walked to Brierly and Ellie. He hugged both of them, then climbed onto the wagon and threaded the reins through his fingers. He smiled at Brierly. "Good luck with Garrick. He can be a bear at times."

Davy pulled the team in a tight circle and left behind the grove of trees and the only father he'd ever known.

When we could no longer see the wagon, Garrick slumped onto a log and dropped his head into his hands. He choked back a sob, and Brierly wrapped her arms around his head. I sat on the grass by Ellie and waited.

Garrick might have lived in the past for as many years as he'd lived in his own time. Things were simpler here. You built a cabin. You planted seeds. You harvested. You went to work. And as long as you had family, food, shelter, and warmth, you were happy. There were no complicated world issues. Or at least without modern communication, you didn't have to worry about them, because you rarely knew what happened outside of your community. He would be returning to the political unrest over the war in Vietnam and the sobering reality of his own draft notice.

THIRTY-TWO

1968

Garrick took a deep breath and rose to his feet. He smiled at Brierly. "I guess we'd better go."

"If you're sad about leaving, I can't see why we don't stay here. You love it here," she said.

He shook his head. "This isn't where I want us to raise our children."

She ran her fingers along his arm and squeezed his hand. "Whatever you think is best."

Garrick pulled out his counter and picked up the two packs containing the few belongings they were taking with them to 1968. I offered Ellie my hand and pulled her to her feet. We stood next to Garrick and put our hands on his arm. The air shimmered around us, and we left the grove. I didn't think we needed to shuffle anymore, but I guess it was habit for Garrick. On our first shuffle, I took one of the packs from him and slung it across my back. Within a few minutes, we appeared in the bedroom of his one-room apartment.

Garrick dropped his pack on the bed. I followed his lead. He took Brierly by the shoulders and lowered her onto the edge of the mattress. "Wait here for a minute, dear. Harper, come with me."

I followed him out of the bedroom. Once he closed the door he whispered, "Help me clean up, would you? I should've come back here and gotten everything ready for Brierly." He stooped to pick up a pair of jeans off the floor and then stepped into the bathroom and put his toothbrush and toothpaste in the drawer.

"It's not that messy," I said, handing him the T-shirt that was hanging over the door. "Remember, your mom was here for a week after you got shot."

We moved into the kitchen. "Oh yeah, I forgot about that. I was on spring break the week I was here with the gunshot wound, but I can't remember a single one of my classes. I think today's Saturday, and I've probably got to be in class on Monday morning."

I went to the sink and started washing dishes while Garrick continued straightening up. "You'd better start studying," I said.

"No kidding," he mumbled.

"What are you boys doing?" Ellie called from the bedroom.

"Just a minute." Garrick set a stack of dishes in the sink, then ran a rag over the table and counter. "Okay, you can come out."

I was still scrubbing the dishes as Ellie and Brierly entered the room.

"Welcome home, Brierly." Garrick wrapped his arms around her. "I know this is really different from anything you've seen before, but we won't be here for long. I'll graduate in December and we can move somewhere else. We'll buy a house with a yard. Or a little land and a cow, and maybe some chickens."

Brierly stared down at her feet as he talked. "Garrick, I'm happy to be anywhere you are, but what is this orange floor?"

"Carpet," he said.

I rinsed the last dish and dried my hands on a towel. "Shag carpet—hideous 1960s' orange shag."

"Knock it off, little brother," Garrick said.

Brierly bent over her pregnant belly and ran her hand across it. "Hmm . . . strange." She waved her hand around, looking in awe at the television, the kitchen, the couches. "What is everything else?"

Ellie grabbed Brierly's arm and pulled her into the kitchen. "You'll love living here. Look at this—running water. It comes straight into your house, and the extra goes down the drain. There's a knob for hot and a knob for cold. You pick the one you want and turn it on. This is the stove. No more building fires. If you want to cook, you just turn the dial. This is the fridge. It will keep everything cold—no more trips to the cellar or the icehouse. But follow me. The bathroom is by far the best invention. I'll show you."

Ellie and Brierly disappeared into the bathroom. Garrick didn't look as happy as I would have expected, and I could tell something was on his mind. He slumped onto his green couch. "Why do you need my help?" I asked.

"I've got to answer that draft summons this week, but if I go off and die in Vietnam, I would have been better off staying in Vandalia, or trying my hand at dodging the draft. That's why I need your help—"

I interrupted. "You're not going to die."

He shook his head. "I have to make sure. I want you to go to my parents' house and find out when I get home. It'll drive me crazy leaving Brierly by herself. I can't do it. I'm going to take her forward, to the date I get home. And then we'll have our baby together, just like we've always planned."

I nodded. "I can do that."

Garrick stood and motioned for me to follow. In his room, he tossed me the T-shirt and jeans I'd worn the day I took him to the hospital. I shut his bedroom door and changed my clothes.

"Give me your counter," he said. "Do you remember my dad's shop, where we got the pistols before we went after Ellie and Davy?"

"I remember," I said.

"Think of the shop. And then once you're there, sneak around to the front door of the house."

"Okay." I took back my counter and smiled at him. "I'll be back in a minute." The anxious look on Garrick's face made me feel sorry for him. I didn't envy his position. If the tables were turned and I was forced overseas to fight a war I didn't believe in, I'd be scared too. "Don't worry, big brother. It'll all work out." Out of habit, I pressed Shuffle and Go.

I shuffled through the Arizona desert, the emerald-green hills of Ireland, the woods of Germany, and the Great Plains of Kansas. On my final shuffle I dropped into the Pacific Ocean, biting back a curse at my bad luck and wishing I'd remembered I could skip the shuffling now that Legard and Lord Arbon weren't a threat.

I kicked to the surface, spitting and coughing up water. I put my hand on my pocket and pressed my counter against my leg. I couldn't lose that. When my shuffle time was up, I tried to get my feet under me so I didn't fall on the floor like an idiot as I spontaneously reappeared on land.

The shimmering started. I took a deep breath. I bumped into a table of nuts and bolts next to the old car, but other than that it was a smooth transition. Thankfully, no one was in sight. I stepped away from the puddle of saltwater and walked to the door. After yanking it open, I nearly fell over a man in a wheelchair. "Sorry, sir," I said.

The man grabbed my arm, scowling. "Boy, what you doin' in my shop?"

I blushed at being caught red-handed where I had no right to be. I stuttered out an answer. "I was looking for Garrick's dad. You're Mr. Eastman, right?"

His expression remained stern. "I am, but why didn't you come up to the house?"

"Um, Garrick said to try the shop, that you're always out here."

He narrowed his eyelids as he studied me. "How'd you end up as wet as a used dishrag out here in dusty old Texas?"

I glanced around, doubting there was a river nearby I could have fallen into. "I just . . . I was hot, so I hosed myself off. I hope you don't mind." I rolled my eyes at my own idiocy. By now he surely thought I was the dumbest kid on the block.

He raised his eyebrows. "Well, son, what can I do for you? Garrick's not here."

"Is he in Vietnam?"

"No, of course not. What makes you ask that?"

"He got drafted. The last time I talked with him he had to report for the draft. He thought for sure he was on his way to Vietnam."

"Army wouldn't take him. He didn't pass the medical exam."

I shook my head. "Why? He was perfectly healthy. He would have made a great soldier."

"After getting shot by some thugs, he lost his spleen. The doctors gave him a medical exemption."

I sighed in relief and smiled. "That's good news. So, he never went? You're sure?"

Garrick's father looked at me with raised eyebrows. "Yes, I'm sure my son never went to Vietnam."

I wondered if they knew of Brierly. "Did he ever get married?"

"Yes, he did. It was a bit of a scandal at first, but it sure has turned out well for them. He married a girl named Brierly. I couldn't have picked a better wife for him if I'd done it myself. They have a little boy named Marcus, and Garrick called me last week to tell me they have another one on the way."

I was nearly jumping for joy. I reached into my pocket but stopped myself. "Thank you, Mr. Eastman. You have a great son, and he's been a great friend to me. I'll see you around." I turned and jogged toward the road.

"Who should I tell him called?" his father yelled after me.

I stopped. "Just tell him his little brother was here." I ran around the corner, out of sight, and pressed Return, anxious to share the news.

Breathless, I reappeared in Garrick's bedroom. He sat on the edge of the bed with his head in his hands, his elbows resting on his knees. I pulled off the wet T-shirt.

"You look happy, so hopefully I didn't die over there. What happened?"

I shook my head, grinning from ear to ear. "You don't even go. Your dad said you never passed the medical exam. Without your spleen the army wouldn't take you."

Garrick stood up and cracked a smile. "Are you sure?"

I nodded. "Your dad told me you didn't go. I even asked him twice."

Garrick threw his arms around me. "Thank you."

"You're welcome. I think you're going to have to get married again. Did you think about that?"

He paced his room. "I probably should have come back here when we first thought she was pregnant. Now everyone will assume we're getting married because of that." He stopped and smiled at me. "But hey, maybe the third time's the charm, and at least I don't have to go to Vietnam, right? I can handle a little disgrace. I've been through worse."

"Yeah, Garrick, you've definitely been through worse. Your dad mentioned the scandal. But he also said that when it was all said and done, he couldn't have picked a better wife for you if he'd done it himself. So it'll all work out."

"That's good to know. Tonight I'll make up a good story with Brierly, and we'll go talk to my parents next weekend."

Remembering the phone call Garrick got the last time I was here, I said, "Don't forget to break up with your old girlfriend."

"What?"

"That girl who called you the last time we were here together—when we were looking for Ellie and Davy. You said you needed to break up with her."

Recognition showed on his face. "Shelly? I do need to breakup with her. That's gonna be ugly. I would've been cheating on her to get Brierly pregnant eight months ago."

I finished dressing in my frontier clothes and laughed. "That's what you get for trying to live two lives at once."

"I could use a little sympathy here, and you're laughing at me?"

"I'm sorry, but it sounds like a soap opera to me. Good luck, bro. You're going to need it. Anything else before I go home?"

Garrick opened the door and we left his room. "Nah, I'll figure it out somehow."

We walked into the kitchen. Ellie and Brierly were exploring Garrick's cupboards, and I could tell Ellie thoroughly enjoyed helping her discover the wonders of modern living.

My wife looked at me. "Did you take a shower?"

I smiled. "No, I fell in the ocean. But I'll tell you the whole story later. We should get going. Life's waiting to be lived—for all of us."

EPILOGUE

Seven Months Later

Once again I found myself in Algonia, fulfilling my duties on the Keepers' Council. Garrick and Brierly had showed up in my bedroom at my parents' house on the night of our first anniversary, ready to be summoned back to the new world. In keeping with Archidus' request, they left their baby in 1968 with a sitter. My mom had called, interrupting my candlelight celebration with my wife, to tell me Garrick and Brierly were in her house looking for me. Ellie and I quickly dressed for a trip to Algonia and left to join them.

The next morning, Archidus summoned Garrick and me. Thankfully, he remembered his promise and brought our wives.

The cases we heard in each of the provinces were similar to what we'd dealt with the year before, and nothing out of the ordinary happened. The rebellion in Shuyle had died with Lord Dolosus. From Marcus we'd heard that Legard had worked tirelessly throughout the past year to promote peace between the two countries. Many of the Shuylians held Legard in high regard, and after his example, they more readily embraced the peace treaty and their Algonian brothers. I was relieved to hear it all worked out, especially since I was the one who'd lobbied the hardest for his pardon.

"A penny for your thoughts?" Ellie said, shading her eyes from the Algonian sunshine.

I turned and looked at my beautiful wife, who smiled at me from atop her horse. "Just wondering how Legard is doing, I guess."

"Well, you should know by tonight."

"Yes, I should."

We had passed several small elf villages and were nearing the town where we'd held our council meetings. When I'd left Algonia the year before, Legard was still unconscious, so we'd never had a chance to say goodbye. If he didn't find me first, I'd start looking where I left him the year before—Cecilia's apothecary shop.

Later that night after we'd set up camp and eaten dinner, I walked Ellie back to our tent. For the past few days, she had complained about being tired and nauseous, so I figured all the travel was probably getting to her. It was sure getting to me. I was more than ready to call this council trip a wrap and go home.

I had wanted Ellie to come with me to look for Legard, but she didn't feel well after eating the fish-and-lobster feast prepared by the elves. It was rich and buttery and not what we were used to, so I assumed it had upset her stomach. Once she was settled, I disappeared with my counter and materialized on the porch of the apothecary.

Before I could knock, the door swung open. "I thought I smelled something out here," Legard said with a grin.

He looked good, probably better than I'd ever seen him. I stuck out my hand. "I never thought I'd be glad to see a Sniffer."

He grasped my wrist, then pulled me close and wrapped an arm around my back in a quick hug. "Keeper, what a pleasure to see you again. Please come in."

I followed him through the shop and into the kitchen. "Celia," he called. "We have a visitor."

Cecilia walked into the room, her long, straight dress showing off the roundness of her stomach. "Keeper, what a pleasant surprise. Are you hungry?"

I shook my head. "No, I'm stuffed from dinner." I glanced from Cecilia to Legard, who was pulling out a chair for her. "So are you two . . ."

Legard sat next to Cecilia, picked up her hand, and raised it to his lips for a kiss. "Married? Yes, we are."

"Congratulations."

"Thank you. And she now carries my child, so we are doubly blessed," he said. "If it is a son, we will name him Wickliff in honor of my uncle. A daughter we will name after Cecilia's mother. Of course, the healer who specializes in midwifery could have told us the gender, but since we will experience this just once we have chosen not to spoil the anticipation. Like all parents of our kind, we had hoped for twins, but the healers tell us Cecilia carries one child."

"Still, that's great. I'm so happy for you."

Cecilia reached forward and placed her free hand on mine. "Keeper, please accept my heartfelt thanks for Legard's safe return last year. He has brought me more happiness than I ever would have imagined, and I owe that all to you."

I looked at her contented smile. "I'm glad I could help."

They asked about Ellie, so I described her symptoms. Cecilia insisted I bring her by the next morning for a potion. I tried to refuse, saying it was probably just all the fish we'd eaten in the Shipping Province over the past few days, but it was useless. The healer committed me to an appointment time before I could change the subject. Cecilia left for bed soon after, while Legard and I talked late into the night. It was hard to imagine we were ever enemies.

I shouldn't have stayed so long, because getting up the next morning was brutal. Ellie tried to talk me out of taking her to see Cecilia, but I won out. I figured it couldn't hurt, plus Elf potions had never let me down. Since I was running late, I left Ellie at the apothecary shop after a brief introduction to Cecilia and ran across the town square to the hall where we held our council meetings. I slipped into my seat as Shahzad addressed the first plaintiff.

When I had suggested Legard could transport Ellie back to camp so she didn't have to walk, the look she shot me would have put a layer of ice on the Twisted Faeries hot springs. She knew he had reformed his ways, but she hadn't yet embraced the idea of being friends.

Once the council finished for the day, I set out to find my wife and apologize for dumping her in Legard's hands. I used my counter to jump back to our tent, but she wasn't there. I searched the camp and asked around, finally concluding she had never come back. No one had seen her all day.

Hoping Ellie's illness hadn't gotten worse, I jumped back to the doorstep of the shop and knocked. Legard opened the door and grinned. "You're looking for your wife, I presume?"

"Is she still here?"

He stepped back and held the door open for me. "She spent the day with Cecilia."

I walked toward the kitchen, feeling my pulse quicken as my mind raced. "Is she sick? Can your wife help her?"

"I'll let you talk with her about that," Legard said.

The windows to the kitchen were open, letting the breeze into the sweltering room. No wonder it was so hot. The aroma of fresh-baked bread filled the air.

"This way." Legard led me into a bedroom. His broad shoulders blocked the narrow doorway so I pushed my way past him, expecting to find Ellie in bed. Instead, I saw the two women sitting next to each other pulling needles through a quilt, smiling and talking like they were the best of friends. An intricately carved cradle lay below the open window, and a painted rocking-horse toy stood next to a pile of blocks in the corner. Obviously this would be the baby's room.

"Hey, beautiful, how are you feeling?" I said. "I was worried when I couldn't find you."

"Are you done already? I must have lost track of time." Ellie tucked her needle into the fabric and stood. Cecilia rose and they hugged each other.

"Thank you for your help today," Legard's wife said. "I want you to take a loaf of bread on your way out."

Cecilia wrapped the brown loaf in a cloth and handed it to me. When I asked if she was able to help my wife, she smiled as if she knew all the answers but didn't want to give me a single one of them. "Oh yes, Ellie is just fine. Some things need to run their course and 'tis best to let the body be."

I was starting to get annoyed, especially with Legard grinning like he was in on a big secret. Ellie thanked Cecilia and Legard for their hospitality and promised to return the next morning when I went to the council meetings. When we left the shop, I turned to my wife. "So, what did she say was wrong with you? You look like you're feeling better now."

Ellie tugged on my arm and we began walking down the street. "Nothing's wrong with me, darling, and I am feeling better. Cecilia made a wonderful meal, so my stomach is more settled." She paused to cover her mouth and yawn. "I'm so tired, I feel like it's bedtime."

I yawned too. "If nothing's wrong with you, why are you so tired?"

Ellie grinned at me. "You haven't guessed yet?"

The smell of warm bread beneath my nose did nothing to help my mounting frustration. Starved, I ripped off a chunk of the crust and took a bite. With my mouth half full, I said, "I can't believe you want me to guess. Just tell me."

She laughed and squeezed my arm. "Where's the fun in that? Please, just one guess and then I'll tell you."

I rolled my eyes. "You're getting over the stomach flu."

Again she laughed.

I raised my voice to say, "If you're sick, this is not funny. I really don't get why you're laughing about it."

"Darling, you're going to be a father."

My jaw dropped, and I stopped in my tracks. When Ellie started talking again, I smiled.

"I know this isn't what you wanted, but—"

I leaned forward to slide my hand around the back of her neck and kiss her mid-sentence. It was a long kiss, probably too long considering we were standing in the street of the largest town in the Elf Province. "You're wrong, Ellie. It is what I want."

She exhaled, looking relieved.

"All I want is for you to be happy, and I know this is what you've wanted more than anything. But you should know that I'm happy about it too."

She rested her hand on her stomach. "Seven and a half more months. I can hardly wait."

We continued down the road. Smoke from the cooking fires rose into the blue sky. "I wonder if it will be a boy or a girl," I said.

"According to the elf midwife, it's a boy. She seemed quite certain, and Cecilia said she's rarely wrong."

"A boy? Are you sure?"

"I'm sure she said it is a boy, but I reckon we'll have to wait until the baby's born before we know for certain."

"We can be sure once we get home and you have an ultrasound."

Again Ellie laughed. It had been a while since I'd seen her this happy and lighthearted. "I have no idea what an ultrasound is, but I'm sure you'll show me."

―◈―

We concluded the council's business in the Elf Province and returned to the castle. Madame Catherine, the healer at the castle, confirmed the elf midwife's claim that Ellie was expecting a baby boy. That night as we climbed into bed in Algonia for the last time this year, I said, "Can we name our baby Garrick?"

Ellie smiled back at me. "Of course. He did save your life, after all. I suppose it's the least we could do."

The next day Archidus returned Garrick, Brierly, Ellie and me to my bedroom. As we prepared to part ways, I told Garrick my plan to name my son after him. I thought I saw a tear in his eye, but he quickly pulled me into a hug and thanked me, so I wasn't sure.

After a round of goodbyes, Garrick took Brierly back to 1968 and their son, leaving Ellie and me alone. I took a deep breath and wrapped my arms around my wife, content to let my future play out before me one day at a time.

About the Author

Kelly Nelson graduated from Brigham Young University with a bachelor's degree. She worked for Price Waterhouse as a certified public accountant for four years before starting a horse-boarding business so she could be more involved in raising her family. As an avid book lover, Kelly later decided to pursue a career in writing. In addition to *The Keepers' Council,* her published novels include *The Keeper's Calling* (2012), *The Keeper's Quest* (2013), and *The Keeper's Defiance* (2013). Her extensive travels to England, Egypt, France, Israel, Canada, Mexico, the West Indies, and across the United States have given her a wealth of experience and sparked a love of adventure and history that shows in her writing. Kelly was raised in Orem, Utah, and currently resides with her amazing husband in Cornelius, Oregon. With four awesome kids and a barn full of horses, cats, and chickens, life for this author is never dull.

Learn more about Kelly and her books at kellynelsonauthor.com, or follow her at TheKeepersSaga on Facebook, or @kellynelsonauth on Twitter. She loves hearing from readers and can be contacted at kellynelsonauthor@gmail.com.

THE KEEPER'S SAGA: BOOK ONE
The Keeper's Calling

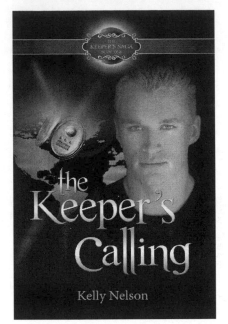

They come from two different worlds.
One fateful discovery will bring them together.
Neither of their lives will ever be the same.

Chase Harper's to-do list for senior year never included "fall in love" and "fight for your life," but things rarely go as planned. Tarnished gold and resembling a pocket watch, the counter he finds in a cave will forever change the course of his life, leading him to the beautiful Ellie Williams and unlocking a power beyond his wildest imagination.

In 1863, Ellie Williams completes school in Boston and returns to the Utah Territory only to discover that her grandfather and his counter, a treasured family heirloom, are missing. When Ellie is abducted and told she must produce the counter or die, an unexpected rescuer comes to her aid.

THE KEEPER'S SAGA: BOOK TWO
The Keeper's Quest

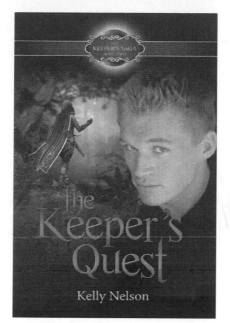

A tragic death. A fatal trap. A daring quest.

I woke to the flash of counter coordinates and a rush of adrenalin. Suddenly, it hit me. I was a pawn in someone's game of chess, and I'd just been moved. Master Archidus required my services. I was a Keeper—the Protector, to be specific. I hadn't wanted this, but I wouldn't shun my duties, either. The other Keeper's life wasn't the only one at stake. —Chase Harper

After a turbulent start to his senior year, Chase expects his life to return to normal now that Ellie Williams is back. But when a Sniffer's trap leads him on a journey spanning two worlds, he soon realizes things aren't always what they seem. Will his calling as Keeper require a sacrifice he isn't willing to make?

THE KEEPER'S SAGA: BOOK THREE
The Keeper's Defiance

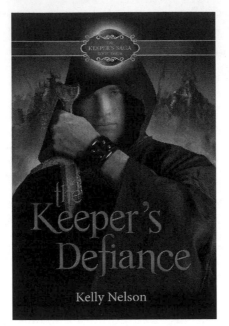

A dreadful dungeon. An epic journey. A lost love.

The scream of a dragon woke me. Wide-eyed, I scrambled to my knees, searching for a place to hide. Then it dawned on me—within the clutches of the enemy, I was perfectly safe from the dragons. —Chase Harper

When Chase found a gold counter buried in a cave, he went back in time, setting in motion events that would change the course of his life and forever alter the destiny of the new world. After he and a small group of soldiers rescue his girlfriend Ellie from the Shuylians, they are overtaken during their race for the Algonian border. Chase falls into enemy hands, leaving Ellie to fend for herself. As time passes, he is believed dead—forever lost. So when Davy, Perception's Keeper, is charged with seeing to Ellie's safety, will his persuasions turn her heart away from Chase?